WERE HOUSE

WERE HOUSE

E. Rose Sabin

Arucadi Enterprises, LLC
St. Petersburg, Florida
2021

WERE HOUSE
E. Rose Sabin
©2015, reprinted 2021
Arucadi Enterprises, LLC
http://www.arucadi enterprises.com

cover art by Igor Desic, ©2021
https://igordesic.artstation.com

ISBN: 0692521364

ISBN-13: 978-0692521366

In all of us, even in good men, there is a lawless wild-beast nature, which peers out in sleep.

--Socrates

1
HOMELESS

My mind roiling with dark thoughts, I walked through a seedy part of town on my way to Lawton's one and only homeless shelter. I had no place else to go. I'd just been evicted from my apartment because, having lost my job, I hadn't paid the rent for several months. I had to walk because I had no money for gas or the repairs my car needed. At least the cool weather of late October made walking pleasant. But the shelter's a bad place for a woman. Lawton winds up with too many of the transients that the larger cities of Tampa, St. Petersburg, and Sarasota, all directly to our north, force out of their areas. My mind busily pictured all the things that could happen in that shelter, even to a girl with a jaguar to protect her. Distracted, I bumped right into a guy coming from the opposite direction.

"Hey, watch where you're going!" My words rushed snarling out before I collected my thoughts enough to realize I'd bumped into him, not the reverse.

Oops! I spoke hurriedly: "Sorry, I wasn't thinking—" Two things kept me from completing the apology. First, he'd marched right on, as oblivious of me as I'd been of him. Second, my *were* sense tingled. *Hey, wake up*, it alerted me. *That guy has an animal spirit too.* I'd spotted another were, and thanks to a special sense most weres don't have, I saw within him the spirit of a large wolf, light gray or maybe even white.

I spun around and tore after him. He'd gotten pretty far ahead of me, but I just planned to keep close enough to follow him. I hoped he might be heading to a place that welcomed weres, a place that had more to offer than the homeless shelter.

With no family or friends to turn to, I longed for a real home. My last boyfriend bailed after I lost my job, and my mother and her new husband had driven off to God knows where in his fancy new RV. But this guy, this *were* might offer help.

I reached an intersection just as the light turned red. Cars flowed past, separating me from my quarry, who'd already crossed the street. I fretted a bit, but if I sped up a little I'd get him back in sight soon enough.

When the light turned, I crossed at a brisk pace but didn't run. No point in alarming anybody. Sure enough, I'd only gone half a block when I spotted the fellow reaching the next intersection, and this time he had the red light. I didn't want to get so close that he'd sense someone following him. Weres generally sense the presence of one of their kind. I slowed down but kept my eyes on him.

A guy in a floppy hat came toward the *were* and bumped into him. As far as I could tell, that person didn't stop to apologize, just darted into a discount shoe store on that corner. The light changed to green, and people waiting headed across the street.

Except for my quarry. He staggered and sprawled

facedown on the sidewalk. I ran to him. A knife stuck out of his back just beneath his left shoulder blade, and blood soaked into his shirt around it.

People gathered to stare. "Call nine-one-one," somebody shouted.

"Don't touch him," another voice warned. "Let the paramedics handle it."

And a question that chilled me. "You do it, lady?" I turned to face the person who asked that. A cop. Where'd he come from so quick?

I shook my head. "I just saw it happen. A guy came around that corner." I pointed. "He had on a hat with a big brim. I couldn't see his face. It could even have been a woman. The person ducked into that building." I pointed at the shoe store. "Maybe he's still in there."

"Can you describe him at all? His clothes, maybe?" I guess it wasn't his job to go after the guy.

I thought. It had happened so fast …

"Is he dead?" somebody asked.

A siren screamed in the distance, coming closer.

"I think he had on a long-sleeved shirt over jeans," I answered the cop, trying to recreate the image in my mind. "Dark plaid with maybe a dark-colored T-shirt underneath."

The cop jotted the description in a notebook but made no attempt either to go after the guy or to check on the victim lying at his feet.

I guess "Let the paramedics handle it" expressed his philosophy, too. Or maybe he figured the guy was dead, certainly a possibility given the pool of blood spreading on the sidewalk beside him.

I longed to slip away and go after the son of a

bitch who'd spoiled my plan, but with the cop standing right next to me and a crowd surrounding us, I hadn't a chance.

"Anybody else see what happened?" the cop asked the crowd.

Nobody answered.

"Come on. Somebody else must have seen the fellow this lady just described." He repeated the description I'd given.

Again nothing but shaking heads. Shows how observant people are. A couple of people did back up my claim to have reached him only after the stabbing. That may not have completely convinced the cop that I hadn't done anything wrong, but it helped.

By this time the ambulance screeched to a halt, and the paramedics ordered everyone to back off out of their way. I watched them lift the guy onto a gurney and get him into the ambulance. The cop stepped away from me to whisper something to the paramedic in charge. The paramedic shook his head and climbed into the ambulance.

I would've gone after the stabber while the cop turned his attention elsewhere, but too many people blocked the way. Besides, like everybody else, I'd hoped to find out whether the victim was still alive.

Even if life lingered, all the blood he'd lost lowered his chance of survival. But weres are tough. Not easy to kill. Not impossible, either.

The cop came back. "Miss, I have to ask you to come to the station with me and give a formal statement."

He stated it politely, but I didn't think he'd tolerate a refusal. A cop car drove slowly to the curb, parting the curious crowd of onlookers. Other cops cleared the street, routing traffic away from the ambulance. It sped off, lights flashing and siren shrieking. My cop led me to the car, opened the door, and pointed me to the back seat. As he did, prickles rose on my arms and neck, an indication of a were close by. I hesitated, but when I tried to look around, the cop shoved me into the car, giving me no chance to study the crowd and try to spot the person I'd sensed.

On the way to the station I worried about whether the shelter would have a place left by the time I finally reached it. Maybe if I explained to the cop, he'd hurry the paperwork up. More likely it would make things worse.

They couldn't make me out to be a suspect. How could they? I didn't know the guy, had no motive, and I hadn't touched the knife, so they'd find no prints on it but the owner's.

But you never know what cops will do.

2
INTERROGATION

After I went over my story about seventeen times and signed umpteen papers, a different cop drove me to the apartment house I'd lived in until this morning. I figured an admission of homelessness would only add to their distrust, so I provided the old address and pretended that I had no idea who the stuff thrown all over the sidewalk belonged to. I didn't care about anything there. Luckily I'd taken a load of clothes—just about everything I owned besides what I had on—downstairs to the laundry room right after breakfast. While I watched the sudsy clothes swish around in the washer, the landlord went into my apartment, carted out the rest of my belongings, and changed the locks. When I went upstairs carrying my clean clothes, I found the bastard waiting in front of my door, eager to tell me what he'd done.

"You left me no choice, Miss Ramirez," he said. "Anything still out on the sidewalk by six tonight will go into the dumpster for pickup in the morning."

I grabbed my only suitcase, packed the clean clothes in it, and filled a canvas tote with other stuff worth keeping. I stored those things in the trunk of my car. Everything else stayed where the landlord had tossed it. I figured he'd clean it up himself eventually, but he hadn't done that yet.

The cop sat in his car watching me step around the scattered junk and go into the building. I hoped I didn't run into the landlord—at least not until after the cop drove off. When he'd gone I went back outside. By now, feeling the midafternoon heat, I decided I really didn't want to head back to the shelter. I stood on the sidewalk considering my options.

Someone stepped out of the shadows. I'd felt his presence a moment or two before he emerged, when my hands and arms started tingling. *Were!*

Also a hunk--tall, blond, a real hot number. I stuck out my hand and smiled. "I'm Charlotte Ramirez." I extended the hand as common courtesy. The smile was involuntary. I mean this guy was gorgeous!

He didn't take my hand. Didn't smile, either. And very pointedly failed to introduce himself. "You witnessed an attack on ..." he hesitated, "a man."

"A fellow were, you mean." I couldn't resist correcting him.

He shrugged. "As you wish. I've been sent here to bring you to one who desires to question you about the attack."

"Hey, the cops questioned me all afternoon. I don't need more questions."

"Police!" He spat. "The police would not know what questions to ask. They know nothing of our kind."

"Yeah, well, I got no time to answer questions. My landlord locked me out this morning. I gotta get my stuff and find a place to crash tonight."

"If you need a place to stay, the man who wishes to see you may be able to arrange that."

I latched on to those magic words as the best offer I'd had. The only offer. Not a firm promise, though. I hid my eagerness and acted cool. "So who's this man that wants to ask me questions? And why does he think I'll come just because he sends for me?"

"He is the head of our family."

Somehow I didn't think by "family" he meant Mom and Pop, two and a half kids, and a dog. Well, the dog, maybe. I've heard of weredogs. I've never met one, but my acquaintance with other weres is pretty limited. "So this head of your family says 'Come' and expects me to hop to, that it?"

"He hoped you would come willingly, but it would be unwise to refuse."

"In other words, I don't get a choice."

"You have a choice of accepting an invitation and coming as a welcome guest or refusing and being brought in as an enemy. The decision is yours." He smiled. Not a particularly friendly smile, but it melted my resistance.

In my animal form I could've given him a good fight, but I needed a home, so I wanted to find out more about his were "family." Furthermore, with my special sense I could see the animal inside him. I searched my memory of animal photos I'd studied, until I got him pegged. Snow leopard. I could see the big cat inside him, and since just about all the weres you'd come in contact with in the U.S. are of European or North Asian descent, that narrowed it down. Yep, snow leopard. Beautiful animal. Figured. This guy's spirit animal matched him in good looks. It made my decision a lot easier.

"I've got a suitcase full of clothes in the trunk of

my car," I said. " I'd better get it in case this head of your family does offer me a place to stay."

He smiled. A little friendlier this time. "I'll help you with it," he said.

I didn't need help, but what he meant was *I'll go with you so you can't duck out on me.* He followed me into the apartment parking lot and across the cracked asphalt to my old Buick, carefully avoiding the pool of oil that had seeped out from beneath it. "The car needs repair. It doesn't run," I informed him, probably unnecessarily.

He made no comment about the car's condition, just stood close while I fished my keys out of my purse and opened the trunk. He might as well make himself useful. I handed him the suitcase and the canvas shopping bag stuffed with books, photos, and keepsakes. He took them without a word and waited while I retrieved blankets and a pillow. As soon as I closed the trunk, he turned without a word and led me to his car.

Car? It glowed in the sunlight, a bright yellow work of art! I stared.

He smiled. A real smile. "You like the Lamborghini?"

"Wow! I've never seen one."

"A Lamborghini Murciélago, to be precise." His voice dripped pride. He opened the door—not out but up, so it looked like a wing.

"Looks like a bird," I said. "A great big canary."

He frowned, then laughed. "How about a bat? Murciélago is Spanish for 'bat.' Actually, though, they named it for a bull named 'Murciélago'."

"A bull named 'Bat'? *Why*?"

He didn't get a chance to answer. The shiny yellow surface showed, along with our reflections, the reflection of my ex-landlord rushing toward us, calling out my name. I turned to face him.

"Miss Ramirez, I want that trash cleaned off my sidewalk and your car removed from the lot. If it's still there tomorrow I'll sell it for parts and apply whatever I get to your back rent."

He might as well go ahead. I doubted he'd get enough to cover the towing charge. I needed a car, but my old thing did me no good without a way to get it fixed or put gas in it.

Before I could speak, my companion said, "You need not concern yourself. The vehicle will be removed."

Ex-landlord stared wide-eyed, clearly impressed by the guy and the car. He didn't back down. Not right away. "Who are you?" he asked.

Leopard Guy took his time about answering. First he assisted me into the car, a two-seater, so low to the ground I had to fold myself into it. Then he walked to the back, opened the trunk, and tossed in the suitcase and shopping bag. I caressed the buttery-smooth leather upholstery while I waited. He came back, took the blankets and pillows from my lap, and tossed them into the trunk too. Only then did he turn to the landlord, who'd waited all this time, absorbing the sight of the car with me in it. I leaned out to hear the conversation, but Leopard Guy didn't say a word, just handed over a business card. I couldn't see the printing on it, but ex-landlord looked at it, looked at Leopard Guy, nodded, tucked the card into his shirt pocket, and walked away.

I'd have loved to know what was on that card, but I didn't ask. Since he hadn't even bothered to tell me his name, I figured I didn't rate high enough in Leopard Guy's book to be entrusted with any personal information—at least not until I'd gone through the coming interrogation.

We tooled along in silence. I *couldn't* speak, too awed by the fancy dashboard and the low way the car rode, like a racecar. When we left town and headed south on Highway 41, the speed took my breath away. I braced myself with a hand against the dashboard every time he swerved around a car in front of him. He must have noticed, but he didn't slow down until we turned off onto a narrow blacktop that didn't look like it got much traffic, and then off that onto a driveway that wound through trees and around a little pond and beneath more trees to a house completely hidden from view from the highway and the blacktop in spite of its size. The sprawling two-story place could house a football team or two.

"Looks like you've got a really big family," I said as we came to a stop.

"You could say that." He got out and hurried around to lift open the door for me.

Not certain how to get out gracefully, I accepted the arm he offered and let him help me.

Keeping his hand on my elbow, he hurried me toward the house, opened the front door, stood aside to let me enter, and followed me in.

He guided me through a foyer into a large living room boasting two extra-long sofas, a couple of lounge chairs, two wing-back armchairs, and a fireplace with a marble mantel. We were the only people in it. And next thing I knew, I stood there alone while Leopard Guy went to fetch the man who'd sent for me.

Maybe he thought driving a Lamborghini excused him from being polite. He hadn't invited me to sit down. I wandered around the room, taking it all in. Mostly brown and beige, the two sofas and several chairs demonstrated good taste without sacrificing comfort. Lots of throw pillows with green, leafy designs created a woodsy appearance. My jaguar approved. The room would make weres feel comfortable. So why was nobody in it?

Probably all off watching TV or playing video games in other rooms, I decided, seeing no television set in this room.

I strolled over to the fireplace, its clean state not surprising with the weather still too warm for a fire. Two tall brass candlesticks with green candles sat on the mantel, one on each side of the gold-framed picture hung just above the mantel and bathed in a golden glow from the candle flames. The arrangement suggested an altar. Drawn to it, I puzzled over the mixture of animals in the painting until a deep voice behind me said, "You like the art? Interesting, *ja*?"

I turned. I hadn't heard him come in. People generally can't sneak up on me like that.

An old man. Thick white hair. Walrus mustache, otherwise clean-shaven. Clear blue eyes. Shoulders slightly stooped, thrusting his head forward like the animal inside him. Some kind of bull. Big. And powerful.

While I studied him, he studied me. Could he see me the way I saw him? Most weres don't have that talent, but his penetrating gaze made me nervous.

"The painting," he repeated, "you like it? It is called *The Peaceable Kingdom*. Fitting, *ja*?"

That "*ja*" again. German, but aside from using *ja*, he didn't have much of an accent.

I gathered my wits enough to answer. "It doesn't look all that peaceable—all those animals together like that. That wolf's staring at the lamb like it wants to eat it. And the bear in the background looks ready to take a bite out of the cow."

He laughed, a deep, hearty laugh. "Perceptive, *ja*, I like that. The animal nature is not so easily tamed. *We* know that all too well. Thank you for coming. Dimitri tells me you came despite needing to find lodging for the night. It is good of you."

Dimitri. At last I knew the name Leopard Guy never bothered to tell me. "He didn't give me much choice," I said.

He chuckled. "If you had refused, he would not have forced you to come."

"That's not the impression I got."

"Ah, but he is like the leopard in the painting, you see." He pointed again to the picture he'd called *The Peaceable Kingdom*. "Powerful but dignified and serene."

I shook my head. "Doesn't look serene to me. Not with its ears erect. And isn't that a bone right by its tail? And if it's not dangerous, why are those two kids cowering in the ravine?"

He laughed heartily. "Most perceptive. So. Please sit and describe in detail the act of violence you witnessed this afternoon." He settled into an armchair, and I sank down onto the closest sofa.

I launched into the same tale I'd told the cops. He interrupted after just a couple sentences.

"Miss Ramirez, I want you to speak as a were. This is not a police interrogation. As were you are more observant than you acknowledge and than the police would have guessed. Please describe your every impression."

I held a mental debate with myself and decided to be completely honest. After all, I wanted shelter from this man. I wouldn't get it if I didn't cooperate.

"I didn't have my mind on where I was going, and I bumped right into him. It took a few seconds for me to sense that he had an animal spirit within. A wolf, to be exact."

He leaned forward, intent now. "How would you know that?"

"It's a talent I have. I see the animal inside the person. I caught only a glimpse of his. But I'm sure."

"All weres can sense others of their kind. But to see the animal within? That's not possible."

"I can, though. Apparently I inherited the ability from my Mexican shaman father." Dimitri had snuck in and sat where maybe he thought I wouldn't see him, but I had. I gestured toward him. "Take him for example. He has a snow leopard."

I enjoyed the surprised look on Dimitri's face. I'd shaken him for once.

Not the old man. "What am I?" he asked.

I looked again at the animal. "Looks like a bull, but bigger and the horns are too long." I shook my head. "I'll say a bull, but that's not quite right."

Now the old man looked impressed. "Close enough," he said. "An aurochs. They are extinct now, though scientists believe they can recreate them. But I," he said, sticking out his chest and laughing, "*I* am not extinct."

"Decidedly not, Grandfather," Dimitri put in. "But shall we not hear the rest of her story?"

"Yes. So the victim carried the spirit of a wolf. Could you tell its color? How exactly do you see the animal spirit?"

"It's ghostlike," I said, considering. "And I don't really see it *inside* the person but kind of superimposed, like a transparent overlay. But the colors do show. I saw the man's wolf as light gray, almost white."

I got the impression that description disturbed Dimitri, but he didn't say anything, and the man he'd called Grandfather went on with the questioning.

"And what about the person who stabbed him? Was that person were as well?"

"I didn't get a close look, but I didn't get a sense of wereness and saw no animal in the man. I keep saying 'man,' but it could have been a woman." I explained about the cap that shadowed the face, the loose-fitting plaid shirt, and the brief glimpse I'd had.

"So. We must consider the reason for the attack by that person, man or woman. Robbery? A random act? Or a deliberate attack against a were? Again, your impressions."

"I don't think it was a random act. He stabbed and ran, too quick for a robbery. He couldn't have expected to have time to take anything, stabbing a man on a street corner in broad daylight like that."

The grandfather rubbed his chin, considering. "If he knew he was attacking a were ..." His voice trailed off. He shook his head. "So few know about us, what we are."

Another moment of silence passed. Then he asked, "What about the were? Is there a chance the paramedics may have saved him?"

"He was still breathing when I reached him. I couldn't tell how far the knife went in. I couldn't hear what the paramedics told the cop. They worked on him up to and while they put him into the ambulance, had an IV going and an oxygen mask on him. That's all I know."

Dimitri shifted in his seat. I caught the slight movement out of the corner of my eye. His grandfather noted it, too. "Something, Dimitri?"

"I assumed he'd been killed. I hadn't considered the possibility that he might survive. We should learn—"

"Ja. Do you know where they planned to take him? Which hospital?"

"No idea."

"The police must have looked for identification. Did they find any?" Dimitri asked. "Did they get his name?"

"The cop who talked to me didn't check. The paramedics may have, but I doubt it. They looked too busy just trying to keep him alive and get him into the ambulance."

"But other police must have come onto the scene," the old man observed.

"They did, but the first cop whisked me off to the station to answer questions and sign a statement, so I don't know what the other cops did. The ambulance pulled away as we left. I couldn't see what direction it took."

"So we must make discreet inquiries. We must also discover the were's identity. That he has a wolf spirit narrows it down. Describe him again, please."

I'd paid closer attention to the animal spirit inside him than I had to his outer appearance, but I did the best I could. "Taller than me, but not as tall as Dimitri." I looked at Dimitri as I spoke, judging his height. And I surprised a look of … what? Startlement? Worry? It interrupted his veneer of coolness too briefly for me to be sure.

Dimitri met my gaze and frowned. I looked away from him, back to the grandfather. I wondered what bothered Dimitri. He hadn't been the attacker, but the idea that the were might still be alive seemed to have shaken him. Not disappointed him, I didn't think — just shaken him.

How did he and the grandfather know about the attack, anyway? It couldn't have been on the news so soon. And how did he know where to send Dimitri to get me?

I asked the grandfather those questions.

"As for your second question, that I cannot tell you," he said. "It must remain my secret for now. As for how I knew about the attack, one of our family members chanced on the scene and observed the paramedics at work. Unfortunately that person did not witness the stabbing or see the perpetrator. However, he worked his way near enough to the ambulance to sense that the victim was were. He couldn't see the victim. The paramedics blocked his view. He phoned me in some alarm, wanting to know if any of the family members were missing. But no, all were accounted for. So, please, continue describing him. Include every detail you can recall."

A quick glance at Dimitri showed him leaning forward, listening intently as I did my best to remember details. "He was young," I said. "Needed a shave. Could have used a haircut, too."

"Color of hair?" the grandfather asked sharply.

"Umm. Not sure. Not blonde. Darkish. Not black, I don't think."

"Skin color? Complexion?" the old man shot the further questions at me.

I shook my head. "Didn't really notice," I admitted. "I mean, he wasn't dark-skinned. I'd say he looked pale, but being stabbed probably explains that."

Dimitri gave a snort, maybe of disgust, and got up and left the room. The grandfather didn't act like he noticed, just asked, "What was he wearing?"

I closed my eyes, trying to recreate the scene in my mind. It had happened so fast. And my attention had been drawn to the killer. Nothing about the victim's clothes stood out in my mind. Except the blood soaking his shirt. The shirt …

"The shirt looked wrinkled and not too clean, kinda like he pulled it out of a hamper or something."

"The description doesn't fit anybody I know," the old man said slowly, more to himself than to me. I pictured him trying my skimpy description on all the weres in his clan, drawing a blank, and trying to figure out whether the fault lay in my description or the were was a stranger to him.

I sat quietly, letting him think about it while I tried to recall any other detail that might mean something. A girl about my age, early twenties, came into the room. Her shoulder-length brown hair fell in soft waves around a face with hazel eyes and a turned-up nose. I judged her pretty but lacking in the manners department. She breezed past me and handed the grandfather a stack of photos. "Dimitri said you'd want these," she said, exploding my theory that Dimitri had left out of disgust with me.

Or maybe not. How'd he known the old man wanted the photos? And what gave the girl her chilly attitude? She'd never seen me before. Maybe Dimitri had told her something about me.

"Rhonda, please meet Charlotte Ramirez. Miss Ramirez, this is Rhonda Ashford, whom we know as Ronnie."

I waited to see whether she'd make a move to shake hands. She didn't, so I didn't. I did say, "Pleased to meet you."

She nodded coolly and said nothing.

The animal spirit I saw within her puzzled me. It slept, curled into a tight ball, making it impossible to identify. I'd never seen anything that peculiar before.

"You may go," the grandfather told her in the way he might speak to a child.

Without a word she turned and stalked off.

"You must forgive her," the old man said, when she had left the room. "She is out of sorts today. It's the time of month, nothing more. Now," he continued, keeping me on task, "please look through these photos and see whether you recognize the injured were in any of them. Most are of members of this were clan, but I doubt he is one of ours. Still, it is best to be certain. Many of our members are out of the house for the day, working, although …" he paused, frowned and shook his head. Without completing his sentence he handed me the photos, giving me more to think about than Rhonda and her sleeping animal.

Before looking at the photos, I wanted to know something. "You introduced me to Rhonda, but you haven't told me your name. I only know that Dimitri calls you Grandfather, and you're the head of this clan."

"Forgive me, my dear, for that rude omission. I am Martin Blass. I am indeed a grandfather, but Dimitri calls me that as an honorific. As do Rhonda and others in the household. We are not related except by virtue of being were."

So he wasn't really Dimitri's grandfather. Or Rhonda's. And Rhonda and Dimitri weren't necessarily related.

"Grandfather" recalled me to my task by saying, "Please, examine the photos."

I started through the stack, peering closely at each one, studying faces. I easily recognized Mr. Blass in several, usually with a sweet-faced older woman, probably his wife. I spotted Rhonda more than once, and Dimitri appeared in a few, including one of him standing in front of the Lamborghini, a big grin on his face. As I neared the end of the stack, seeing the same faces over and over without spotting the guy, I figured I never would. And then I did, in a photo at the bottom of the stack. "Here." I pointed to a guy standing beside Dimitri and Rhonda with a hand on the shoulder of a pretty Black girl. "That's him."

Grandfather Blass took the photo from me and studied it for several moments, frowning. He looked up. "You're certain? There can be no mistake?"

"It's not a close-up, but it's clear enough. Yeah, I'm certain."

"Dimitri!" His bellow startled me so much I dropped the pics.

Dimitri rushed in, calling, "Grandfather! What is it?" even before he reached the old man's side.

"Look at this picture! This is who she saw get stabbed. This!"

I looked up from gathering the spilled photos to see Dimitri's pale face turn even whiter.

"It can't be!"

"She says she's certain."

Dimitri swung around to face me. "You're mistaken! Or lying. You can't have seen this man."

"Does he have a twin?" I smarted off. I don't like to be accused of lying.

"He does not," Grandfather Blass answered, while Dimitri just glared at me. "Could he merely resemble the man you saw stabbed?"

He handed the picture back to me to look at again. Hoping I'd changed my mind? I hadn't.

Three other people had filtered into the room. I didn't turn around to see who they were.

"I'm sure," I said. "I got a good look at his face when the paramedics turned it toward me to give him oxygen."

"That's impossible," Dimitri growled. "Marko died two years ago."

"They never found his body," Grandfather Blass said.

"But if he didn't die," Dimitri said with what sounded almost like desperation, "if he somehow survived, he would have contacted us. He'd never have gone two years without letting us know he was alive. It couldn't have been Marko she saw."

"What's this about Marko?" a deep voice asked. Its owner came forward to peer at the photo I'd handed back to the grandfather. A tall man with light brown hair and blue eyes. Looked to be pushing fifty, but it's hard to tell with weres. And within him, filling him, I saw a large, dark-furred bear.

"She's identified Marko as the man she saw get stabbed," Grandfather Blass said. And to me, "Miss Ramirez, this is my son, Jeffrey Blass."

He gave me a nod and took the photo from his father's hand. As he gazed at it, I saw the bear lean forward to look as well. And I swear it recognized the man and became so eager to break out that I imagined I could hear its growls.

"He couldn't. Be alive. After all this time. And let my son, let Gene, be accused— No, I can't accept that. And now, what? Stabbed? Dead? No."

The bear strained to leap free. I backed away, not certain a jaguar could take a bear.

A dark-skinned girl who looked no more than nineteen ran up to the grandfather. I recognized her from the photo. The Black girl with Marko.

"What's wrong? Are you all right?" She directed her question at the grandfather, but without waiting for an answer she turned to the man with the bear. "Jeffrey, what's happening?"

He held out the snapshot and growled.

"Easy, my son," Grandfather Blass said.

"She swears she saw Marko this afternoon," Jeffrey's voice rumbled. "Saw him get stabbed!"

The girl looked at me, her eyes wide. She screamed.

"Lisette, be calm. Nothing is proved as yet," the grandfather told the girl, patting her on the shoulder.

Jeffrey collapsed onto the sofa, eyes vacant, staring.

And the bear broke out.

3
WERE CLAN

Human and animal natures coexist within us weres. When we're stressed or angry or scared, the animal nature becomes strong enough to draw substance from the human body, leave it, and take physical form. This leaves the human weak, sometimes even unconscious, while the beast prowls free. But we can also let out our animal nature deliberately and remain conscious, with some control over the beast.

Jeffrey's bear had escaped that control. The girl Lisette cowered behind the grandfather. I might have let my jaguar out to defend her, but I guess Dimitri had the idea a bit sooner. His snow leopard emerged and leaped on the bear's back. Its claws left bloody trails through the bear's hide.

A huge boar thundered toward them. A lynx bounded into the fray, caught the leopard's tail, and clenched it in its teeth. A fox darted about, nipping legs and tails.

A wolf bounded in to add to the confusion. A dark wolf. It let out a howl and went after the fox.

My jaguar wanted out! I had all I could do to restrain her. "It's not our fight," I told her. "I don't know whose fight it is or why it's happening. I don't think they know themselves."

"Enough!" The grandfather's bellow thundered

through the room, halting the action. But only for a moment. The wolf growled and dashed after the fox. The snow leopard turned on the lynx. The bear lumbered toward the wolf. The boar charged the snow leopard.

And into the middle of it all pushed the big bull, snorting and bellowing. Not a bull. What had the grandfather called his animal? Not an ox but something that sounded like that.

The girl Grandfather had called Lisette crouched against me, I guess because I seemed to be the only one who hadn't changed. Her animal crept out. I couldn't identify it. Gray with black spots, it looked like a cross between a cat and a weasel. It ventured only a few steps from Lisette, whose body sagged against my legs. It surveyed the scene, retreated, and faded back into Lisette, smart enough to know that its small size wouldn't give it much of a chance in that crowd.

Into the midst of the snarling, biting, howling, tearing bunch marched a small, gray-haired woman smacking anything in reach with a big wooden spoon. I judged her either the bravest old woman I'd ever seen or completely nuts.

Nuts or not, her method worked. One by one the animals backed off and slipped back inside their humans. Finally only the bull-thing remained, standing eye-to-eye with the old woman. I feared for her life. But the bull or ox or whatever backed off, and in a moment the grandfather rose from his chair and went and took the woman into his arms.

Apparently in no mood to cuddle, she pushed him aside and demanded, "Martin, what is the meaning of all this?" Giving him no chance to answer, she turned in a slow circle, shaking her spoon at the humans seated or standing around the room. "What were you all thinking, attacking each other?" she scolded them as she might scold naughty children. "We are a family. We do not do such things."

Besides the ones I'd met—Dimitri, Jeffrey, and Rhonda (who must have slipped into the room and watched the fun)—there were several new folk. I checked each one to see which animal went to which person.

I spotted the lynx in a middle-aged woman. Blonde, probably bleached, but no dark roots showed, fancy hair-do, not a hair out of place. Her hairdresser must love her. And her clothes weren't shabby, either. Stylish to the max. She sat by Jeffrey, and by the concern in her face I guessed she was his wife. The younger man beside them hosted the boar.

The fox, who'd been more an annoyance than a threat to anybody, had retreated into a young guy now talking to Rhonda. He kind of resembled her—a little taller, same hazel eyes, but his brown hair held red glints, his features similar to Rhonda's but sharper. Not bad-looking, but not what I'd call handsome. As for Rhonda, I checked, and her animal had not uncurled. It looked like it slept through all the excitement. Odd.

A young guy leaned against the mantel glaring at everybody except the old woman who'd broken up the fight. The dark wolf had come from him.

Every one of them sported embarrassed looks, some with red faces, others with bowed heads, all cowed by the woman's scolding.

Lisette got to her feet and stepped forward, away from me. "It's her fault," she said, pointing a beautifully manicured finger at me. The little traitor. She'd been happy enough to huddle against me while the battle raged.

The old woman turned not to me but to the grandfather. "Who is this woman?"

"Velma, let me present Charlotte Ramirez, the young lady who witnessed the attack on a were today." To me he said, "Miss Ramirez, please meet my wife, Velma Blass."

I nodded, having got the idea that these people didn't like shaking hands.

"You're were," she stated. "But your beast didn't join this free-for-all," she continued. "Why does Lisette blame you for it?" Eyes drilled me like blue arrows.

Lisette spoke up. "She claims the man who got stabbed was Marko."

"Marko! But Marko is dead."

"She identified him from this photo." Grandfather Blass showed her the picture.

"She must be mistaken." She turned to me. "You are mistaken." As though I hadn't gotten it the first time.

Grandfather Blass shook his head. "I do not think so. She has a special gift—she sees the animal within us. She saw a wolf within the man."

"That means nothing," Grandmother Blass insisted. "Many weres have wolf spirits."

"The color she described fits Marko's wolf."

"The wolf's color is not unusual."

While the grandfather and grandmother held their

debate I looked around. Rhonda had left the fox guy's side and gone to Dimitri. She draped herself over him and shot a defiant look my way. I got the message. She'd marked her territory.

He put an arm around her. "I'm okay, Ronnie," he told her. "Stop fussing. I just can't believe Marko's alive. Or was until this afternoon. And didn't get in touch with me … with any of us."

I didn't hear her response, though I noticed she didn't move away.

Wearing a worried frown, Jeffrey's fashion-plate wife clucked over him, patting his arm and whispering into his ear. Dimitri's leopard had clawed his bear badly enough that Jeffrey would feel the pain of those wounds. His own back could well be bleeding if the leopard's claws had sunk deep enough into the bear's back.

Jeffrey and the wife stood up and left the room, he leaning on her arm. And, yes, streaks of blood did mark the back of his shirt. Dimitri turned to look, and I didn't miss the smirk that came over his face.

Grandmother Blass cleared her throat. "I sent Ronnie in to tell you all to come to supper. Now the food's getting cold. You must all be hungry, so go to the table and start on the salad while I warm up the rest."

To me she said, "You'll take supper with us and stay here tonight as our guest while we try to sort all this out."

Her inflection and stern look made it more an order than an invitation, but I welcomed it anyway. I'd no sooner heard the dinner announcement than my stomach growled embarrassingly, reminding me that I'd had no lunch and only a Pop-Tart for breakfast.

We trooped after the grandmother into a large dining room, its table set with pretty china plates and silverware that gleamed like sterling. Not that I cared, as long as the food tasted good and there was plenty of it.

While others took seats, I stood there wondering whether I'd find a place, since the grandmother hadn't known about me when she set the table. A hand grasped my elbow. "This way," a voice said.

I turned away from the table and saw the guy with the black wolf. His sullen look had been replaced by a friendly smile that lit up his face, making him almost as good-looking as Dimitri. Dark-haired while Dimitri was fair, his eyes, blue like Dimitri's, but warm, not icy like Dimitri's. He pulled out a chair and seated me, every bit the gentleman. I wouldn't mind getting used to that kind of treatment.

He sat beside me. "I'm Gene," he said. "Your name is Charlotte?"

"Yes, but everybody calls me Sharl."

"Sharl it is, then. Have some salad."

He grabbed the bowl and used tongs to lift salad from it onto my plate. Someone passed me a pitcher of dressing, and I doused my salad and dug in.

"I hope you're right about Marko," Gene said. "I don't know if you've heard, but a lot of people, including some here at this table, think I murdered him. The police couldn't get enough evidence to charge me, but that hasn't changed some people's minds."

I hadn't noticed Lisette sitting nearby until she

slammed her fork down on her plate. "I knew you'd grab at her story to declare your innocence. Again. I don't believe her or you."

An ominous hush fell over the group. I could sense the animals stirring. Getting ready for another battle?

"Enough!" Grandfather Blass shouted. "We'll have no discussion of this at the dinner table." He stood abruptly and swept his gaze over all those at the table. "Miss Ramirez will remain here while she investigates this matter further. She will discover whether the stabbing victim is indeed Marko."

He turned his gaze on me and addressed me directly. "Miss Ramirez, Marko's surname is Pavich. You must learn whether he survived the attack or has died. And if he is Marko Pavich, a member of our household, you must help us find and bring to justice the person who did the stabbing."

I choked on a piece of lettuce. When I could speak I asked, "How am I supposed to do all that?"

"I do not know, but you must find a way," the grandfather said, sinking back into his chair. "Until you do, you will be held responsible for what has happened here this afternoon. You have brought us both hope and despair, and you have reopened wounds that had finally healed. So you owe us a blood debt."

I knew all too well what that meant. Weres live by their own unforgiving code. It didn't matter that I'd caused the turmoil in perfect innocence by identifying the stabbing victim as a person who they all thought had died two years ago. My identification of the victim had caused the animal spirits to break loose and attack each other. I didn't understand the reason for that reaction. Shock, maybe? Disbelief? Gene and Lisette seemed hopeful. Dimitri looked angry and skeptical. I couldn't read the others, but for whatever reason, the news disturbed them all.

Even though I couldn't possibly have expected the brouhaha that broke out, if I failed to do what the grandfather demanded, at the least I'd get the boot and at the worst forfeit my life.

I should have gone to the homeless shelter.

4
NIGHT PROWL

Despite my hunger, I can't say I enjoyed the dinner. I had no complaint about the food, which included two kinds of meat, a delicious pork roast and a marvelous platter of rare roast beef, accompanied by potatoes, carrots, green beans with mushrooms, and beets, all yummy. A salad of greens with cheese and anchovies. Weres needed that kind of food after their animals had been out and battling one another, and everyone ate heartily.

My jaguar hadn't taken part in the battle, but she'd have work to do soon, and I didn't want to send her out hungry. So I ate enough for both of us, trying to ignore the currents of anger and suspicion that kept all the beasts riled and restless.

Gene tried to make conversation, but I wasn't in a talky mood. Lisette's glares didn't help any. How did I know she wasn't right about Gene? Two male wolves in a household could spell trouble. Certain trouble if the household included a female wolf, but if I'd met all the residents, Gene hosted the only wolf. Whatever the kind of animal I saw curled up in Rhonda — or Ronnie, as Grandmother Blass had called her — it wasn't a wolf.

During the meal Gene did help me get everybody straight. The guy with the boar he identified as his older brother, Cameron. Heavier built than Gene but also good looking, though he could have stood to slim down some. "Cameron's a photographer and works for a studio, but also does work on his own as 'Cameron the Camera Man.' Cute, huh? He's married, but" Gene hesitated, then added with a frown, "his wife, Joy, isn't were."

He'd intended to say something else but thought better of it. "Where is she?" I asked because I didn't see anybody but Grandmother Blass who didn't have an animal within.

"At work. She's a dispatcher for 9-1-1. She has the five p.m. to midnight shift this week."

I sensed that Gene didn't like Joy. Not wanting to ask about it, I changed the subject. "So how are you and your brother related to the others?"

"As grandsons of Grandfather and Grandmother Blass," he said, "we and our parents, Jeffrey and Helene, make up what I guess you'd call the nucleus of the Blass family. All the others joined the clan by virtue of being were."

Helene. So Gene's mother was the woman decked out with the fancy hairdo. But I didn't see her and Jeffrey here at the meal, so I asked Gene about that.

"Mom's upstairs tending to Dad," he said. "Grandmother took their meals to them there."

"And none of these other people have any blood relationship to you or any of the others?"

"Only Roy and Ronnie. They're brother and sister—twins—but not related to our family by blood. They're what you'd call honorary cousins. So's Lisette. And Dimitri."

When he added Dimitri's name, Gene's tone

turned bitter and he scowled. So. He didn't like Dimitri and didn't try to hide it. Peaceable kingdom my hind leg!

"And Marko, if he's alive? Another honorary cousin?"

"Yep. He and Lisette had a thing going."

I'd guessed that. I still wondered what kind of connection linked Marko and Dimitri, but I didn't ask. We both fell silent to concentrate on our food.

After dinner Gene invited me to watch TV with him in the family room. Most of the others seemed to be going there, but I politely declined. I'd had enough "peaceableness" for one night. I didn't say so, of course. I just said I needed to be alone to think how to go about the assignment the grandfather had given me.

Grandmother Blass understood. She pried me away from Gene and showed me to a first-floor guest room with its own adjoining bath, which she made certain held a good supply of towels and washcloths, plenty of shampoo and conditioner, and everything else I might possibly want. Someone had brought my suitcase and tote bag out of the Lamborghini and put them here, where they looked pitifully shabby in the big, beautiful room. But they held my clean clothes and make-up and stuff. I assured Grandmother that everything was perfect and there was nothing more I needed. She took a bit of convincing, but finally she left.

At last I was alone.

I showered, put on my gown, and went to the window. It looked out on a grassy area with trees close by. Good. I opened it before getting in bed. A very comfortable bed. I sank down into the softness. "Okay, sweetie," I said, "time for you to go exploring."

I pulled the covers up under my chin and relaxed. My jaguar jumped out, ran to the window, leaped over the sill, and headed off.

My mind went with her, sensing her actions, while I lay still, not sleeping but in a kind of trance.

The jaguar lands on the ground, sniffs the air, looks around, ears alert. Avoids the driveway and takes a direct route to the road through trees and shrubs. Scouts along the road, climbs a tree with overhanging branches, crouches on a limb.

Jumps into the open bed of a passing pick-up. Crouches low, out of sight of the driver.

In town the pick-up slows, stops. She leaps out and dashes from the street into the shadow of buildings. Slinks from shadow to shadow, cautious, alert.

She finds the corner where the stabbing happened. A streetlight sheds light on the spot. She waits patiently in a dark doorway until she sees no people nearby, then dashes to the spot, smells the blood. Sniffs the road.

A shout! Someone sees her! She darts away, weaves through shadows.

Ahead! A small park. Grass. Trees.

She climbs a tree, lies still.

No one follows. She waits, not moving. Watches the street.

No people. She jumps down, runs back to the corner where a bloodstain remains. Sniffs it. Sniffs the street. No trail. She knows his scent now, though, and will remember it.

She sniffs around the blooded spot and around the door into the building near it. She wants to circle the building but can't. No space between buildings. She turns the corner. Another door. She sniffs around it. Still no scent she recognizes. Nothing to give any hint of the person who stabbed the were.

Her tail droops. She trots back to the park. Takes shelter in the shadow of a tree.

After a while she returns to the corner. No people around now. She sniffs to tease out scents. Finds one familiar odor among so many. Faint but she knows it well. Her person.

Another scent. Stronger. More recent.

Leopard! Hunting her?

She scouts around, picks up and follows the trail. It leads back to the park. She doesn't go there. She spots a building with an awning she can climb to. Flattened on the awning, she watches and waits.

His light-colored coat makes him visible to her, though its dark spots hide him from careless human eyes. He walks slowly, gracefully, swishing his tail. He passes below the awning on which she perches. She hears him stop, sniff. She tenses, ready to pounce. He pads on. She watches until he recedes into the distance. Curious, she jumps down and follows. Stops. A new scent. Not leopard. Not cat at all. Wolf!

She flattens herself against the side of the building. She hears the leopard hiss, hears the throaty snarl of the wolf. The growl of the leopard.

Slowly, cautiously, the jaguar advances. She hears growls, snarls, thumps! Clicks of nails on cement.

She stops, looks. Two bodies grapple, roll. One light-colored, the other dark. Easy to distinguish the dark wolf from the white leopard with dark spots. It is not her fight, but the jaguar draws closer.

She sees the wolf's long muzzle, sees his teeth clamp down on the leopard's paw. The leopard's claws rake the wolf's belly.

The leopard is on his back, the wolf has his jaws at the leopard's neck. The leopard tries to break free, but the wolf is large, strong. If it sinks its teeth deep into the leopard's neck …

She leaps, comes down on the wolf's back. Now her jaws clamp on the wolf's throat. She can kill with one powerful bite.

The wolf whimpers and rolls off the leopard. The leopard struggles to his feet. Her hold is tight but she doesn't close her jaws. She lets the wolf throw her off, lets him rise.

With jaguar on one side and leopard on the other, the wolf, his belly bleeding, growls and leaps away. He runs off, disappearing into the shadows. She does not follow. She knows whose wolf he is.

Blood stains the leopard's coat. One front paw lifts off the ground. The jaguar's only wound is a torn and bleeding ear. The leopard licks away the blood. The jaguar's tongue cleans the gashes on the leopard's neck.

The two great cats leave the battle scene. The leopard leans against the jaguar for support. They have a long distance to cover. The jaguar could travel the distance best alone, but she stays with the leopard. They avoid lighted areas, keep to shadows and shelter of buildings until they reach the edge of town. They do not venture onto the road but find concealment in the weeds and shrubs that line it.

The sun rises before they reach their destination. The leopard, though weak and limping badly, leads the way to a special entrance at the rear of the house. They are safe!

I sat up and looked at the clock I remembered seeing on the nightstand. I stared at the numbers, unbelieving. Two in the afternoon. I'd not only missed breakfast, I'd also slept through lunch.

I was famished! I also wanted to know Dimitri's condition. He might still be asleep after what his leopard had suffered. And Gene! The wolf had been his. Had it really tried to kill the leopard? Or only intended a warning, not wanting the leopard to help me find Marko?

I couldn't tackle these thorny questions on an empty stomach. I got up, washed, dressed, and headed downstairs. Didn't see anybody until I reached the kitchen, which was spotless, nothing like my apartment kitchen. The cabinet fronts gleamed, the fridge likewise. The floor looked freshly scrubbed. Grandmother Blass was sitting at a table going through what could only have been a recipe box. Planning supper, I supposed.

She looked up. "Ah, Charlotte. Come in. We thought we should let you sleep late. Dima told us you'd had quite a night. You and Dima must have had the same idea about checking the area for familiar scents. Smart but dangerous. Did you learn anything?"

"Dima? You mean Dimitri?" I wanted to avoid her

question until I knew more of what Dimitri might have told her. I couldn't believe he'd risen before me. And he obviously hadn't spilled out *all* the night's events. Gene was Velma Blass's grandson. She wouldn't be so calm if he'd told her what her grandson's animal had done.

"Dima's what we all call him," Grandmother Blass explained, setting aside her recipe box. "All of us except Martin. My husband tends to be more formal."

"Oh." I pulled out a chair and seated myself at the Formica-topped kitchen table. "Well, Dimitri — Dima — helped me, but we couldn't find a trace of the, uh, stabber." I'd almost said "killer," but I reminded myself that we didn't know whether the guy they called Marko was dead or alive.

"Of course you couldn't. You were foolish to try. With all the people that must have passed on a busy street how could you expect to find a scent you barely caught at the time — if you did that."

The jaguar had been hunting for a scent she'd recognize. Someone from this Were House. But I hesitated to tell Grandmother Blass that. She regarded all these people as her family.

"Dima's leopard might have had a better chance," Grandmother continued, "if the person who did the stabbing was someone he knew. But really, I can't think that would be likely. Of course, if he caught the victim's scent and it was Marko, he'd recognize that."

I wondered whether he had. With all the blood the victim had spilled, the scent wasn't hard to pick up. Probably Dimitri had sent the leopard out to discover whether the victim's scent was familiar and also in hopes of finding another scent he recognized — that of the killer. Could Gene's wolf have been trying to prevent that?

I didn't think so. The stabber hadn't been were. Of that I felt certain.

I also felt certain Dimitri hadn't told her about the wolf's attack. I wished I knew just what he *had* told her.

"Really, Charlotte, you should not have sent your jaguar on such an errand. You took quite a risk, sending her into town like that. Suppose she'd gotten lost! If Dimitri's leopard hadn't found her and led her back here, she could have wandered around, been caught, and possibly even shot. And then, well …

No need to finish the thought. All weres knew what happened when their animal self died or got killed. The person would remain in a coma from which he'd never wake up. My teacher had said once that the person could be saved if somehow a second animal spirit could be induced to take up residence in him. I never heard of that actually happening, but my experience isn't that great. There's a lot I still don't know.

But I did have a better idea now of what Dimitri had told her. Making himself—or his leopard, anyway—to be a hero. And I couldn't contradict his story, though my jaguar had saved *him*. I said nothing, and to my relief she dropped the subject.

"Let me fix you something to eat, dear. You must be hungry."

"I'm starving," I admitted, as grateful for the change of subject as for the promise of food.

She got up and went to the fridge, took out containers, and busied herself at the stove and countertop. I was tempted to get up and see what she was fixing, but I made myself stay seated.

"I hope you don't mind that Dima told me your animal is a jaguar," she said while she worked. "You hadn't told us, and it surprised me. It's very unusual, you know. All our animals are of European origin. Weres seem to have originated in Europe."

I shrugged, though she wasn't watching me to notice. "I would have told you I had a jaguar spirit if you'd asked. My father is Mexican. Mestizo. So the wereness must come from the Hispanic side and the jaguar from the Mayan. I haven't seen him since I was three, but I understand he's some kind of shaman."

"Ah, I see."

To head off further questions about my background and also to take my mind off the food smells that rose from the stove, I asked, "Grandmother Blass, how is it that you live with weres and know all about them but you aren't one?"

She turned and smiled. "I was raised among weres. Both my parents were, so I carry the genes. My children—mine and Martin's—all inherited those genes. I don't know why I got left out. When I was young it bothered me terribly, but not now. I know how poor Ronnie feels, though."

"Ronnie?"

"Rhonda. Roy's twin. She's like me—not were."

"But she is! I can see her animal. It's curled up inside her, so I can't tell what it is. Not a large animal, I don't think. I wondered why it didn't come out yesterday when all the others did."

Grandmother Blass turned and stared at me. "Ronnie has an animal spirit? You're certain?"

"Absolutely. I can't identify it because its head was tucked down partway under its body, but I saw it clearly. It's gray with white on its neck."

She dried her hands on her apron. "We must tell Ronnie!" she said, heading for the door.

"Wait!" I got up and went toward her. "Maybe telling her isn't such a good idea. If it's never come out, maybe there's some reason it can't."

She stood in the doorway and considered. "I don't understand why it wouldn't have come out," she said slowly, more to herself than to me. "But you're right. Before anyone speaks to Ronnie about it, we need to consult Martin."

Off she went. I'd have to get my own lunch.

I got out a plate and served up the meat and vegetables she'd heated for me. I'd just got back to the table and dug in when Grandmother Blass returned with the grandfather and a man I hadn't met before, another were. The wild stallion inside him moved restlessly, eager to be out.

He didn't look the stallion type. Gold-rimmed glasses bridged his long nose, the lenses magnifying his eyes. He was stocky, not tall, and his hair was thin and graying.

"Miss Ramirez," Grandfather Blass said, "let me introduce another of our family. Please meet Professor Georges DuChamps. Professor DuChamps teaches courses in folklore and mythology at our local university. He is interested in your ability to see the animal in each of us, and now you claim that Rhonda has an animal within. We do not know how that can be without her being aware of it."

And they expected me to know?

"Can you see my animal?" the professor asked, testing me.

I nodded, smiling. "A horse," I answered. "A wild one, I'd guess."

He turned to the grandfather. "You didn't tell her?"

"No, indeed. She knew nothing of you until we entered the kitchen just now."

"Fascinating. I must investigate this phenomenon."

So now I was a phenomenon.

"Tell me about this animal you see in Rhonda Ashford," the professor demanded.

I told him what I could, which wasn't much. I explained how the animal's position didn't let me see it well enough to identify it. "It's not a large animal, though. Not compared to most of ours."

"Her brother Roy's fox isn't large. Could the animal you see be another fox?"

I considered that and shook my head. "The body isn't shaped like a fox."

"Can you tell the color?"

"Gray. Some white on the little I could see of the head."

"Why doesn't she know she has this animal?" Grandmother Blass wondered. "How is that possible?"

The professor stood silent, head bowed, thinking it over. When he raised his head, he stood, feet apart, cleared his throat, and spoke like he was lecturing his class. "The animal in us usually makes itself known at puberty. But it surely doesn't enter us only then. We must have it within us from childhood, but it is hidden to us until it emerges the first time. We all know of instances when a young person becomes confused and panicky at this occurrence."

He paused, shut his eyes, and rocked back and forth, maybe recalling his first time. I sure remembered mine. It frightened me so bad I fainted, and my mother found me passed out on the sofa. It freaked her out. She thought I'd drunk something or taken drugs. I couldn't convince her I hadn't, especially when I told her this huge cat had leaped away from me and out the window. It didn't help that I acted groggy and slurred my words. She went out of the room to call a doctor, and while she did that, my jaguar returned. I didn't tell her. She carted me off to the hospital emergency room. They couldn't find anything wrong. Tested me for drugs—all negative. Mom swore I'd been faking to get attention.

The professor had started lecturing again. I'd missed the first part, too involved in my memories.

"... assumptions may be wrong. We recognize other weres, but we can't tell whether a child will become were until either an animal emerges or one doesn't. We assume that if one hasn't emerged by the time the child reaches adulthood, that child is not were. It seems that in Ronnie's case that isn't so." He paused and rocked back and forth again, but continued sooner this time. "Or it may be that the animal did emerge, and for some reason the experience was so traumatic that she has repressed the memory and become insensible to the presence of the animal within her."

"Then we must help her acknowledge it and let it out," Grandmother Blass said.

"That may be difficult," the professor said. "We must proceed with great care. I do not think we should hurry to speak to Ronnie about this."

"Speak to me about what?"

We all whipped around. Ronnie and Dimitri were standing in the kitchen doorway, Dimitri's arm around her waist.

Shaking off Dimitri's encircling arm, she repeated, "Speak to me about what?"

5
BULLETS

Grandfather Blass stepped forward, clearing his throat, ready to tell her! Not a good idea until we knew why it had never emerged.

I ran to Dimitri, threw my arms around his neck, and gushed, "Oh, Dima, I've been wanting to thank you for sending your leopard to protect my jaguar last night and lead her safely back here."

His face reddened; I'd embarrassed him. I didn't care. My act had the desired effect. Distracted from her question, Ronnie glared and yanked my arms away from Dimitri. He stepped back in a hurry, afraid, I guess, I might attack again. At least I'd let him know that I'd backed up his story.

"What do you think you're doing?" Ronnie demanded. "What are you talking about?"

Perfect! "So Dima *didn't* tell you!" Let her think we'd been discussing the previous night's activities when she and Dimitri arrived on the scene.

Dimitri glared at me. I guess I blew my chances with him—if I ever had any. Nothing new. I'm good at that sort of thing.

Grandmother Blass slipped between Ronnie and me. "Now, Ronnie, Dima's leopard and our new friend's jaguar had a bit of an adventure last night. Nothing serious."

The hell it wasn't! The leopard looked about to get himself killed when my jaguar saved him. But of course Grandmother didn't know that, and I sure wouldn't tell her. I kept my mouth shut.

Ronnie craned her neck to glare at me around Grandmother. "Why'd she let out her whatever it is?"

"She was trying to do what Grandfather ordered," Dimitri said quietly. So maybe he wasn't mad at me after all.

"So what'd she think the jaguar could do?" She pointedly directed the question at Dimitri, not at me.

But I answered. "I thought she might find traces of a scent she recognized. In case the killer — or would-be killer — is somebody from this house."

"Well, it didn't find any such thing, did it?" Ronnie said, eyes glittering. "Nobody in this house is a killer. You're stupid to think that."

"Now, Ronnie, she doesn't really know us," Grandfather put in.

"And as the police always say, no one is above suspicion," Dimitri added, probably thinking of Gene. No matter how composed his outer self appeared, his leopard poised, tense, ready to spring. Holding it in check had to take a real effort.

"But no one in this house would do such a thing," Grandmother added, probably also thinking of Gene.

"And Charlotte said the stabber was not were," Grandfather reminded the others.

"I don't believe anything she says," Ronnie put in, glaring at me again.

"That's okay, Ronnie," I said, smiling sweetly. "You can think whatever you want. You don't have to believe me when I say that my jaguar really enjoyed the jaunt home with Dima's leopard." As I spoke, I moved closer to Dimitri and put my hand on his arm.

The animal within her twitched but that's all. At least that indicated that it lived. I'd wondered.

Ronnie didn't just twitch. She grabbed my arm and yanked me away from Dimitri. "You're not a part of this family." She spat the words. "Keep away from Dimitri. You have no rights here."

"Sorry, didn't mean to encroach on your territory, Rhonda." I used a tone that meant the opposite of my words, and I pointedly avoided using her nickname. I guess everybody in the room could see I was plenty pissed with Ronnie.

"Now, dears," Grandmother cajoled, again getting between us, "remember, in this house we form a peaceable kingdom."

"Yeah, well, she better watch herself. I may not be were, but I do know how to use a gun." With that grand pronouncement, Ronnie flounced from the room.

"Oh, my," Grandmother said. "I do wish Ronnie would learn to curb her temper."

"I will talk with her," Grandfather said and went after her.

The professor wandered out, too, leaving me, Dimitri, and Grandmother alone. Shaking her head, Grandmother walked to the table and started clearing the dishes I'd used. Something I should have done.

Before I could move to help, Dimitri took my arm and drew me close. "Be careful, Charlotte," he whispered while Grandmother ran water into the sink. "Ronnie can be dangerous. And Roy, too. Her enemies usually become his as well. Please don't give them reason to oppose you."

Grandmother turned from the sink, leaving water running. "Dima," she said, "you toy with Ronnie's feelings. You must heed your own warning."

Interesting. Though Grandmother wasn't were, she had excellent hearing, as most weres did.

She turned back just long enough to cut off the water before continuing. "We need to settle this question about Marko. The two of you need to find the stabbing victim, learn whether he's still alive, and whether it is Marko. That's not something your animals can do. Go now. Check the hospitals and the morgue."

Neither of us argued or questioned Grandmother's right to give us orders. I might have explained that my leopard had tried to find a trace of the stabber, but Dimitri took my arm and guided me to a side door that led into a laundry room and through it into the garage.

"Gene drove the Lamborghini this morning. We'll take the BMW." He led me to a red convertible.

"So … the Lamborghini isn't yours?"

"No, sorry. It belongs to the family business. As do the other cars here." He opened the door and I slid into the passenger seat.

We tooled out of the garage and down the winding driveway, and if I hadn't ridden in the Lamborghini yesterday I'd feel I was riding in great style now. As it was, I felt pretty good, hitting the road in this jazzy red convertible, seated next to this dream of a guy. Not a bad way to start the afternoon.

I'd barely framed the thought when a loud crack

drove all thoughts from my mind. Something whizzed past me, shattering the windshield. Dimitri shouted, "Get down!"

More cracks. The car sped, swerved. I braced myself. Dimitri grabbed my shoulder, raised me up just before the car hit the tree and the airbags burst out, pinning me against the seatback.

The next thing I knew, the airbags deflated, leaving me coughing in a cloud of powdery stuff. I brushed it away, thankful I hadn't been killed in the crash. Dimitri groaned. He must be hurt!

Another groan and a faint mutter. "I've totaled Grandfather's car."

That was his worry? After somebody tried to kill us? And might succeed, if we couldn't get away.

Angry, my jaguar strained to get out, to hunt. No one had ever shot at us before.

"This would not be a good time to release your beast," Dimitri said, his tone surprisingly gentle.

I looked over at him. Blood soaked his right sleeve, flecked the front of his shirt.

"You're hurt! In the crash? Or did you get shot?"

He shook his head. "A bullet winged me and I have small cuts from glass. But most of this blood is yours. *You* were shot, Charlotte. I need to get you to the house."

Me? Shot? He must be crazy. I'd feel it.

"You're probably in shock," he said in that same gentle tone.

"I'd know if I'd been shot," I insisted.

He reached over and touched my shoulder, just below the collarbone. I screamed as pain shot through my shoulder, down my arm, and across my chest.

"Shhh! Sorry! I just wanted —"

More gunshots. I screamed again.

I awoke slowly, my mind muddled. What was I doing in bed? Why had I been sleeping?

My jaguar!

No, I felt her right where she belonged. Had she been out? Was that why I'd been asleep?

I got my eyes open. A woman bent over me. "Ah, you're awake. Good."

Like waking up was a major accomplishment. I had questions to ask, but I couldn't get words out past my dry throat and my thick tongue.

The woman filled a water glass from a pitcher on the table by the bed. She stuck one of those bendable straws in it and held it to my mouth. I drank. The cold water revived me and eased my throat. My brain cleared a little.

I'd been in a car with Dimitri. And gotten shot!

Now I lay in bed, in a different room from the guest room where I'd slept last night, and with a woman I'd never seen before taking care of me.

A tall, skinny woman with birdlike features and a rather long neck. How appropriate. Within her I saw a bird. A crane.

I'd never seen a werebird. I giggled. And winced. Moving hurt my shoulder.

"Easy," said the bird woman. "You'll be fine, but you had a bit of surgery to remove a bullet. That's why you're in an upstairs bedroom. It's close to the room outfitted for emergency surgeries. I'm Henrietta, a nurse. Luckily I'd just gotten home when Dimitri brought you in. Grandfather needs to know you're awake. He'll want to talk to you, if you feel up to it. He can't stand the thought of somebody shooting a guest of his house."

My tongue decided to cooperate enough to allow me to ask, "Did they find who shot at us?"

"No, but … let me get Grandfather. He can answer your questions better than I can."

She hurried from the room like a bird taking flight.

Still laughing inwardly at the similarity between Henrietta and her crane, I wondered whether anyone saw a likeness between me and my jaguar. I didn't have spots, not even freckles. My tan skin I inherited from the Mexican father I scarcely remembered. His animal, a coyote I'd been told, and mine came from his Indian forebears.

I thought again about the first time my jaguar came out and how scared it made me. I thought I must be dying and the big cat had arrived as a weird guide to the other world. That I didn't die left me confused. I didn't tell the doctors or anybody about the jaguar when Mom dragged me to the emergency room. They'd think the same as Mom—I'd taken something that gave me hallucinations.

It didn't frighten me quite so much the second time it happened. I tried to tell Mom about it again. Big mistake! Not only didn't she believe me, she told me off for "indulging in flights of fancy," and said at thirteen I was too old for such nonsense.

I never spoke about it again. Mom and I never got along after that. She considered me just a typical rebellious teen. Me, I resented that I couldn't talk to her about the things that mattered most. Not just the jaguar. I wanted to know about my father. She never answered any of my questions. Never would tell me anything about him. Or why she left him. Well, I showed her. That Saturday she went to the salon for a permanent. Knowing how long that would take, I grabbed the chance and went through all her papers. I found her final divorce decree. It had my father's full name on it. Emilio Francisco Ramirez Tamay. First time I knew it. The Tamay was from his Mayan mother.

I learned that from my uncle. I found out about him in those papers. A scrap torn from a notepad had the name Rodrigo Ramirez scribbled on it and "Emilio's brother" and a phone number.

I had an uncle! I called the number and talked to him! He's a mechanic in a big repair shop in Atlanta.

Mom had plans for my summer vacation. She meant to stash me in some camp where I'd supposedly learn to get along with people. I had other plans. I skipped school the last day and headed for the bus station, clothes in my backpack. I ran away to meet my uncle.

From my uncle I learned that my jaguar meant that like my dad, I had an animal spirit within me that marked me as being were. My uncle isn't were, but he knew about them. He understood all my confusion and fears. He knew somebody who could answer all my questions better than he could. A were!

Pierre probably saved my life. He taught me so much! Wish I'd met him earlier. He was old then. Dead now. I'll never forget his patience and all the lessons he taught me. He made me go back home before summer ended. Said I needed to finish high school. I could get through it now that I understood my nature. And I needed to be patient with Mom, because she didn't know anything about weres.

I tried. I really did. I guess things improved a little between us. But I never felt really comfortable with Mom. I needed to be with other weres.

And now I am. And somebody wants me dead.

6
NETTED

Henrietta fluttered back into the room, followed by Grandfather Blass and, wouldn't you know it, the professor.

Grandfather Blass came to my bedside and took my hand in both of his. "I so deeply regret your injury. It should never have happened. We pride ourselves on being civilized. I have not yet decided on a punishment for the Ashfords, but—

"Whoa!" I withdrew my hand. "The Ashfords. That's Roy and Ronnie?"

"Yes. We all heard Ronnie's threat. Dimitri has stated that shots came from more than one direction. So apparently Ronnie enlisted her twin's aid in this nefarious deed."

"Has Ronnie confessed?"

"No, she has denied it most vehemently. But we heard her threaten you and—"

"She is not guilty!" Dimitri declared, walking into the room. Far from looking cool now, he looked furious.

Grandfather Blass turned to confront him. "How can you say that? We witnessed her furious outburst at Charlotte."

At least I'd graduated to Charlotte from Miss Ramirez.

"We all say things we don't mean sometimes when we're angry."

"She said she had a gun," the professor put in. "When someone threatens to shoot a gun, and shortly afterward shots are fired, isn't it natural to assume that the one who threatened did the shooting?"

"She would not have carried out the threat," Dimitri insisted. "And she had no reason to shoot *me*."

"Even after you went off with Charlotte?" Grandfather Blass said.

"The shots came from more than one direction."

"Roy would have supported his twin, would he not?"

"Not for no reason," Dimitri said. "And I'd judge more than two shooters shot at us. I believe a group ambushed us."

"A group!" The professor's eyebrows arched upward in an expression of astonishment.

Grandfather Blass stroked his mustache. "Are you sure that your fondness for Rhonda has not colored your perception?"

Yeah, I wondered that too. Although I wouldn't have expressed it in such flowery words.

"If I thought Ronnie capable of shooting with intent to kill, I would certainly say so."

Ouch! That didn't tell me how Dimitri really felt about her. He'd gone back to being Mr. Cool.

Grandfather turned to me. "Charlotte, you also get the impression that there were more than two shooters?"

"Sharl passed out before the worst of the shooting," Dimitri said quickly.

"The last thing I heard just before I passed out was a bunch of gunshots. They sounded close, almost like we were surrounded. How did you get us out of there, Dimitri?"

"I dragged you out of the car onto the ground — I was afraid the car might catch fire. I lay flat on the ground beside you while the shooting continued. And, Grandfather, while I was waiting to see whether it was safe to try to make it to the house, I gathered up some shell casings that were lying by the car. They're not from the small handgun Ronnie carries, nor are they from any weapon Roy owns. They're from a high-powered rifle." Dimitri pulled them from his pocket and handed several to Grandfather, who inspected them as Dima continued speaking to me.

"I feared the people who were shooting would come close and kill us both. The firing stopped, and I waited for the sound of footsteps. I heard nothing. I called the house on my cell phone, and Cameron answered. Speaking very quietly, I described our predicament but advised him not to let anyone leave the house immediately, or the shooters' would target them. Good thing. I guess they'd heard the shots and were getting ready to investigate. I kept the phone open and waited. It remained quiet, so I took a chance and got up slowly. Nobody shot at me, so I picked you up and carried you toward the house. Grandfather met me at the door and helped me get you inside, where Henrietta cared for you until the doctor arrived."

"You took a big risk, leaving the car." Grandfather Blass said.

"I had to. I was worried about Charlotte. She was

losing quite a bit of blood, which is why she passed out."

"Ah, of course."

Of course? Well, maybe. But I hoped it meant more than just an attempt at gallantry. And apparently I just fainted rather than having been shot again, as I'd thought. "So a doctor came here to the house?" I asked, curious. "Is he were?"

"She. Dr. Horshaw is Henrietta's mother. She is not were, but she knows about us. We can trust her. She would never betray us."

"We needed her to remove the bullet and check the extent of damage," Dimitri put in. "Fortunately the bullet missed your heart and lungs. You'll recover quickly."

"Fortune favored you both, *ja*?" Grandfather Blass shook his head. "To think, on our own property, people with guns. Killers."

"I find this most strange," the professor said. "Who would do this? Why?"

"Has someone discovered what we are? And thinks us a threat?" Grandfather Blass wondered. "But we have hurt no one. And we have kept our nature a secret."

"Somebody found out," I said. "I can't help thinking it's related to the stabbing I witnessed."

"We had just set off intending to search hospitals, looking for Marko," Dimitri said slowly. "But who knew that?"

"Nobody. Just Grandmother Blass," I said.

"We'll have to ask her if she told anyone," Dimitri said.

I sat up, and Henrietta immediately stuck another

pillow behind my back. "Dimitri, even if she told someone, no one would have time to get a bunch of people out here and into position to shoot at us when we drove out." I puzzled it out as I spoke. "I think they must have just been waiting for anyone to leave the house. But why? It doesn't make sense."

"It does not indeed," Grandfather Blass said. "The fact remains, however, that you could both have been killed. We must get to the bottom of this. It must not happen again."

I couldn't agree more, but I didn't see any solution to this mystery. The whole thing was crazy from the time I witnessed the stabbing right up until now.

"I think I should complete the errand Sharl and I were on, looking for Marko," Dimitri said. "He must be found."

"Hey, I want to help with that," I protested.

"You aren't going anywhere today," Henrietta stated, her hands on her hips in a way that made me imagine her arms as wings.

"I'll take Lisette. And Gene. If Marko is alive, Gene deserves to know it." Dimitri paused, then added, "I can't go anyway until Gene comes back with the Lamborghini."

I'd seen two other cars in the big garage when we set out. Couldn't he take one of those? But I kept my mouth shut. I'd already noted that Dimitri had a passion for flashy cars. At least he hadn't suggested taking Ronnie. Maybe he just didn't want to risk *her* getting shot.

"I will speak to Velma and find out whether anyone else knew of your errand," Grandfather Blass said. "Follow Henrietta's instructions, Charlotte, and you will recover more quickly." He left without waiting for my response, which was just as well, because I was too pissed about Dimitri setting out without me to be polite.

I could go with him, I don't care what anyone says. Weres heal fast. My shoulder ached, but it wouldn't hurt me to ride in a car and then walk through hospitals.

But I refused to beg.

The professor came to the bedside and took my hand. He squeezed my fingers and said, "I regret your horrifying experience. I'm greatly relieved to see you recovering nicely. In Henrietta you have a superb nurse."

I smiled and thanked him. I just wanted him to go away so I could talk to Dimitri. But he lingered, and Dimitri gave a little wave and left the room. I stopped smiling.

"Miss Ramirez," the professor hesitated, "or … may I call you Charlotte? You are part of our family now, it seems."

I am? Did getting shot qualify me?

I didn't say anything, but I guess he took my silence to indicate approval. "Charlotte, I am puzzled," he continued. "After apparently trying to kill you and Dimitri, the shooters left when they had almost succeeded. They had you trapped in the car, vulnerable, and with no help arriving from the house. The shooters, whoever they were, must have surmised that you had no guns, since you would have returned fire if you'd been armed. They could have approached and killed you both, and then made their escape. Why didn't they?"

I had no answer, and I guess he didn't really expect one. He continued, "I suppose they could have believed you already dead — either shot or killed in the car wreck. But one would have expected them to check."

"Yeah, well, I'm kinda glad they didn't."

"Oh, of course. We all are. But if we cannot understand what they wanted, what motivated them, we cannot predict when or how they will try again."

"Georges, you are tiring my patient," Henrietta said. "You must leave." She flapped her arms and shooed him from the room. She looked so like a crane defending its nest I had to laugh. She was an odd character. I liked her.

After chasing the professor into the hall, she closed the door. "That Georges," she said, and sighed. "He's a smart man without a shred of common sense. You don't need to hear his speculations now. What you need is to rest."

So saying, she removed the pillow she'd stuck behind my back, practically stuffed me back under the covers, and ordered me to go to sleep.

I pretended to do that. I needed time to think about what the professor said and about why Dimitri and I were still alive. The professor had a point. Whoever had ambushed us could have finished us off. Easily.

I should have loosed my jaguar. Wouldn't want to risk her getting shot, though. I guess Dimitri didn't let his leopard out for the same reason.

Now, though … the shooters had disappeared. Trapped here under Henrietta's watchful eyes, I could go nowhere. But the jaguar could sniff around, maybe learn something. I just had to get rid of Henrietta for about five minutes.

"Hey, Henrietta, I think I'd sleep better if I had my own pillow. It's with the blanket and stuff I brought with me. It must be in the guest room downstairs."

She came to stand beside the bed and peer down at me, frowning. "The pillow you're using is of fine quality and hypoallergenic."

"Oh, well, but I'm so used to my own. Couldn't you get it for me?"

"I suppose. I hate to leave you, though."

"Why?" I whined, trying my best to look pitiful. "I'm okay, and I'm not going anywhere. I'm sure I'd go right to sleep if I had the pillow."

I sounded like a three-year-old. But it worked. Giving me a last, worried look, Henrietta turned and left the room.

No time to waste. I got out of bed, and opened a window, stifling a scream when that action sent a blaze of pain through my shoulder. I hurried back in bed, closed my eyes, and let my jaguar free, hoping when Henrietta returned, she'd think I'd just fallen asleep.

The jaguar avoids the drive and trots through the trees and brush to the wrecked car. She circles it, sniffing, widens her circle until she catches an unfamiliar scent. Human. She continues her prowl, catching other scents, many. All human but none she recognizes.

She's moving quietly, belly low to the ground. Alert for any noise, any hint that the humans are still present.

She nears the place where the driveway joins the wide road. The scent is strongest here. Wary, she crouches low.

She hears the beat of wings. A large crane swoops down beneath the trees, lands near her. It approaches, flaps its wings. Its beak jabs toward her, forcing her to back away.

It wants her to return to the house and to her human.

She snarls, not ready to return. The crane backs off. Not far. It jabs toward her again.

Her attention is on the crane. She poises, ready to pounce. Not to injure. She knows whose this crane is, where it has come from. She means only to frighten it, show it she will not do what it wants.

They are under tall trees, the branches high above them. From those branches a net drops over them! The jaguar tries to free herself. The net tightens. The crane grabs at the netting with its beak, tries to flap its wings.

Their struggles are useless. The net has closed tightly around them. They're held fast!

The net rises into the air, carrying them with it. The scent of human male grows stronger. She cannot see its source. If she could twist around, she might see it, but her motions only draw the net tighter.

She hears a motor. The net lowers. They drop heavily onto the bed of a truck. Men laugh. The truck lurches into motion. They are jostled about. The crane makes small, hurt cries. The jaguar sees that one of its wings is bent by the net.

She growls. The truck speeds, the net rolls around in the truck bed, knocking her and the crane against one side and then the other. One sharp turn hurls the jaguar against the side so hard she's stunned.

She is still recovering her senses when the truck slows to a stop. Another car pulls in behind the truck. Men climb into the truck bed and hoist the net out. They drop it on the ground. The crane doesn't move. Does it still live?

The men drag the net across the ground. More bumps and scrapes. They drag it over cement and into a big closed-in space that smells of cars. No cars are in it. They pull the net into the middle of the place. They're laughing. One kicks her through the net. They put on a light and pull down a heavy metal door. She knows this by the sound it makes as it clangs shut. She's not facing it.

The men stomp around a bit and leave through a different door, one that she can see until they turn out the light. Then it is too dark even for the jaguar to see much.

Not too dark for her teeth to find the netting and bite down. Ugh! Metal threads. Hard to bite through. She must, though. She has to free herself. And help the crane.

7
JAGUAR

Couldn't think. Couldn't move. My strength mostly with my jaguar. Had to get help. How?

Someone. In the room. Have to focus.

"Charlotte? Where's Henrietta?"

Can't answer. Can't do more than blink.

"Martin! Martin, come! Quickly!"

Grandmother Blass. Calling Grandfather. Good. They'll help.

Footsteps. Grandfather coming?

"Grandmother, what is it? What's wrong?" Not Grandfather. Dimitri.

"She's sent out her jaguar, I suspect," Grandmother said. "And I can't find Henrietta."

Dimitri swore. Mr. Cool? Not now.

Someone else came in. "What's happening? I just found Henrietta passed out on the bed in my room. I can't wake her." I recognized Helene's voice.

"Your room's close to this one," Dimitri said. "That must be why. She sent out her crane and expected to be right back. She didn't want to be far from her patient."

"Maybe she will be right back. Let's wait a bit before we do anything," Helene's suggestion wouldn't help.

I managed to shake my head and mouth, "No." It

took a lot of effort, but I got another word out: "Trap."

"Her crane's trapped?" Dimitri's voice was sharp.

I could only nod in answer.

"Your jaguar, too?"

Another nod brought fresh pain to my shoulder.

Their questions and the pain distracted me. Jaguar needed help. Had to concentrate on her.

Grandfather came in. Listened while they filled him in. Understood more than the others.

"We must leave Charlotte alone and confer elsewhere," he said and herded them all from the room.

I closed my eyes and let my mind drift into the jaguar's thoughts.

The jaguar rests, recovering from the weakness that stopped her work. Her strong teeth have parted two strands, but she must make the hole larger. Again she bites into the net. And again. The strand parts. She works on another section. It parts too. Now! She wriggles through.

She noses around the net, finds the strands that wrap around the crane's wing. Again she bites. Careful of the wing, she parts the strands below it. Taking the net in her teeth, she pulls it gently away from the wing.

Now she can reach a paw in and lift more of the net away from the crane. She has to bite again and again to make the hole large enough to free the crane.

The crane does not help her. It does not move. Awkwardly she pulls the bird free of the net. With her nose she pushes the net away. She and the crane are still trapped in this dark place. But she can find by scent if not by sight the door the laughing men went through. She sits near it. She waits.

The door opens. A man pokes his head through but steps back. His hand reaches out, gropes the wall. Light floods the garage. The man steps through the door.

The jaguar leaps. She hurtles against him. Her weight topples him. He falls back. Her jaws crush his throat. Blood spurts.

Other men come running.

"Grab the guns."

"Lord, that thing's killed Josh."

The jaguar strikes again. "Urggh." The man's final sound.

Shouts. A scream. A shot that misses.

An open window. The jaguar leaps through. Another shot shatters glass.

No matter. She is free. And night is falling fast.

She runs. Crosses a large grassy area, zigzagging to make it harder for the bullets volleying past to strike her. Beyond the grass are trees. Many trees. She climbs one. From its branches she leaps to another tree. And another.

"Where'd it go?"

"I can't see. It's too dark."

She leaps farther from them, keeping to high, sturdy branches. Still, a branch cracks beneath her weight.

"There! I heard it!"

A shot follows the shout, but she has leaped away.

Her night vision is better than the humans'. She could get away from them. Easily.

She cannot take the easy route; she has to stay close. She has to rescue the crane. If it still lives.

So instead of putting more distance between her and the house she escaped from, she draws nearer, creeping from branch to branch until she reaches a tree on the verge of the grassy area.

She lies flat on the branch and watches.

Lights gleam in the windows of the house. Shadows pass across them. The house still holds people. Not all are hunting her here under the trees. A siren sounds, coming nearer.

"God help us!" comes a nearby voice. "Somebody's heard the shots and called the police."

"We'll tell 'em we surprised a burglar and chased him into the woods. We can't let 'em in the house. They'd see it wasn't nothin' human killed Josh and Dan."

"What're we gonna do about them? About the bodies?"

"I don't know. We'll leave that up to the reverend."

"Dan's got nobody but a sister, but Josh is a family man. Was, I mean. He had a wife and three kids."

"They gave their lives for a good cause, riddin' the world of demons. Reverend'll make 'em understand that."

The voices fade as the men move on across the grassy field and back to the house. The jaguar understands little of what the voices said, but they are lodged in her memory. Her human will understand.

She does understand that more men might be coming under the trees with lights and guns. She needs a safer refuge.

Next to the house is a taller building with a high, peaked roof. Between that building and the house is a space with flowers, a footpath, and two trees. One tree is small and spindly. The other is large enough to climb, tall enough to hide in. From it she can watch for a chance to get in and rescue the crane.

She only has to reach the tree.

8
SACRIFICE

My jaguar rested ... not asleep ... watchful ... but relaxed. Letting me think and speak ... not clearly. Hard to put words together. Had to try.

Nobody here. Had to call out. They wouldn't be far.

"Hey!"

Steps. Someone heard.

Grandfather.

"Charlotte? Did your jaguar return? No?"

"Waiting ... Crane ... Hurt ... Bad."

Grandfather pulled a chair, sat close ... head near mine ... listening. "Can you tell us where they are?"

I shook my head. "Caught us in net ... Thrown in truck ... Long drive ... Dumped in garage ... Dark."

"They're there now?"

"Crane is. I'm free. Resting ... Waiting ... Try to rescue crane."

"Your jaguar is still in the dark garage?"

"Killed two men. Got out. Waiting in tree."

"Can you describe the place?"

"White house, big. Red tile roof. Woods in back. Tall building next to it ... Not house. Church, I think. Men talked ... about a reverend."

"Hmm. That gives us something to go on. Are you getting that, Dimitri?"

"Every bit."

Hadn't heard Dimitri come in. Had to tell him …

"Lost her. Something must be happening."

Danger! The jaguar stares downward, every sense alert. Wolf! But not the dark wolf. This wolf has a light coat, easily seen even in the darkness. Has it seen her? Caught her scent?

She is safe. The wolf cannot climb the tree. But the wolf is not safe from the men. And the crane is not safe from the wolf, if it should find a way to get to her. The dark wolf would not, she is certain, harm the crane, but she cannot be sure about this one. Whose wolf is it? Is it the wolf from the man who'd been stabbed? She will know if she can catch its scent.

She does not want to leave her perch, but she must. She must lure the wolf away from the house, from the men, and from the crane. She does not fear the wolf, and she does not want to kill it.

She sees no men nearby. Some have gone back into the woods with the police. Others remain in the house. She does not know how many. She must act while none are close.

She leaps from the branch and bounds toward the wolf. He snarls and runs—toward the woods instead of away as she expected. She vaults across the space between and leaps onto the wolf's back. He snarls and stops. His scent confirms what she'd thought. The wolf carries the scent of the stabbed man. She clamps her teeth into the ruff of his neck, her aim not to kill but to turn him.

It works. He turns away from the woods, and tries to shake her off.

"Hey! Look!" a man shouts. "There's the cat-demon! And a demon wolf!"

They were seen. She presses her paws into the wolf's side, urging him to run, then sliding off him so her weight won't impede him. He dashes between the house and the other building, past the tree where she'd found refuge. She stays with him.

Shouts follow them but no shots. They round the corner of the large building. Its door opens. A man steps out. He holds a gun. She nips at the wolf's side, driving him to run faster. Sirens sound.

She needs to hide. She pulls away from the wolf. He half turns but runs on, out toward the street. She lets him go. She's done her best to keep him away from the humans, but now she has to protect the crane. The bird, not the wolf, is her responsibility.

She looks back toward the large building she's run past. The man who came outside watches her. He doesn't have the gun in his hand now.

Ahead of her rises a low wood fence. She jumps it easily. On the other side are plants too small to hide her. She runs along the side of the fence for a short distance, and then jumps back to the other side, landing in an open paved space. A parking lot. It stretches from beside the tall building to its rear. She is exposed, no place to conceal herself in the large open space. She races to one of the few cars in the lot, crouches behind it, looks to see whether anyone is near and has seen her. Seeing no one, she dashes on across the parking lot and behind the large building. When she reaches the grassy lawn behind the house next to the building, she slows. Watching for the men who'd gone into the woods, she sneaks along until she is beneath the window she'd leaped from. It's still open. She listens. No sound comes from within.

She leaps to the sill, clings there, looking inside. It is too dark to see much, but the absence of light means no one is in the room. She jumps down to a table and then to the floor, and pads softly to the door to the garage. The door is closed. She pushes hard against it. It swings open, dropping her down the steps into the garage.

She freezes. Did anyone hear?

Moments pass. No footsteps. No voices.

She eases further into the dark garage. She sniffs, finds the crane's scent. It no longer lies on the floor. It crouches on its legs, trembling. Afraid. Hurting. Too injured to stand or fly. But it lives. Somehow she must get it out of this place.

Leaving the crane, she sniffs and feels her way around the garage. She reaches the side wall and finds something—boxes, by their shape and feel— stacked against it. Exploring these boxes, she finds those on the bottom are flush against the wall. A careful climb onto them reveals a space between smaller boxes and the wall, a space big enough to hide in. If she and the crane can hide there, the men may think they have escaped. They may open the garage door and give them a chance to flee.

But how can she get the crane into the hiding place? And if she does, and the plan succeeds, how can she get the crane out and safely away? It is not too heavy to carry in her mouth, but carrying it in that way in its present condition would probably injure it further.

Maybe her human can think what to do. She

squeezes herself into the hiding place and sits quietly, eyes closed, nearly dozing.

Grandfather still sat beside me. On the other side of the bed Grandmother stood, holding my hand. I struggled to sit up and speak.

"Easy, Charlotte," Grandmother said, squeezing my hand.

Grandfather held a glass of water to my lips. I swallowed. The water made it easier to speak.

"Crane," I said, "alive but hurt ... bad. Jaguar can't carry her ... Needs help."

"Can you give us any idea where they are?"

"Garage ... attached to house."

"That's the house you described, *ja*?" Grandfather asked. "Next to a church?"

I nodded.

"Dimitri and Gene are searching for it. There should not be many places fitting the description you gave."

"Can you tell us anything more?" Grandmother asked.

"My jaguar snuck back into the garage. Found the crane ... hurt too bad to move. It's dark. Jaguar's found a hiding place. Won't leave the crane. Doesn't know what to do."

"Never mind." Grandmother patted her hand. "Dima will find the place."

"Dangerous. Men ... guns." I sank back against the pillows, unable to go on speaking. My jaguar needed my full attention.

Light floods the garage. Two men come down the

steps and cross to where the crane sits. "At least we got this one. It'll have to do for now," one says.

"We'll get the big cat-demon. The wolf-demon, too. We just have to be patient. The sacrifice may draw 'em out."

One man walks over to the boxes where the jaguar hides. She tenses, ready to spring. He takes something from a box at the top of the stack and walks away. She relaxes a bit.

He holds a length of cloth. He and the other man scoop the crane up and onto the cloth. They carry it between them. They go up the steps into the kitchen. They don't close the door to the kitchen. She hears another door open, close.

As soon as it is quiet, she leaps from her hiding place and dashes to the kitchen, finds it empty. She sees the door they must have gone through. The door leads outside, but it is closed.

The window is still open. She jumps to the table and from it out the window. She easily locates and follows the men. Darkness conceals her. The trail leads to the front door of the large building. Light spills from that door. Voices sound from within.

She creeps close, staying in the shadows.

At the edge of the open door she stops and listens. Men are speaking, but the voices sound distant. The men seem to be well away from the door. She risks a peek inside.

That peek shows her one large room with rows of seats on either side of a wide central path. She pulls the word from her human's mind. *Aisle.* At the end of that aisle on a raised platform is a table. The crane lies on the table. A man in a white robe stands behind the table. He holds a knife. Two other men stand at either end. Other men—four or five—stand near the rear of the room. They have guns. She ducks back out of sight.

She retreats from the door and hunkers beneath bushes. No one comes outside. The man in the robe means to kill the crane. She must find a way to stop him.

A car pulls up in front of the building. Two men get out. Dimitri and Gene.

They look around, head for the door. They don't know about the men with guns.

She comes out of her hiding place and runs to them.

"Charlotte's jaguar!" Dimitri says.

"Good. We've found the place," Gene says. "Take us to Henrietta's crane."

She starts toward the door, stops. She can't let them walk into a trap.

"We're armed," Dimitri tells her.

But they are only two men.

A low snarl comes from nearby. She looks. The wolf has returned, its light coat easy to spot. "That looks like Marko's wolf," Dimitri says. "That must mean he's still alive."

So now they are four: two men, a wolf, and a jaguar. Better.

But only she knows what to expect.

She races to the door and through it. The man in white is speaking, his knife held high in both hands.

She leaps forward. A shot. Loud. It misses her, not by much. She slides under a seat, wriggles forward, staying low. Men shout, look for her.

More shots. Growls of a wolf. She dares not rise up to look. She continues to move toward the front, scooting from beneath one row of seats to the next.

From beneath the foremost row she gathers herself for a leap but the sound of a shot stops her. The white robe sprouts a red bloom. Looking surprised, the man folds slowly downward. The knife falls from his hand.

Dimitri hurries to the table. He picks up the crane and holds it in his arms. The jaguar creeps out and looks behind her. Gene holds a gun on several men. The wolf has a man down and is tearing at his throat.

Sensing no immediate danger, she goes to Dimitri, rubs against his legs in thanks for saving the crane. He smiles.

She turns, sees one of the men Gene is holding at bay shove another toward Gene, then dive at Gene's legs, unbalancing him. She bounds down the aisle and leaps on the man. Her teeth bite deep into his neck. She laps the warm blood.

Growls close by. The wolf has claimed other prey.

"Enough!" Dimitri's voice. "You've killed them. Leave them now."

She lifts her head but does not rise. The wolf continues tearing at his kill.

"The crane's nearly gone. If we don't get her back to Henrietta right away, we'll lose them both."

The jaguar rises and moves away from the man. The wolf ignores Dimitri.

"Marko. Come," Gene says. He places a hand on the wolf's head.

The wolf snarls and snaps, just missing his hand. Gene jumps back, shaking.

"Come, wolf. We do not eat flesh," Dimitri urges.

The wolf *is* eating the flesh. Dimitri shakes his head. "We'll have to leave him. He's gone feral."

Gene nods and heads out the door.

"How many got away?" Dimitri asks as he follows with the crane. The jaguar pads after him.

"Three, I think," Gene answers. "I took their guns. When the jaguar rescued me, they ran for their lives."

"They'll be a danger to us, but we have no time to hunt them down. Gene, you drive."

They reach the car. Gene opens the front and rear doors, and Dimitri gets into the back, holding the crane. The jaguar leaps into the front and hunkers down on the passenger seat. Gene hurries around to the driver's side.

As he starts the car, a man steps out of the shadows. He holds an iron bar. He's screaming, "Demons! Fiends of hell!"

He hurls the bar at the windshield. The glass shatters. The car lurches forward, smashes into the man. Covered in shards of glass, the jaguar cowers on the floor.

She awaits the crash.

9
AFTERMATH

I'll never know how Gene kept from crashing the car. I felt my jaguar's fear, experienced her relief when the car swerved onto the road and pulled over to the side while Gene collected himself, got out, and shook off the pieces of glass, pulling out many embedded in his flesh.

He brushed off his seat and got back in, and my jaguar licked the blood from the cuts on his hands and arms until he told her to stop so he could drive. She did, and busied herself licking her own wounds, stopping only when she cut her tongue on a sliver of glass.

Gene's hands shook so badly I wonder how he managed. Dimitri couldn't help. He had all he could do to protect the crane and keep it alive while they headed home.

My mind was so with my jaguar I was unaware of anything going on around me in the house. I heard voices only dimly as though from a great distance. I kept my eyes closed to avoid the dizzying feeling of seeing things here and at the same time there, through my jaguar's eyes.

When they arrived and my jaguar bounded from the car, shook herself to clear off the glass in her fur, and bounded into the house and up the stairs to my bed, I felt great relief. I opened my eyes to see her race through the door into my room and leap toward the bed.

She faded in midleap as I reabsorbed her essence. I didn't absorb the glass shards still clinging to her fur. They remained on the quilt along with dirt and a bit of blood that wasn't hers.

Grandmother Blass carefully gathered up the quilt and carried it from the room, leaving me covered only with a sheet. But she returned in minutes with another quilt.

"I don't need that," I said. "I'm getting up. How's Henrietta? Did the crane make it?"

"Yes, thanks to your jaguar. Henrietta's mother is with her. You stay right there." As she spoke, she unfolded the quilt and put it over me. I let her, enjoying the new experience of being fussed over.

"She's very weak," Grandmother continued. "The crane was badly injured, and of course Henrietta has absorbed those injuries. Her mother says she'll heal, but it will take a few days."

I'd forgotten about Henrietta's mother being a doctor, the doctor who'd tended me.

"Henrietta would have died along with her crane. We'd have lost them both if it hadn't been for your jaguar." She bent and kissed my cheek.

Of course my jaguar had to save the crane. My conscience was really kicking me. I felt obligated to say, "If I'd followed her instructions and not let my jaguar out, she wouldn't have been hurt."

"You must not carry guilt. You could not have known that Henrietta would send her crane after your jaguar. Henrietta has always acted on impulse, and she is often overly protective of her patients. But having only just met her, you did not know those things about her."

She made me feel better, but she also aroused my curiosity. How did Grandmother Blass know so much about what I'd done and what had happened? I hadn't been in any condition to say much since releasing my jaguar. I certainly couldn't have told anyone. And neither could Henrietta. Yet Grandmother seemed to know all about it, as if she'd been there. She must have some kind of sixth sense.

I'd have asked about it, but Gene burst into the room, dashed to my bedside, and planted a big kiss first on my cheek and then on my lips. My response was entirely involuntary. I think.

"Sharl, you were great!" he said. "We'd've been killed if it hadn't been for you. For your jaguar."

"You were darn good yourself," I responded, my cheeks hot, probably blushing. "I'll never know how you kept from crashing the car. You were all covered with glass and blood, and I thought we were going to die."

"Superficial cuts. Had a hard time steering with the wheel slick with blood. But never mind that. I've got good news." Somehow he'd gotten hold of my hands and was holding them tightly in his.

"What news?" Grandmother Blass's question reminded me of her presence.

Grandfather entered in time to answer. "We may have located Marko. Georges called an officer friend of ours on the police force, and the friend checked and found which hospital they took the stabbing victim to. Georges told him he thought he might

know the victim. The bad news is that Marko, if it is
he, is in a coma. He carried no identification, so they
know him only as 'John Doe.' Not only did he lose a
lot of blood, but he hit his head on the pavement
when he fell. He has a severe concussion. Dimitri and
Rhonda have already left for the hospital. The officer
Georges spoke with has arranged permission for
Dimitri to see Marko just long enough to identify
him. The police will be present, of course. They have
kept him under guard for his protection, since the
perpetrator has not been apprehended."

I didn't miss that he said "Dimitri will be allowed
to see him" and not "Dimitri and Rhonda." So why
was Ronnie along?

"I wasn't trusted to go," Gene said bitterly, his
hands tightening around mine.

"Now, Gene, that is not true," Grandfather
soothed. "Dimitri has known Marko longer than any
of the rest of us and was closer to him. And you were
getting your cuts tended to. You've had quite an
evening. It is late. You should rest. And so should
Charlotte."

I'd lost track of the time. I looked around and
spotted a clock on a table. Almost midnight. "Will
they let them into the hospital this late?"

"The police are most eager to identify the victim
so that they may find clues that may lead them to the
perpetrator. They will meet Dimitri and Ronnie and
escort them to Marko's room, but only Dimitri will be
allowed to enter unless there is doubt about the
identification. In that case they may call Ronnie in to
verify it."

Grandfather's explanation may have made sense

to the rest, but not to me. "Why'd he take Ronnie? Why not take Lisette?"

"Ronnie had not yet retired. She was dressed and ready to go. Lisette was in bed, asleep."

Ready to go? Of course she was.

All this time Gene hadn't let go of my hands. It's good he didn't know how my thoughts lingered on Dimitri.

But maybe he did. He said, "Dimitri feels sorry for Ronnie because she isn't were."

I was tempted to tell him she *was* were, but I held my tongue, knowing the professor was studying the problem of why the animal spirit might remain asleep. I'd been informed that Grandfather would decide when and how Ronnie should be told about it.

"I must go and see how Henrietta is doing," Grandmother Blass said. "Martin, Gene, you should leave, too, and let Charlotte get her rest."

"No, it's all right," I said. "I want to know how Henrietta is, too. Let me come with you." I started to get out of bed.

"Stay here," Grandmother ordered sharply. "I'll come and tell you. If she can leave Henrietta, Dr. Horshaw would probably like to check you over. You stay right in that bed."

Gene grinned and sat on the side of the bed. "I'll see that she does."

Grandfather frowned and said, "No, Gene, you leave. I'll stay with Charlotte until Velma returns."

Grudgingly Gene released my hands and walked slowly to the door. I felt sorry to see him go.

I liked Gene. Liked his good looks. Loved the contrast between his dark hair and blue eyes. I found

him pleasant, easy to talk to. And clearly interested in
me. So why couldn't I stop thinking about Dimitri?
Why did Dimitri turn me on?

"Gene is quite taken with you," Grandfather
observed.

I didn't want to pursue that, but I did want
something else. "Do you think I could see Henrietta?"
I asked. "I can't rest until I see for myself that she's
going to be okay."

"I will ask Dr Horshaw if she would mind if you
went in just for a moment or two." Grandfather left
the room but was gone only a minute or two.

"The doctor has no objections. Henrietta has
awakened and asked to see you."

I got out of bed and into my robe and slippers
before you could say "Boo!"

The room was right across the hall from mine.
Helene's, they'd said. Not Helene and Jeffrey's. I
wondered about that.

I guess they hadn't wanted to move Henrietta
when her condition was so grave.

She lay in the bed, eyes barely open. Waiting for
me. "Charlotte." In a voice hardly more than a
whisper she said, "So glad you're all right."

Thinking of me after all I'd put her through? "I'm
glad you're going to be okay and so sorry I didn't
follow your orders."

"Wouldn't have known …" Her voice trailed off.

A woman stepped out of the shadows. She was
tall and slim like Henrietta, but no crane or other
animal spirit hid inside her. "Please don't tire her. She
must rest." She came to me and shook my hand. "I'm
Dr. Horshaw, Henrietta's mother — and her doctor."

"I'm grateful to you for patching me up. And sorry I got your daughter into so much trouble."

"But I understand you also saved her. Thank you."

"And now, thanks to you, we know more about who our enemies are and where they are based." I hadn't known that Grandfather had followed me into the room until he spoke.

"And there are fewer of them," I added grimly.

"Yes, and the police will be looking for the killers. We must be very careful."

"It was self-defense," I said. "They meant to kill Henrietta's crane and my jaguar. To sacrifice us." I shuddered, picturing the crane on the table, the reverend standing over her with a big knife. "What kind of church has sacrifices? What kind of reverend …?" I shook my head. I couldn't finish.

"My poor crane," Henrietta murmured. "If you hadn't saved her …"

"Hush, dear. It's over. Go to sleep." Her mother smoothed her forehead and kissed her cheek.

To me and Grandfather, Dr. Horshaw said, "You need to leave now. In the morning she'll feel more like talking."

I went back to my room. Grandfather came with me only as far as the door. "You are all right now? You can sleep?"

"Yes, I think I can." Suddenly, I could hardly stay awake. The relief of seeing for myself that Henrietta was alive and beginning to recover let me feel my own exhaustion. Grandfather closed the door, and I stepped out of my slippers and tumbled into bed, still wearing my robe.

I fell almost immediately into a light doze from which I was jarred by a loud scream. Had I dreamed it?

The second scream told me I hadn't.

10
NIGHT OF HORROR

I got up, pulled on my slippers, and ran into the hall. Dr. Horshaw came out of the next room at the same time.

"Who screamed?" we both asked. I was relieved to know the screamer hadn't been Henrietta or her mother.

Grandfather thundered up the steps with Grandmother following on his heels. So neither of them had screamed.

Nor Gene. He came down the hall toward us.

"Check on your parents," Grandfather ordered Gene. "I'll check on Cameron and Joy."

My intuition led me to follow Grandfather. He knocked on a door, listened, and pushed the door open.

Blood everywhere!

The light gray wolf tore at someone on the bed. Someone else was moaning.

Grandfather slipped down, his back against the wall. His aurochs thundered out just as a lynx darted into the room.

I slumped to the floor and let my jaguar loose.

A dark wolf leaps to the jaguar's side. They advance on the gray wolf.

The gray wolf stands over its prey, snarling and baring its teeth. The lynx creeps along the other side of the bed, poised to leap. The aurochs stands at the foot of the bed, lowers its massive head, hooks its horns beneath the bed, and heaves.

The bed flips on its side. Wolf and victim slide onto the floor. The jaguar and the dark wolf land on the gray wolf at the same time. The lynx follows. The jaguar's jaws find the wolf's throat. She's poised to bite down, hard.

The Grandfather's voice stops her. She looks around. The aurochs is gone. The Grandfather stands in the doorway.

"Do not kill!" he shouts. "Subdue it, but do not kill."

The jaguar releases the wolf's throat. Her weight and that of the dark wolf hold it down. The lynx crouches beside them.

On the floor is a bloody corpse. A woman's. From a dark corner creeps a man. He is bleeding badly.

The doctor comes into the room. She glances at the wolf, takes in its victim, and hurries to the bleeding man. "Get these creatures out of here so I can work on Cameron," she says.

To the lynx the Grandfather says, "Go back to Helene. Now!"

The lynx hesitates, then slowly obeys.

To the jaguar and the dark wolf he says, "Hold the wolf down while I fetch help."

He hurries from the room. Moments later the jaguar hears the clop of hooves. A horse prances into the room. The Grandfather walks beside it, brings it to a stop.

"We must bind the wolf and lift it onto the horse's back. You must hold it still so that we can do so."

The jaguar understands. She mouths the wolf's neck but does not bite down. The threat plus her weight across his body keep him lying still. The dark wolf growls from behind her, adding his weight to hers.

Someone brings rope. The dark wolf and the jaguar shift positions enough to allow someone to bind the wolf's front legs together. They shift again to allow its hind legs to be bound. The jaguar rises first, followed by the wolf. A loop of rope joins the two bindings. "He is secured," the Grandfather says. "You may return to your hosts."

The wolf grumbles low and angry, but he, like the jaguar, obeys the Grandfather.

I pushed away from the wall and got to my feet. Not far from me Gene was doing the same.

Someone near us was sobbing the word, "Why? Why?"

I turned. Helene clung to Jeffrey, repeating the question over and over. He stroked her back, not trying to answer. Probably he had no answer. I remembered the words the jaguar had heard Dimitri say in the church: *The wolf has gone feral.* I didn't know that could happen. But if its host was in a coma, possibly near death, and in no condition to direct his wolf, then maybe …

I could hear the clop of the horse's hooves but couldn't see where it had gone. Grandfather must have followed. Jeffrey, too, left Helene and headed after Grandfather and Georges's horse.

Grandmother went to Helene and patted her shoulder. "We'll find out why. But at least Cameron is alive. I'm going to see what I can do to help Dr. Horshaw."

She passed Gene and me on her way into the death room. "Good work, both of you," she said without stopping.

Helene turned and walked away. I didn't see where she went.

Gene came to me, shaking. "Cameron and I don't always get along, but he's my brother. To see him hurt like that. And Joy killed ..." He shook his head.

I hugged him. "I never got to meet Joy. I'm sorry."

Truthfully, I wasn't sure of that. Knowing Joy would have made the bloody scene even more horrible. "She wasn't were, I think you told me?"

"Not were, that's right." Gene leaned against the wall. "Very few weres live in this area outside the family. And it's hard to find a nonwere who can accept what we are. Besides the fact that we try to keep it secret."

"But she knew? Before she married Cameron?"

"Yes. She knew."

I waited for more, but there was no more. Gene stared off into space, saying nothing, a faraway look in his eyes.

I guess Dimitri was right about Marko's wolf going feral. We might know more about that when Dimitri returned with Ronnie. I couldn't get over being angry that he'd taken her along.

My jaguar didn't like it, either. She stirred within me. Wanting out.

Georges and Grandfather came down the hall,

distracting me and my jaguar. Good thing. I hoped they'd gotten the wolf confined someplace it couldn't escape from.

"How is Cameron?" Grandfather asked as he reached us.

Gene just stared into space acting like he hadn't heard, so I answered. "Dr. Horshaw's working with him. Grandmother Blass is with her. You could probably go in."

"Better not," Grandfather said. "Dr. Horshaw does not like anyone hovering over her when she works. And she rarely pauses to answer questions. When she can leave her patient, she will come and give us a report."

Apparently, Grandmother didn't hover.

I went to Gene and touched his arm. His wolf, I saw, was asleep. That could explain Gene's daze.

"I'm exhausted," I said. "You must be, too. Why don't you go get some sleep? I'm going to."

He focused bleary eyes on me and nodded. Georges stepped to his side and took his arm. "I'll see you to your room," he said.

"Cameron."

His brother's name seemed to be all he could manage, but the professor got it. "We'll come and wake you as soon as there's news," he promised.

Gene said nothing more, and Georges walked him to his room. Grandfather watched, and then turned to me. "Gene is suffering. If Cameron does not recover …" He shook his head sadly.

I didn't know what to say. Fortunately, Dr. Horshaw came out at that moment.

"I've got Cameron stabilized for now," she said.

"He can be moved to another room. I don't want him to wake and see what's left of his wife. We have her body covered, but he'd know what was under those sheets."

Grandfather swallowed. "My poor, poor boy," he said. "Georges will help me move Cameron as soon as he returns from getting Gene to his room. But where shall we take him?"

"Grandmother Blass said to put him in Henrietta's room, since Henrietta is using Helene's and Helene is helping me."

"Helene will stay in my … in our room tonight," I heard Jeffrey say. I hadn't seen him come back.

Georges returned, and he and Grandfather busied themselves with their new task, Dr. Horshaw advising and accompanying them.

I headed to my room, looking forward to some much-needed sleep. I wasn't sure I'd be able to sleep after all the horrors I'd seen but I meant to try. As I passed the stairwell, I heard footsteps and waited to see who it was.

Dimitri came into view, Ronnie clinging to his arm like a leech. Dimitri put his hand on the newel post and pulled himself up onto the landing. Dark shadows under his eyes showed that he, too, needed sleep after all he'd been through. And he—and Ronnie—didn't yet know about Joy and Cameron. Ronnie glared at me. She'd probably expected some other family member to greet her.

Dimitri'd stopped, still leaning on the post. "It was Marko, all right. Got to tell Grandfather. He still up?"

"Yeah, he'll be here soon."

"We'll go find him," Ronnie said, brushing past me, pulling Dimitri after her.

"Better wait. There's been a—" A what? An accident? A killing? I was too tired to think. I shouldn't be the one delivering the news.

Dimitri turned back to me, suddenly alert. "What happened?"

"Marko's wolf. It came here, got in somehow." I paused, willing Grandfather and Georges to get back and take over.

"Doesn't matter. What happened?" Dimitri's tone told me to quit stalling.

"He got into Cameron and Joy's room. He ... he mauled them both." I tried to stop there.

"And?" Dimitri's eyes were hard.

"Joy's dead. Dr. Horshaw is caring for Cameron."

Ronnie screamed and rounded on me. "This is all your fault. Everything was fine until you came. Since you got here we've had nothing but trouble. You've brought death into this house."

She tried to leap on me, but Dimitri restrained her. She fought to free herself. And within her, the animal stirred. Would it come out?

I backed away. I did *not* want to let my jaguar out. Whatever the animal I saw in Ronnie, it was smaller and, I was certain, a lot weaker than the jaguar.

We'd had enough killing tonight.

Ronnie was screaming, "Let me go. Let me at her." Dimitri could barely hold her.

Grandmother came running. So did Lisette. Where'd she come from? I'd forgotten about her. She had on a floor-length nightgown. Could she possibly have slept through all the noise?

"Here, what's going on?" Grandmother demanded, hurrying to confront Ronnie.

Ronnie's screams must have roused Roy, too. By now the whole house was awake. Roy pushed Grandmother aside, hauled back, and slammed his fist into Dimitri's face. I guess he misinterpreted Dimitri's attempt to hold Ronnie back. With both hands needed to hang on to her, Dimitri couldn't defend himself. So when Roy readied his arm for another strike, Dimitri let Ronnie go.

Ronnie shoved Grandmother to get to me. Grandmother would have fallen, but I caught and steadied her. Lisette, bless her, grabbed Ronnie from behind, jerking her backward.

That did it! "Ha, Ronnie! Go ahead, let your creature loose, and I'll turn my jaguar on it. Then we'll see—"

"You dare mock me? You know I don't have a 'creature'," Ronnie yelled, jerking free of Lisette.

"Oh, yes, you do! Can't you feel it? It's stretching, trying to get out."

"Bitch!" She reached around Grandmother, ready to claw my face.

And collapsed.

And suddenly everyone became very quiet and stared at the animal that emerged.

"It's a badger!" Grandmother exclaimed.

"She *is* were." That was her brother, who'd left off his fight with Dimitri to gape at the creature.

Dimitri edged nearer for a better look. "Damn!"

The animal stood in the middle of the group, looking confused and scared. And I couldn't control myself, I started to laugh. And laugh.

The creature had such a cute face. A white stripe ran from its long snout back between its ears to its neck. Other white stripes ran along the sides of its face below its ears and also ended at its neck. The rest of its body was gray.

A badger, Grandmother had called it. I'd never seen one. A werebadger. Imagine! I was practically shrieking with laughter.

The poor badger scrunched down, scuttled back to Ronnie, and faded into her.

"You scared it!" Lisette accused.

"I'd say we all did," Dimitri said, his voice a bit muffled because his jaw was swollen.

I found that funny, too. Couldn't stop laughing. Grandmother shook my shoulders. "Charlotte, get hold of yourself." Her stern voice only made me laugh harder, tears running down my face.

Grandmother slapped me. Hard. I hiccoughed and took a deep breath. Stopped laughing.

Ronnie sat up, looking dazed.

Lisette screamed. I saw the bear lumbering toward us. It advanced, teeth bared, eyes spitting fire.

Grandmother stepped out into its path. "Go back to Jeffrey," she ordered. "Everything is under control here. Go! Back!"

Afraid for Grandmother, I sat down, ready to let my jaguar out. But the bear stopped, eyed her for a few seconds, and turned. It went back, as ordered.

I wasn't the only one who let out a big sigh of relief.

Ronnie, though, was wailing. She got to her feet, went to Dimitri, threw her arms around him, and sobbed into his shoulder.

I couldn't figure out why she was bawling. She'd just found out she was were. Shouldn't she be happy?

And why did she have to soak Dimitri's shirt with her stupid tears when her brother stood right there next to him?

Then I heard what she was getting out between big, gulping sobs. "She … she … laughed … at … my poor … my badger. She laughed!"

"She didn't mean to," Grandmother said soothingly.

Ronnie wasn't soothed.

"I … hate … her. Why did … she … laugh?"

I shouldn't have laughed. I knew that. And Grandmother was right. I didn't mean to. I couldn't stop because I was so damn tired. But I didn't intend to explain that to Ronnie.

Grandfather came huffing and puffing down the hall so like the aurochs within him that I almost started laughing again, but the grim expression on his face stopped me.

"What is going on?" he demanded, his voice low and filled with fury. "Do you not know we have injured family members? How are they to sleep with all this racket? What is the matter with all of you? Velma, why have you not kept them quiet?"

"I never got the chance," she said in the sudden silence. "By the time I got here, they were in such a state no one would listen."

"Dimitri, I am eager to hear what you learned at the hospital. And instead of coming to me, I find you involved in a brawl. Charlotte, I thought you were going to bed. Lisette, what are you doing out of bed at this hour?"

"I wanted to hear about Marko," she whined.

"All right. Everyone. Go downstairs. Immediately. To the living room. Dimitri will make his report. And you will tell me what all this commotion was about."

Like naughty kids, we hung our heads and traipsed downstairs, no one speaking, no one looking at anyone else. Only when we got to the living room and found seats did I look around and see that not only all of us "noise makers" were gathered here, but the professor had joined us along with Grandfather. After that quick look, like all the others I fastened my gaze on Grandfather.

11
GRANDFATHER'S PROCLAMATION

We waited for Grandfather to speak. He took his time, making me more and more nervous, and I'd guess most of the others felt the same.

Finally he said, "Children, this house has not been a 'peaceable kingdom' this night." His gaze flicked briefly to the painting over the mantel. "We have serious problems to face. We must face them together. We must not be divided.

"So, I will hear what provoked the unseemly disturbance upstairs. And I will hear Dimitri's report on Marko. We will have an orderly discussion and make informed decisions."

Ronnie pointed at me. "She provoked the —"

"Rhonda," he interrupted, "we will have no such accusations. Put aside your anger, and let us have no more outbursts. Each of you will speak in turn as I give you leave to speak.

"Dimitri, your report now."

Dimitri cleared his throat and began: "Ronnie and I arrived at Community General Hospital and went inside, where we informed the attendant that the police were expecting us and asked her to notify them of our arrival."

So Dimitri was careful to include Ronnie in his report, though Grandfather had pointedly not included her. He continued, "A police officer came to meet us. After checking our identification, he escorted us to the floor Marko was on and asked Ronnie to wait at the nurses' station.

"He accompanied me to the room where the patient lay, hooked up to monitors and IVs. It was Marko, no question. I was only allowed to stay in the room long enough to identify him. Back in the hall, the officer informed me that when Marko fell after being stabbed, he hit his head on the curb. He's being kept in an induced coma to allow the swelling of his brain to subside. He is by no means out of danger, but the officer said the doctors seem optimistic. However, due to his condition they have, of course, been unable to question him, so they were most eager to question me and Ronnie not only about his identity but regarding his family, his habits, and any known enemies."

His glance cut to Gene and back to Grandfather so quickly that I wondered who else had even noticed. I felt sure Gene had.

"We told him that everyone had believed Marko drowned after a boating accident two years ago, though his body had never been found," Dimitri continued. "We had no indication throughout the past two years that he was alive."

We. He insisted on including Ronnie, though I was willing to bet that on their whole trip he did all the talking. She was just along for the ride. Or whatever.

"He wanted to know the details of Marko's supposed drowning, and I gave them to him. I saw no reason not to, since it was all on the record."

Grandfather nodded his approval. I'd like to have

heard those details, but since everyone else was familiar with them, I wasn't going to hear them. Maybe I could get Gene to fill me in later.

"We asked how to get permission to move Marko to a hospital where he could be seen by his own doctor. They told us we'd have to consult with the doctors who've been treating him, but the police officer didn't think it would be safe to move him any time soon."

"And Dr. Horshaw does not have privileges at Community General?" Grandfather must have already known the answer because he went right on. "We must find a way to get Marko's wolf back to him. Marko will not wake until we do that, and the wolf is extremely dangerous without his conscious guidance. You know," Grandfather looked directly at me as though he thought I might not know what he was about to reveal, "if a were animal is separated from its host for several weeks or months, it usually dies, but in some cases it gains independent existence as a feral creature. That seems to be what has happened here."

I knew that. It was one of the things my mentor taught me. But the wolf hadn't been out for weeks or months. It had been in Marko when he got stabbed. Even if it had come out right afterward, maybe when they were transferring Marko from the ambulance into the hospital, it had only been out a couple of days. But I didn't try to contradict Grandfather. I had all I could do to keep awake. Hard as I tried to keep them open, my eyelids kept wanting to close. I'd just about lost the struggle, when Grandfather called my name. Oh-oh! He'd caught me napping.

"Charlotte, what do you think? How can we return Marko's wolf to him before it is too late? If it is not too late already, and I must hope that it is not."

I had no idea, but I didn't dare say that. "We can't smuggle the wolf into the hospital," I said, thinking fast. "We would have to smuggle Marko out. And bring him here."

"Ah," Grandfather said. "A fine suggestion."

My pleasure at having won Grandfather's approval soured when Ronnie burst out with, "Don't trust her! She knew I'm were and didn't tell me! And when my ... my badger came out, she laughed at it and scared it back inside. She laughed, Grandfather!"

"I'm sorry," I said quickly. "I just ... I was so tired. It wasn't funny, I just couldn't stop myself."

"So your animal finally awoke and emerged, eh?" Grandfather asked, ignoring my feeble attempt to apologize.

"Yes, but she scared it, and what if it never comes out again?" Tears rolled down Ronnie's cheeks and she leaned against Dimitri for comfort. What a drama queen!

Dimitri slid his arm around her and said, "We're all exhausted, Grandfather. Not acting rationally. I'm sure Sharl meant no disrespect."

"Possibly not, but it is very serious if the animal — a badger, you say? — fears to reemerge."

"She had no right to laugh," Ronnie persisted, the tears flowing faster.

Grandmother came to my defense. "Charlotte was hysterical, and no wonder after all she'd been through."

"But she brought it all on herself. She caused all

the trouble," Ronnie accused. "If she hadn't disobeyed Henrietta and sent her off on an errand and let out her jaguar, Henrietta's crane wouldn't have followed and they wouldn't have got caught and—"

"And we wouldn't have found the people who've tried to kill us," Gene said.

"Maybe," Ronnie said. "And maybe the wolf wouldn't have followed us here and killed Joy and nearly killed Cameron."

Oh, God! I hadn't thought of that.

"You don't know that the wolf followed us," Dimitri said. "It's Marko's wolf. It knows where the house is. Maybe it thought Marko would be here."

"It's gone feral," Gene pitched in, speaking to Grandfather. "You said it yourself."

"In that case it may be too late to restore it to Marko," the professor said.

Grandfather frowned. "We must trust that it is not too late. The wolf, though restrained, will remain extremely dangerous until he can reunite with Marko.

"So," he paused and looked at me, "there is truth to what Ronnie says—you should not have disobeyed the orders left by your doctor and conveyed to you by your nurse. You have, in truth, put us all in grave danger.

"I gave you the assignment to find the stabbing victim. You identified him, but it was not you who found him. So I give you a new assignment. Devise a plan for smuggling Marko from the hospital and getting him back here without making his condition worse."

I gasped. How was I going to do that?

"You must rest first. I understand that. We all need sleep, though some of us have a most unpleasant task to perform first. We must dispose of Joy's body. It cannot be taken to a funeral home because the manner of her death would bring an unwelcome investigation that would reveal our were nature. Joy must be buried where she cannot be found. You have no part in that, Charlotte. Get what sleep you can in the few hours of night remaining. That goes for all of you. Georges will assist me in doing what we must. And the story will be that Joy left abruptly, and we have no idea where she has gone."

He stood, a signal the conference had ended. We all got to our feet. Ronnie and Lisette were both glaring at me, and Gene had reverted to the numb state he'd fallen into earlier.

But Grandfather had one thing more to say to us. He gestured toward the painting over the mantel. "Remember, all of you, this is a *Peaceable Kingdom*."

Ha!

I headed for the stairs. Gene stumbled against me as I passed him. I steadied him and slipped my arm around his waist. He leaned against me. We stood like that while Dimitri and Ronnie passed us. Dimitri paused. I thought he wanted to say something, but Ronnie tugged his arm and drew him on to the stairs.

Lisette passed us, too. "Bitch!" she whispered, but I heard.

Gene heard, too, and seemed to pull himself together. "Shut up, Lisette!" he hissed. "We wouldn't know about Marko if it wasn't for her."

"We haven't got him back yet," Lisette said,

turning to glare at us. "Do you really think she can do what Grandfather asked?"

"I have a better chance than you would," I retorted before Gene could speak.

"Children! Upstairs!" Grandfather's gruff voice cut off any further exchanges. With a toss of her head Lisette turned and climbed the stairs. We followed more slowly, Gene still leaning on me. Hearing no one on the steps behind us, I turned enough to see that Grandfather had paused at the foot of the stairs and was speaking very quietly to the professor, while Grandmother stood behind them. Waiting, I guessed, to see what they were going to do about Joy.

My room was just off the stairs, and when we reached it, I said, "Gene, you want to come in?"

He squeezed my arm. I took that as a yes. I closed the door behind us.

Was I doing this because I feel sorry for Gene? Or to make Dimitri jealous? At this point I didn't care.

Gene sat on the edge of my bed and watched while I got undressed. He fumbled with the buttons on his shirt. I went to him, helped him get out of his clothes. As tired as we both were and given Gene's dazed state, I didn't expect this to lead to anything. I figured he just needed to be with someone right now.

We tumbled into bed and lay close to each other, and I closed my eyes, relaxed, ready for sleep. My head was against Gene's shoulder; his hand rested on my side. He stroked my bare skin, found my breast, caressed it.

I shifted to one side. He nibbled my earlobe. I swung around to face him. He pressed his lips into the hollow at the base of my neck, moved down until his lips closed around my nipple. It hardened as his tongue teased it. His hands moved down along my thighs, parted my legs.

"No, Gene. No."

I didn't convince him—or myself.

His tongue was warm on my breasts. His fingers probed, stroked. My "No, no" changed to "Yes. Oh, yes!"

He slid inside, and I rose to meet his thrusts. My fingers dug into his back as I rode the rising wave until he came, pulled out, and left me panting and sobbing and wanting more.

He collapsed beside me and his breathing slowed, evened. He'd fallen asleep!

For me sleep didn't come.

12
RIVALS

I hadn't meant to hook up with Gene. It was the stress of all that had happened, the evening's horrors, the anger and hatred I felt from Lisette and Ronnie.

I kept hearing Ronnie: "This is all your fault. Everything was fine until you came. You've brought death into this house."

Was she right? Had I brought all the trouble?

Coming here wasn't my idea. I'd been ordered to come. So why should I feel guilty?

I *did* bear the responsibility for the injuries to Henrietta's crane. And I *had* laughed at Ronnie's badger. And by identifying the man I saw stabbed, I'd stirred up a whole lot of bad feelings.

Those feelings had lain there beneath the surface. I hadn't created them. So why should I feel guilty?

I should and did feel guilty about having sex with Gene not out of affection but to satisfy my own need. I tried to tell myself it was a response to his need after what he'd been through—nearly getting shot, having to run down in his car the man who was trying to kill us, seeing his brother hurt and his sister-in-law killed.

No. I can't think about that. I need to get my mind on something else. Like how to do the job Grandfather expects of me. If I can come up with a plan and if it works, maybe I can stop feeling guilty. Maybe.

I only slept a couple of hours. When I woke up, in late morning, Gene had gone. Before falling asleep I'd come up with a plan. It depended on getting Dr. Horshaw's help. So I got up, showered, and looked for something to wear that wasn't all wrinkled from being stuffed into a laundry bag too long. I settled on a black miniskirt and pale pink peasant blouse. After dressing, I headed for the kitchen, where I found Grandmother fixing lunch or late breakfast. The woman seemed to spend all her time cooking for and cleaning up after this brood.

"Good morning, Grandmother. Where can I find Dr. Horshaw?"

Grandmother looked up from the pot she was stirring. She frowned as she took in my outfit but answered, "She's gone home to get some rest after being up all night caring for Cameron. She got him stabilized. Then she checked on Henrietta, who's doing much better. She needed a couple hours of sleep before seeing some patients who have appointments. She'll be back midafternoon."

Great! That would give me time to eat breakfast and enlist help. I sat down, and Grandmother set a plate of eggs and bacon in front of me and followed it with a cup of hot black coffee. Just what I needed! I stirred a spoonful of sugar into the coffee, took a sip, and picked up my fork.

"Ah, Charlotte," Grandfather strode into the kitchen, scowling. He waved a newspaper. "Have you seen this?"

I shook my head.

"This will spoil your appetite, I fear." He spread the paper out on the table beside my plate and pointed to a photo in the center of the front page. It showed the interior of the church where my jaguar and Marko's wolf, along with Dimitri and Gene, had our nearly fatal adventure. Of course the photo didn't show the church the way we'd left it—littered with corpses. The bodies had been removed. Chalk marks showed faintly on the floor of the aisle.

Massacre in Church, the headline screamed. Below that, in smaller type, *Four killed, one wounded*.

Four killed. I did some quick math. There had been four men down inside the church, the man outside that Gene ran over, and the two men my jaguar had killed to escape from the garage. Those two may have been disposed of before the police arrived. But if the count of four included the man outside, then someone inside the church must have survived. I read the article.

A grisly scene greeted police who were called to investigate a hit-and-run that left a man dead on the side of a residential street. The crash occurred in front of the nondenominational Christian Witness Church.

Hoping to gain information about the crash and finding its doors open, police entered the church. Inside the sanctuary they found three men dead and one severely wounded. The wounded man has been identified as the church pastor, the Rev. Hanley Carlisle. The identities of the dead men have not been released. The police did reveal that the pastor and one of the dead men inside the church had been shot, but they refused to comment on the cause of death of the other two, saying only that it was under investigation.

The police have yet to determine whether the hit-and-run death is connected to the deaths inside the church. The car would have a badly damaged front end and a missing windshield. Anyone seeing or knowing anything about such a car is asked to get in touch with the police department immediately.

Telephone numbers followed.

After reading through the report twice, I looked up at Grandfather. "Can they find the car? Will they find us?"

"They won't find the car," he said without the slightest trace of doubt. "As for finding us, I don't know. The pastor who survived may be the one who planned the ambush that caught your jaguar and Henrietta's crane and was quite likely also responsible for the shots fired at you and Dimitri. We must assume he knows exactly who we are—and what we are. He can lead the police right to us if he chooses to."

Wonderful! We may all spend the rest of our lives in prison. "What are we going to do?"

"I am thinking on that." Grandfather took a seat opposite me, beckoned to Grandmother. "Coffee, please."

She set a steaming mug in front of him. He blew on it and put it to his lips without benefit of cream or sugar. Grandmother picked up the newspaper and read the article, shaking her head as she did so.

"The first thing we must do is retrieve Marko," Grandfather said. "That is your task, Charlotte. Have you decided how to accomplish it?"

"I have a plan, but I need to ask Dr. Horshaw—"

"The doctor is not to be involved," Grandfather broke in, glaring at me over the rim of his cup. He might at least have heard me out.

"She wouldn't be," I said. "I only need her to get a couple of outfits—scrubs, like orderlies wear. And an order form that we could fix up to look like Marko was being transferred to another hospital for specialized treatment. She'd have nothing to do with the actual grab. She wouldn't show her face in the hospital where Marko is."

Grandfather sipped his coffee, considering. Finally he said, "No. The risk is too great. If you are apprehended, the outfits could possibly be traced to her."

"Now, Martin, it's not a bad plan," Grandmother said, putting the newspaper back on the table. You should leave it up to Emmaline to—"

"You know how good-hearted Emmaline Horshaw is. And she would feel obligated because of Henrietta. No. I will not permit it." He slammed his mug down on the table, sending coffee splashing over the side.

"Martin!" Grandmother scolded, wiping up the spill with a paper towel. "You're being foolish. We are all in danger, and you say we must get Marko before doing anything else. And that Charlotte must do it. Very well then, don't put roadblocks in her way. Her plan is good. Do you have a better one?"

Scowling, Grandfather pushed away from the table. "It is her job to come up with a plan," he grumbled.

"She's done that," Grandmother persisted. "Now let her carry it out."

I dug into my eggs and bacon. No way would I butt into their argument. Yes, it concerned me, and that's exactly why I kept quiet. I didn't stand a chance of winning against Grandfather. But Grandmother did.

Grandfather stalked to the door. There he turned and glared at Grandmother. "You think it is right to involve Emmaline?"

"I think if you don't give Emmaline a chance to make up her own mind, and she learns of it, she will not be pleased. And if you hinder Charlotte in this way, we may all suffer."

I don't know what Grandfather would have said. Gene slouched in, pushing past Grandfather as if he didn't see him. He had on jeans and a dirty T-shirt. He pulled out the chair opposite mine and slumped into it, looking like a corpse somebody had propped up there as a joke.

Some joke!

Grandfather didn't seem to notice his grandson's state, but Grandmother did. She hurried to Gene and put her hands on his shoulders. "You didn't get any sleep again, I suppose," she said, massaging his shoulders. "Your grandfather didn't, either. That's why he's being so cranky this morning."

She raised her eyes to me as she said that. I didn't have much sympathy. Gene had got a lot more sleep than I had, but I could hardly tell Grandmother that. I just kept my mouth busy finishing my eggs.

Grandmother spoke to me directly. "Do what you have to do, Charlotte. I'm sure Dr. Horshaw will be glad to help."

Having eaten all the breakfast I wanted, I stood up. "When will she be here?"

"I don't know, but you can call her on her cell phone. I'll give you the number."

Gene didn't look up or act like he knew what was going on around him until I called Dr. Horshaw on the kitchen phone and explained my need. Then he sat up straight and listened.

As Grandmother had predicted, Dr. Horshaw was willing to help me. She'd arrive here in an hour or two. We'd go through my list then, and she'd tell me whether she could get the things I needed.

"I'm going with you, Sharl," Gene said.

"You don't look—"

"I know how I look. Doesn't matter. I'll be okay."

I didn't say anything. He wasn't the companion I would have preferred, but I doubted Dimitri'd be available.

Gene took the piece of buttered toast Grandmother offered, saying, "At least get something into your stomach." He ate it quickly, and stood up.

"Let me know what the plans are," he told me as he left the kitchen.

"He feels so guilty," Grandmother said when he was well away. "He and Cameron had fought just before you came here. He told Cameron some things about Joy that, well …" She hesitated, then continued, "they were true enough, but it wasn't the way Cameron should have learned them."

Grandmother gathered my dishes and carried them to the sink, rinsed them, and put them into the dishwasher. I waited, hoping to learn more, but apparently Grandmother figured she'd said enough. My place here wasn't secure enough to let me ask a lot of questions.

I stood, stretched, and headed for the stairs, no particular destination in mind. Just restless.

Halfway up the stairway I met Dimitri coming down. His face lit up. "Sharl! I was just looking for you."

"You were?" Be still, my heart!

"I wanted to ask your plans for getting Marko out of the hospital. Whatever you come up with, count me in."

"I have a plan, but it may be dangerous." Why did I think that would deter him?

It didn't, of course. "All the more reason I should help," he said, gazing at me with those ice-blue eyes.

"Gene's going to help me. He insisted."

Dimitri frowned. "Do you think that's a good idea?"

"I think it's something he needs to do."

"That may not be for the reason you think." He looked upstairs and down. No one else was in sight. Even so, he lowered his voice to a whisper. "You know Gene was blamed for Marko's supposed death. He was accused of murder. The charge was dropped because of lack of evidence, but he's remained under suspicion."

"But Marko's not dead," I said, shifting around to lean against the railing. "That should clear him."

"Of murder, yes. But not necessarily of attempted murder. Nobody knows what happened on the boat that day. Nobody but Gene—and Marko. We know what Gene told us—that with the boat on autopilot he'd gone to use the head, came up, didn't see Marko, and looked all over the boat before deciding Marko had somehow fallen overboard. He turned the boat around and tried for several hours to find him but couldn't—but without Marko to corroborate his story, well, it's just that—a story. It may or may not be true."

"Well, when Marko recovers, he can tell you."

"That's my point. Gene may not want Marko to recover."

"You don't know that—" I began indignantly.

"No, I don't. But consider this. For two years we've thought Marko dead. He's never contacted anyone here to let us know he was still alive. Why? Why hide from us? Unless letting us all think he was dead was his way of keeping safe."

"That doesn't make sense. If Gene had tried to kill him, why wouldn't Marko come back here and accuse him and let the family protect him from Gene."

A bitter smile accompanied Dimitri's words. "Gene *is* family, Charlotte. He's a biological Blass grandson, not an 'honorary' one like Marko, like me, like Lisette, like Henrietta. Like you."

"And like Roy and Ronnie," I added thoughtfully. "Okay, I get that. But would it really make a difference?"

"Of course it— Hush! Someone's coming." He came down two more steps, grabbed my arm, and hustled me down the rest of the steps, into the dining room, and through it into the kitchen.

"Dima," called a voice I recognized all too well. Ronnie! "Dima, where are you?"

Dimitri hustled me past Grandmother, who pointedly took no notice, and through the door into the garage. By this time we were practically running.

"In here." Dima opened a door and pulled me into a small toolroom. He closed the door behind us without turning on the light, leaving us in complete darkness. He drew me against the wall next to the door, pressed a finger against my lips, and held it there.

Ronnie's footsteps tapped loudly against the cement floor of the garage. "Dima, are you in here?" she called. "Dima?" Her steps drew closer.

The door opened but we hid in a shadowed corner. I held my breath. If she came into the room to look, she'd see us even without turning on the light. And what a fit she'd pitch!

But she stepped back outside, closing the door. We stayed statue-still until her footsteps faded into the distance. The toolroom was hot and stuffy, but the heat I felt wasn't just from the close quarters.

Dimitri took his finger from my lips and cupped my chin in his hand. His lips pressed against mine. His tongue explored my mouth. My arms slid around his waist. If the fireworks had gone off outside my head instead of in it, the toolroom would have lit up like Times Square on New Year's Eve. What brought this on? Didn't matter. I didn't want it to stop.

I was gasping when we finally came up for air. His arms went around me, hands clasping my butt. His breath heated my face. My shoulders pressed against the wall, my back arched. He lifted me up. My legs wound around his, my hands dug into his shoulders. His mouth was back against mine; my teeth nipped his lips. His hands slid up my thighs to the edge of my panties.

I was so ready! Forget the dark, stuffy toolroom. For all I cared we could be on a beach or in a forest. Or on a comet racing among stars. The only two people in the universe.

His mouth drew free of mine. "Sharl," he whispered, his voice caressing my ear, promising, offering ... "Sharl, I *will* go with you to Community General."

The stars crashed down around me. My feet hit the floor.

"Is that what this is about?" I went from trembling with desire to shaking with rage. I pushed him away from me and groped for the door. "That was what this was for? To get me to take you instead of Gene?"

"No, Sharl. No." He sounded so contrite. The worm! "I just ... just got carried away. So close to you ... I lost control."

The oh-so-cool leopard guy lost control? Hah! "You were playing me." I found the doorknob, got the door open, stepped out into the garage.

"No ... it's just ... not the way ... not the place. I wanted ..."

"You wanted to break down my resistance," I snapped, sudden tears filling my eyes. "And you damn well did. And then— Why did you think you could work me that way?"

"Gene did."

I stared at him, speechless. He knew I'd slept with Gene. And thought ...

I spun around and stormed from the garage through the kitchen, empty thankfully, and up the stairs to my room, flung myself across the bed, and sobbed.

13
THE PLAN

I didn't know I'd fallen asleep until I woke up to someone knocking at the door. Dimitri?

It must be. I got up and yanked open the door.

Dr. Horshaw stepped back, startled, I guess, by my expression. "I thought you were waiting for me. And I want to check your shoulder, see how the wound is healing," she said.

"I'm sorry. I thought … I was expecting someone else. How's Henrietta?"

"Doing much better. In fact, she's well enough to look after Cameron." She bustled in and had me lie on the bed while she removed the bandages from my shoulder. "I've spoken to Grandmother Blass. I'm not sure what Grandfather has asked you to do is possible, but I'll help you in any way I can. After all, you saved Henrietta's life."

"Thanks, Dr. Horshaw. You're being very kind, considering that my actions put Henrietta in danger."

"Nonsense. You did what you thought right. Henrietta decided on her own to send her crane after your jaguar. A rather foolish decision, in my opinion."

"But I tricked her into leaving me alone so I could let my jaguar out. I knew she'd object if she knew what I was going to do."

"Forget all that. Tell me what you need."

Her willingness to help and her insistence that she didn't blame me for what happened to Henrietta's crane pleased and relieved me. I lost no time explaining my plan and listing the items I hoped she could get for me.

"I can do all that," she said. "It will take a bit of time. I'll try to have it for you tomorrow by midmorning. Today you still need to rest and let that shoulder finish healing. If you weren't were, you'd need much more time, but I'm sure you realize that. I'm always amazed at how quickly weres recover from serious injuries. Cameron would be dead if he didn't have his animal spirit to help him heal. Instead, he's already wanting to be up on his feet."

That was good news. And I didn't object to waiting another day before attempting to steal Marko out of the hospital. My shoulder wasn't bothering me, but I hadn't recovered in other ways from the last horrendous adventure. I needed more rest and time to steel my nerves for the next endeavor.

I went downstairs and found Grandfather Blass in the living room reading. I explained the delay.

As much as Grandfather had been against my plan, he now was impatient and upset about having to postpone it one more day. "I'm worried, Charlotte. Very worried. I have a presentiment, a feeling, *ja?* that we face terrible danger. That trouble will strike us very soon."

I couldn't disagree. I could only point out that we had to have the help only Dr. Horshaw could provide, and she couldn't get what we needed before tomorrow.

Tired as I felt, I was also restless. I disliked waiting as much as Grandfather. I needed something to do. I'd seen nothing of Dimitri since the scene in the toolroom. Gene, too, seemed to be avoiding me. Grandmother said he was catching up on his sleep, adding, "And you should be catching up on yours."

But if I slept any more during the day, I wouldn't sleep tonight. I wandered around the house, exploring parts I hadn't seen. Downstairs I found a game room and a computer room where I surprised Jeffrey. He'd been working on something he apparently didn't want me to see, because he minimized the window as I approached and said, "Oh, hello, Charlotte," in a dismissive tone that clearly meant, "Goodbye, Charlotte."

"Didn't mean to disturb you," I said. "I didn't know anyone was in here. How's Cameron?"

"Doing better, thank you." He sat stiffly, all too obviously waiting for me to leave before returning to whatever it was he'd been doing. The room was lined with bookshelves, and I'd have loved to find a book to read to take my mind off the interminable waiting. But rather than add another member to the Enemies of Charlotte Society, I left to continue my exploration.

Beyond the computer room along one side of the hall were two more bedrooms with baths. Across from them was a large walk-in linen closet. I walked in. With its wide shelves lining both sides from floor to ceiling I could be prowling through a linen store. Sheets, pillowcases, blankets, bedspreads, and bed skirts were all neatly arranged on the shelves along one side, while the other side held tablecloths, place mats, napkins in one section and towels, face towels, and washcloths in another. The aisle between the shelves ended in a blank wall—no shelves there, just a grate on the wall about eye level. Curious, I peered through it and got a view of a good portion of the kitchen. I could see Grandmother Blass seated at the table going through her recipe file, probably planning tonight's dinner.

Not interested in watching, I left the linen closet and walked past it to the last room off the hall. That room was long and narrow and carpeted, but furnished only with a single lounge chair. I entered and regarded its rear wall. I recognized the room as the one Dimitri's leopard and my jaguar had come into using the secret entrance for the were animals' use. Secret because neither here nor outside the house could anyone tell that an entrance existed. Yet when the door opened, it opened widely enough to allow even the aurochs to pass through.

I'd like to discover the key to opening it. Dima's leopard had made the door open when he and my jaguar returned. I guess the secret was only revealed to permanent family members. Would I ever be one?

Maybe I could figure out the key. The latch had to be something easy for any of the animals to use. Which meant it had to be close to the floor or ground and easily manipulated by a paw or hoof or beak.

I walked to the back wall and studied the area just above the floor. The latch couldn't be on the floor because the carpet would cover it. And it had to be something that could be pushed or kicked.

I couldn't spot anything. But I knew who could.

I sat in the lounge chair, relaxed, and let out my jaguar. She walked to the wall and sniffed along the baseboard. She stopped, and through her eyes I saw the merest indentation about a foot above the floor. She didn't use her paw; she stuck her nose into the indentation and pressed upward. A tall, wide panel swung open. She looked back at me, wanting to go out but knowing I wanted her to return to me.

I let her go—just for a few moments. I wanted to know how to close the door and also how to open it from outside. I might need that knowledge.

She'd gone only about a yard away when the door swung closed automatically. She walked a bit farther, but then returned to the wall. Again, no door was visible. Through the jaguar's eyes I watched her prowl along the wall, moving slowly.

Ronnie entered the room, stopped short when she saw me. Distracted, I missed what the jaguar did to make the door swing open. Ronnie stared as the jaguar entered and stopped. The panel swung closed.

Hands on her hips, Ronnie glared at both of us. The jaguar growled low and ran forward. Ronnie gave a little scream and retreated to the hall.

The jaguar ran to me and faded into me. I sat up and turned toward Ronnie, who lingered in the doorway. "Did you want something?" I asked sweetly.

"What was your jaguar doing out?"

"Just getting some air." I flashed her a false smile.

She sniffed. "I thought maybe it needed to get away from you for a while. Wouldn't blame it." With that, she turned and stalked off.

I waited a few minutes to be certain she'd gone before leaving the room. Ronnie was nowhere to be seen. Good!

Deciding against doing any further exploring, I returned to my room and stayed there until dinnertime.

Dinner was awkward. No one had much to say. Ronnie avoided looking at me throughout the meal. She chatted quietly with Roy. Gene didn't show up. Helene and Jeffrey came and reported that Cameron was much better and would be up and around in another day. Henrietta's absence I understood to be due to still not being fully recovered from her crane's ordeal.

Dima sat beside Lisette, carefully avoiding both Ronnie and me. He spoke to Lisette in a low voice, but I made out Marko's name and something about tomorrow, probably telling her about the plan to steal Marko from the hospital. I couldn't hear any of her responses.

Grandfather and Grandmother were uncharacteristically quiet, their conversation consisting mainly of such things as "Please pass the green beans," "The roast is quite good tonight, my dear," and "Do you think the carrots need more salt?"

Professor DuChamps arrived late and apologized for his tardiness but didn't explain it. Instead, apparently unaffected by the gloomy mood, he proceeded to entertain us with the silly mistakes he'd come across in grading his students' papers. His stories might have been amusing under other circumstances, but this evening they didn't do anything to lighten the mood.

No one lingered over dessert. We all excused ourselves as soon as possible and went off in different directions. I went to the computer room where I'd seen the bookshelves, found a short romance novel, and spent the rest of the evening reading in my room and wishing the clock would speed up so tomorrow would come and then get over with.

Time crawled. I slept fitfully, but I got enough sleep. And when I went down to breakfast, Grandmother greeted me cheerfully.

She held out a stack of clothes and a file folder.

"Dr. Horshaw brought these for you," she said. "She's tending to Cameron."

"Oh, good." I took the green uniforms and the folder. "I didn't expect the things so soon. When did she bring them?"

"Early this morning, on her way to the hospital. Eat quickly and get ready. Dimitri had your car fixed and filled with gas. It's in the garage. You'd better use it. It's less likely to be recognized than any of ours. Gene will go with you." She gave me a look that dared me to object as she said that.

I just nodded, gulped down a bit of breakfast, and carried the things Dr. Horshaw had brought up to my room.

I set the stuff down on the bed and immediately looked into the folder. It held authentic-looking authorization papers for the transfer of patient Marko Pavich to Howell Memorial Hospital. The Howell administrator's signature was at the bottom along with a doctor whose name I didn't recognize. I had no idea whether the signatures were forged or genuine. Dr. Horshaw's signature or name appeared nowhere in the papers.

I put them back into the folder and looked at the clothes. The crisp white nurse's uniform had to be for me; the other two outfits were green orderly uniforms. So it seemed that both Gene and Dimitri would be going with me, and I had no say in the matter.

As I held up the nurse's outfit, a paper fell out. I picked it up and read the typed message:

An ambulance will pull up to Community General Hospital, the west side entrance, at precisely 12:15 this afternoon. The driver will be on a tight schedule. You MUST have Marko on a stretcher at that door at that time, ready to be loaded into the ambulance. The driver will open the doors, and your crew will wheel the stretcher into the ambulance. One of you will accompany Marko. The others will follow by car. Three blocks from Howell Memorial, on the corner of Grace Street and Holly Drive, is the Stanton Goodman Nursing Home. The ambulance will pull into the driveway beside the nursing home, and you will pull your car up behind it. You will have to lift Marko from the ambulance and transfer him to your car very quickly, then leave immediately. Back out of the drive while the ambulance drives forward and out the rear exit. You drive in the opposite direction from Howell and take back roads to the highway, then drive the speed limit to the Were House. (Better not let Dimitri drive!) Phone the house when you're on the highway so they'll be ready to get Marko from the car and get him inside the house and into bed. I'll get by this evening to check on him.

Good luck!

Dear Dr. Horshaw! She had it all worked out. I never expected to be handed a detailed plan like this. Now came the hard part: putting it into practice.

14
GETAWAY GONE BAD

I checked the time: 10:25. I'd have to hurry. But then I thought of something else we might need. Blankets. I got into the nurse's uniform, put on makeup, and hurried to the linen closet I'd spotted yesterday on my tour of exploration.

I grabbed two blankets off a stack and reached for a towel, just in case. Voices came clearly through the grate at the rear of the closet. I walked to the back wall and peered through the grate. Grandfather and Grandmother were seated at the kitchen table. They were talking about me.

"Now, Velma, of course you're worried," Grandfather was saying, "but Charlotte seems to be a competent and courageous young lady. I believe she will do what she's set out to do."

"I know she is those things," Grandmother responded. "But so much can go wrong."

"So much already has. Yes, it's a risk, but it's one we must take. We must get Marko to his wolf." With a scrape of his chair Grandfather stood and pushed his chair in against the table.

"I know." Grandmother sighed. "I just wish—"

"She's not doing this by herself. Dimitri and Gene will watch out for her." Grandfather's voice faded as he walked from the room.

I needed to hurry. I shouldn't have stayed to listen. Gene and Dimitri would watch out for me? As though I couldn't watch out for myself? But it did warm my heart to know Grandfather thought those things about me. I hoped they were justified.

I gathered up my bundle and hurried to the garage, reaching it by 11:35.

Gene was waiting. Dimitri too. I tossed an orderly uniform to each one, smiled at Gene, ignored Dimitri. I understood that Gene and I would need his help to carry out the plan, but I didn't have to like it.

I almost didn't recognize my old car. Not just because it'd been cleaned and waxed. Dents had been hammered out, scratches painted over. The tires looked new. The exhaust pipe no longer hung an inch above the ground. And was that a new rear bumper?

"So what's the plan?" Dimitri asked. He'd put his uniform on over his clothes, as had Gene.

I pulled my thoughts away from the car to answer. Facing Gene, I read Dr. Horshaw's note.

"Not much time," Gene said.

"Better let me drive." Dimitri opened the driver's door and slid behind the wheel, had the key in the ignition and the motor humming before I could figure out a way to stop him.

I got in the back seat, so did Gene, and we roared out of the garage and down the driveway.

"Whatever you do, don't get stopped by the police," I warned as we swung out onto the highway and headed for town, the old car buzzing along at a speed it hadn't been capable of in years.

Dimitri didn't answer. Nor did he slow down.

Gene gripped my hand. He hadn't said a word

since I got to the garage. What had Dimitri said to him?

And does he regret what happened night before last?

Do I?

No time to think about that. I have to think about the plan when we reach the hospital. If we make it there without getting stopped by the police or without crashing into anything.

Why is Dimitri acting like such a jerk?

Guess I should be glad he didn't bring Ronnie along.

We got to the hospital quicker than I would have thought possible. Finding a place to park near the ambulance entrance took a while, though. I'd chewed two nails to the quick by the time we finally pulled into a place where we were close but not conspicuous.

"I'm going to wait in the car until you come out with Marko," Dimitri announced. "Since I've been here before, I could be recognized."

Gene opened the car door and got out, still without a word. "You really think there's danger in that?" I asked, suddenly wanting Dimitri at my side.

"Of course," came his curt reply.

I shrugged. No time to waste arguing. I followed Gene from the car and into the hospital. We took the elevator to the fourth floor. Gene still hadn't spoken and I wanted to ask what was bothering him. I thought of what Dimitri had said about Gene not wanting Marko to recover. But if Dimitri really believed that, would he have stayed in the car?

I tried to recall the scene of the stabbing. Could Gene have been the guy who did it? I didn't think so. Gene was tall, and to my best recollection, the stabber hadn't been. It had happened so fast, I couldn't be sure of anything, but my impression was that the would-be killer had been shorter than the victim. And without an animal spirit.

We left the elevator, and I headed for the nurse's station, Gene following.

I reached the station. Good—only one nurse was behind the desk. I handed her the papers and asked, "Is the patient, Marko Pavich, ready?"

She gave me a blank look. "Ready? For what?"

I acted surprised. "You weren't notified about the transfer?"

"What transfer? I haven't received any sort of notification about that patient."

"You should have. I assumed … but all the paperwork is there." I pointed to the papers she held but hadn't looked at. "We're running a bit late." I sounded apologetic. "I expected he'd be ready."

"He's in a coma. Moving him would be dangerous. I don't understand this at all."

"We're aware of the coma. He's to be taken to Howell Memorial so a specialist there can examine him. The ambulance is waiting."

She glanced over the papers as I spoke. Without looking up, she said, "I'll have to check this out with security. He's a crime victim. They had a police guard on his room until this morning."

So the room wasn't guarded now. Great! "Of course I know that," I said, thinking fast. "The police are eager to question him, find out if he knew his attacker. They're all for this move."

"Well, then, you won't object to my checking it out."

I was really coming to dislike this prig of a nurse.

"How long will it take? We're short of time."

"Shouldn't take long." She turned to her phone.

I looked around, hoping Gene would have an idea. He wasn't there!

When did he leave? And why?

I couldn't go hunt for him. Nursezilla had already reached someone and was starting to explain the problem.

"Code Blue! Room 413. Code Blue! Room 413," blared over the speaker system. The nurse dropped the phone and came around the desk.

"Wait right here," she ordered and ran past me.

I had the horrible thought that 413 might be Marko's room. And that Gene had done something to—

Gene stepped out into the hall from a room just two doors away. Not the room the nurses were rushing to. He beckoned, and I hurried to him.

"He's in here," Gene said. "And I have a gurney."

"How—"

"I saw an orderly wheeling a patient into a room down the hall. I followed him in and said I needed the gurney stat. As soon as he'd lifted the patient off it and onto the bed, I grabbed it." He'd led me into the room as he spoke. "I've got Marko ready. Had to unplug him from the oxygen and take out an IV, and that set off a beeper, so we've got to get out of here with him before somebody comes and checks."

Words failed me. I gave him a quick hug.

On the bed lay the man I'd seen stabbed. His cheeks were sunken, his skin and lips bluish-gray. Afraid for a moment that he'd died, I looked closely and, to my relief, saw the slight rise and fall of his chest.

Gene pulled back the sheet, and I grasped Marko's legs while Gene got his hands under his arms. "Ready? Lift," Gene said, and we picked him up and placed him on the gurney. At that moment, Gene's cell phone rang. I grabbed the sheet and put it over Marko while Gene answered.

"On our way," he said into the phone and clicked it shut. "Dimitri says we need to get him to the ambulance *now*. The driver's ready to leave."

We guided the stretcher toward the door. It opened just before we reached it, and a security guard entered the room. "Stop!" he ordered. "I can't confirm your authorization."

The nurse must have gone back to the station and reported us.

"I don't understand," I said. "The papers are in order. The ambulance is downstairs waiting."

"It'll have to wait. You aren't cleared to remove the patient."

Gene sat down in an armchair in the corner of the room. Guessing why, I moved to block the guard's view of that corner. "You're endangering the patient by delaying us," I said. "He needs oxygen. We'll hook him back up as soon as we get him to the ambulance."

The guard gave me a funny look but never got a chance to object. Gene's wolf bounded at him, knocked him flat, and held him there while I stuffed a towel in his mouth and looked around for something to tie him up with.

No time. I picked up the bedpan from the table by

the door and banged the guard over the head with it as hard as I could. Twice. That only stunned him, but it gave time for the wolf to return and Gene to stand up and come and grab up the guard and hit him hard enough to knock him out. He dragged him into the patient bathroom and closed that door.

"Come on," he urged. "We're gonna be late. Let's hope Dima can stall the driver."

I grabbed my end of the gurney, and off we went again. We reached the staff elevator and pushed the Down button. The doors opened right away. We wheeled the gurney in and pressed the button to take us to the ground floor. But before the doors closed, Nursezilla barged in.

"Where's the guard?" she demanded. "He hasn't reported back to me."

She glared at me. Gene grabbed her arm and pulled her into the elevator. I stabbed the button to close the door and slumped to the floor to let my jaguar out. The jaguar leapt on the nurse. She fell heavily to the floor. Not hurt; she'd fainted. As the elevator stopped, the jaguar returned to me.

Leaving the nurse propped in the corner of the elevator, Gene and I wheeled the gurney out, and I pushed the button for the sixth floor. The elevator doors closed and the elevator ascended, carrying Nursey safely away. As we rushed to the side exit I prayed silently that the ambulance had waited.

Dimitri jogged toward us and took Gene's end of the stretcher. "Not a minute to lose," he grunted as he pushed the gurney toward an open ambulance door. "Gene, get the car started. Sharl, you're going to ride in the ambulance."

"Why me?" I squeaked.

"Because you're the nurse."

The driver stood by the door, and I guessed Dimitri's explanation was for his benefit. *The driver must think I'm a real nurse.*

I couldn't object. Not with the driver helping get the stretcher into the ambulance. I climbed in, the driver went to his seat, and we sped out onto the street. And all I could do was look at Marko and will him to keep breathing.

At least we'd made it this far. We'd got him to the ambulance and were zooming toward the rendezvous at the nursing home.

Was anyone following us? I hoped Gene would stay right behind the ambulance. Transferring Marko to the car would be tricky. I wondered how Dr. Horshaw had persuaded the driver to help us. He was risking his job and probably facing a jail term if we got caught.

We were risking our lives. And Marko's.

I fretted and chewed my remaining nails while the ride went on—and on. My watch told me it took eight minutes, but my nerves told me it must have been hours before the ambulance jerked to a stop.

"Open the door and get him out," the driver called back. "I'm staying right here." He had parked the ambulance in a space that couldn't be seen from the nursing home.

I'd just opened the door when my car pulled in behind us. Dimitri got out and ran to the ambulance, jumped in, and picked Marko up. I was ready to help him, but he shook his head and said, "Get in the car." He carried Marko while I did as ordered.

As soon as the ambulance door closed, the driver took off. Dimitri got Marko onto the back seat and climbed in after him. I got in the front beside Gene.

"Go!" Dimitri said.

Gene backed out of the drive.

I turned to look back at Dimitri. He was tucking the blankets I'd brought around our patient. "Marko's still alive, isn't he?" I asked.

"Yes, but he doesn't look good."

What an understatement! I almost wished Dimitri were driving instead of Gene, who conscientiously obeyed the speed limits as Dr. Horshaw's note had insisted. I thought more speed was called for anyway.

I didn't say anything, just kept an eye on the side-view mirror, hoping not to see a cop car. Nobody spoke. The silence was oppressive, but I wasn't going to be the one to break it.

At last we pulled into the were house driveway. My relieved sigh turned into a gasp.

A police car was parked across the entrance to the garage. Gene swore and braked.

"Reverse," Dimitri said. "We need to get out of here."

"But—" I started to tell Gene that my car stalled in reverse but stopped, figuring that must be fixed like everything else about the car.

Gene backed fast around the curves, heading to the highway. The car stalled.

"Damn." Dimitri reached for the door handle. "Get the car going. Drive to the overpass."

"Where're you going?" I asked.

"Nowhere. But my leopard is." Dimitri slumped against the seat.

"No, don't—"

Before I could finish my objection, the snow leopard emerged and jumped through the open door.

I reached around and got the door closed just as Gene got the car moving again. Still backward. It stalled again.

I couldn't stand it. "Gene! Get over and let me drive. This is my car. I know its quirks."

"You need to look after Marko now that Dimitri can't."

"I can't do anything for Marko. Let me drive!" I got out of the car and ran to the driver's door, opened it, and shoved Gene over.

"Charlotte—"

"Shut up! You're wasting time."

I got in, shoving him further with my body. I started the car, shifted into reverse, and took off. Smoothly. No more stalling.

Could Gene have deliberately stalled the car? I didn't want to think so, but I couldn't shake the idea Dimitri had planted in my mind—that Gene didn't want Marko to recover.

Maneuvering around curves in reverse wasn't easy, nor was backing out onto the busy highway. It took all my concentration. It wasn't until I was safely headed forward and up to speed that I could speak.

"Nobody's following us, are they?"

Gene looked behind us. "Don't see anyone that looks suspicious." He stopped and cleared his throat. "Uh, Sharl, I should have let you drive to start with. You're handling this car much better than I could've."

His unexpected apology made me ashamed for doubting him.

"It's okay," I said, giving him a smile. "You were just following Dr. Horshaw's instructions."

"Yeah. I wish she'd told us what to do in case we couldn't get home."

"You could call her."

"Not a good idea. She'd be at the hospital, not where she could talk freely. But I can call someone at home." He got out his cell phone and hit a key.

"You aren't calling the house phone, are you?"

He gave me a scathing look and shook his head. "Dad? What's happening? We have Marko. We got to the house but a police car was blocking the driveway. We—

"No, we backed out. We're on the highway. Sharl's driving. Dima let his leopard out before we left.

"I know, I know. He didn't give us a chance—"

"Yeah, I agree, but you know Dima. I— Oh, okay." He flipped the phone shut and turned to me. "Dad says the place is crawling with cops now. He said for us to keep going and ditch the phone so they can't trace us. He didn't have time to tell me what to do about Marko."

"We'll just have to wait and see what the leopard does."

"Dad says it'll make things a lot worse."

"Did he say whether the cops are there because of last night or because we stole Marko?"

"Didn't have time. Guess we'll find out."

A yell of "No!" from the back seat ended in a terrible choking sound. I looked back. Dimitri thrashed around, then collapsed, his eyes rolled back in his head.

I swung over onto the shoulder and screeched to a halt. Gene and I both got out of the car and opened a rear door. He was closer to Dimitri; I had to crawl over Marko to get to him. Gene was shaking him gently. I reached for his wrist and hunted for a pulse.

I found one so faint I had to check it twice to be certain it was there. "He's still alive."

"But if his leopard —"

"Don't say it." I backed from the car and returned to the driver's seat. "Get in," I ordered Gene. "We're going back."

"Are you crazy? We'll just be arrested — or killed."

"Maybe. Probably. But we're going back."

I put the car in motion while Gene hesitated. He had to jump for the open front door, pull himself in, and then swing the door shut. I watched for the chance to change lanes, found it, crossed to the lane next to the center island. Drove forward until I came to a break in the island for the use of emergency vehicles, and swung the car around in a highly illegal U-turn.

"For God's sake, Sharl!"

I stomped down on the accelerator, swerved around a slower car, and sped down the highway pushing the old car to its limit.

I knew I was being a fool. I didn't care.

15
INDECISION

Gene didn't say anything at first. Too busy hanging on while I swerved around slower cars. But as we neared the turn-off, he got out the words, "Go past. Back way. I'll show you. It's safer."

"Is it quicker?"

"It's no longer."

He directed me past where I'd planned to turn. A cop car turned in just as we passed. Not good!

Gene directed me to get into the right lane and turn off onto a small side road that wound away in the opposite direction from where I wanted to go. Was he deliberately leading me away from the house? Then the road curved back around toward the highway and an underpass I'd never noticed. From there it wound through a low, marshy area thick with trees and finally up onto higher ground.

Definitely not a shorter or faster route than the front drive, but Gene hadn't led me astray as I'd feared. We came out within view of the rear of the house, and Gene directed me to park among trees that hid the car, at least from casual observers.

We got out. "I don't like leaving them here," I said, indicating Marko and Dimitri. "If anyone finds the car …"

"It was your idea to come back. You have a plan?"

"No," I admitted. "I just want to find Dimitri's leopard."

"It may be dead."

"Or badly injured. We have to know."

"*You* have to know. All right, all right," he added hurriedly in reaction to my glare. "You're right. *We* have to know. Follow me. There's a secret entrance, mostly for the animals but we can use it. You aren't supposed to know about it, but under the circumstances ..."

"Stop talking and get moving!"

He led me away from the house to a stone cairn and moved a few stones to reveal a narrow passage leading sharply downward. I followed him in. "It'll be dark," he warned.

I'd already gathered that. I kept one hand on the side as I moved cautiously forward. I could touch the other side, as well. In fact, it was hard not to. The passage was barely wide enough to allow us to get through it. If it was for the animals, the larger ones would get stuck, especially Grandfather's aurochs.

As we moved farther from the entrance, it got darker until I couldn't even see Gene walking right in front of me. This was an ideal place for a trap.

I ran into Gene and almost knocked him down. He'd stopped.

"Shhh," he cautioned. "Listen."

Footsteps! Coming toward us.

A beam of light played over us. Blinded, I couldn't see who was behind it.

A whisper. Lisette's voice. "Gene! You have Marko?"

"He's in the car," Gene replied. "Barely alive.

Dima's there too, and no better off. What happened to his leopard?"

"Dima was a fool to send his leopard out. A cop shot it. Henrietta's trying to keep it alive."

Determined to be part of the conversation, I asked, "How can we get his leopard to him? Or him to the leopard? And the wolf to Marko?"

"You can't. Not with the police all over the house. And what if they find Dima and Marko? You'll make everything worse than it already is."

"The car's hidden," Gene said.

"They're searching the grounds."

"Why are they here?" I asked. "What're they looking for?"

"What do you think?" Lisette asked. Couldn't she answer a simple question?

"It either involves Marko's abduction from the hospital or last night's killings," I said, exasperated.

"Well, guess again," she snapped. "They came looking for Joy because she didn't show up for work. She was a 9-1-1 dispatcher, so of course the police wanted to know where she was."

That was unexpected. "So why wouldn't they just phone?"

"Her supervisor did phone. Roy took the call, which he shouldn't have, and said something that made the guy suspicious. So one police car came, with two cops. They wanted to talk to Joy. When Grandfather said she wasn't home, they wanted to know where she was. They asked to talk to Cameron. Grandfather said they couldn't. They asked to come in, and he wouldn't let them. That made things worse. They called for back-up, and more police cars came. But it would have been okay, 'cause they didn't have a warrant, and Grandfather demanded to see one. One car did leave, maybe to try to get a warrant, I don't know. Grandfather says they wouldn't have grounds for one, and they would all have to leave. Then Dimitri's leopard shows up and a cop shoots him, and the car that left comes back, and everything's a mess. And now you're here, and if they find Marko and Dima ..." Her voice trailed off in sobs.

"And they're searching the grounds?" The car wasn't well enough hidden that a deliberate search could miss it.

Gene made things worse by saying, "I knew we shouldn't have come back here."

Lisette latched onto his words. "See! She messes everything up! Ronnie's right about her. She's brought nothing but trouble."

"I've brought Marko," I reminded her.

"He's barely alive, you said. And we can't get his wolf to him. You've probably killed him. And Dimitri, too. Even though he brought it on himself." She dissolved into tears again.

I felt like slapping her, mostly because I knew she was right.

"Did they connect the leopard with, uh, what happened last night?" Gene asked.

"Don't know. Prob'ly," she said between sobs.

"Bawling won't help," I snapped, almost ready to join her.

"What can we do?" Gene asked.

"What about the house?" I asked. "Are the police searching it?"

"Not yet. Grandfather still won't let them in without a search warrant. They can probably get one now, though." She said it like it was my fault.

It probably was. "Where does this tunnel come out? In the house?"

"No. In the garage," Gene answered. "Next to the toolroom."

Toolroom. That aroused a memory I didn't need now. "Are the police in the garage?" I asked Lisette.

"They looked in it, but Grandfather shooed them away."

"So we can get into the house," I said triumphantly.

"And what? Be welcomed with open arms?"

Lisette's sarcasm cooled my triumph. But I had a plan. Well, half a plan. "We can get Marko's wolf and bring it back through the tunnel. It isn't far from the end of the tunnel to the car. If we can get the wolf back to Marko, he should recover, right?"

"If the police haven't found the car and towed it off. And sent Marko and Dima to the hospital."

"We've gotta take the chance," I insisted, nudging Gene forward, toward Lisette. "Let's go."

"The wolf's gone feral," Gene reminded me. "We can't control it."

"We've got to find a way," I said, determined to carry out my plan.

"Grandfather won't like it." Gene sounded like Lisette now. But at least he kept moving. And Lisette turned and walked forward, too. Probably just wanting to prove her forecasts of doom were right.

We reached a door, and. as Gene eased it open, Lisette switched off her flashlight. Gene peered out.

"Looks like it's clear," he said. We crept out and hurried to the kitchen door.

Locked!

Lisette sagged against it. "I left this open when I came out this way," she said.

A thought occurred to me. "Why did you come into the tunnel? Were you looking for us?"

"Grandfather said you might come that way."

"Then why would he lock the door?"

"He wouldn't. Somebody else must have. To keep the police out."

"Shhh," Gene said and knocked softly on the door.

It opened. Just a crack at first. But when Lisette hissed, "Let us in!" it opened wider.

Lisette slipped in, followed by Gene. I stepped forward, and the door started to shut. I stuck my leg in to keep it open.

"Let her in," Gene said.

I gave a hard push and barged in.

Ronnie jumped away from me and snatched up a knife from the kitchen counter. "You aren't welcome here," she shouted.

"Go to hell."

She lunged at me with the knife. I ducked, caught her arm, and yanked her around, her arm high behind her back. The knife dropped from her hand. Gene grabbed it off the floor.

"Don't be a fool," he told her as Grandfather came into the kitchen. I let Ronnie go. She wouldn't try anything in Grandfather's presence.

"Where are Dimitri and Marko?" he demanded.

Gene answered, explaining again about the car.

"They'll find it," Grandfather declared, scowling at both of us. "And why are you here, making matters even worse than they already were? Wasn't it enough that Dimitri foolishly sent out his leopard and got it shot and put us in deeper trouble?"

"Grandfather Blass, I did what you ordered me to do — got Marko out of the hospital," I said in my most reasonable tone. "Everything went exactly according to plan until we got here and saw the police car. We left, but after Dima let out his leopard we had to come back. He acted impulsively, but he had no idea how bad things were here. He only wanted to help. He was worried about Marko. And he knew we had to get Marko's wolf to him. That can't wait."

"The wolf is feral and very dangerous. The plan was to bring Marko to it. To do anything else would be foolhardy."

"We disconnected Marko from all the tubes and things in the hospital that were keeping him alive," I said. "He'll die if the wolf doesn't get back soon. We can take the wolf through the tunnel. It's just a short jog from the tunnel end to the car."

Grandfather shook his head. "Too dangerous. You couldn't control the wolf. If Georges were here to help — but he's not back from the university. No. It's not wise."

I was done being reasonable. "Wise doesn't enter into it. It's necessary."

"She's right, Granddad," Gene put in. "It's dangerous, yes, but it's the only chance Marko has."

"Then let them do it, pleeease," Lisette begged.

But Grandfather was adamant. "That wolf is more dangerous than I think you realize. Take it into that dark tunnel and it could tear you apart. Charlotte, you and Gene together aren't strong enough to restrain it. A feral werewolf is fiercer, stronger, and more vicious than any normal wild wolf."

"I don't believe that wolf is feral," a man's voice said.

Everyone spun around to face the door. My jaw dropped. Cameron stood in the doorway, leaning heavily on a cane. He bore scars and one arm was still bandaged, but even though Dr. Horshaw had predicted he'd be up and walking today, I could only think of the condition I'd seen him in last. Weres heal fast, but he'd been so near death!

"I think you're wrong to assume the wolf is feral," he said, limping into the kitchen.

Grandmother followed Cameron and guided him to a chair. "Don't tire yourself," she told him. Turning to us, she added, "I think you all need to hear what Cameron has to say."

16
TOO LATE

"**This** isn't easy for me."

Everyone's gaze fixed on Cameron while he stared at the floor. I wanted to yell, "Get on with it."

Finally he spoke again. "A couple of weeks ago I told Joy I wanted a divorce." He paused again, keeping his head down and a white-knuckled grip on the head of his cane. His voice, when he continued, was so low I edged closer to better hear his words.

"I knew living in a household of weres was difficult for Joy. I'd warned her — we all had — that it could cause problems. She thought she could handle it. She couldn't. She hid her feelings from the rest of you, but she took them out on me. Nervous jitters. Restlessness. Anger. And lately, fear."

Another pause added to my own nervous jitters. If we didn't get the wolf to Marko soon …

"In spite of her obvious unhappiness she said she didn't want a divorce. Didn't want to leave. It didn't make sense. Then Charlotte and Gene and Dimitri came back from rescuing Henrietta. 'Back from the slaughter,' as Joy put it. We had a terrible argument. She was crying and yelling that we were 'a bloody bunch of killers,' and now friends of hers were dead."

"Friends?" Gene blurted. "She knew those people?"

Cameron didn't raise his head to meet his brother's gaze. He nodded. "She ... she betrayed us to them. She didn't tell me that. Dad found evidence on her laptop after ... after she died. He would have told you about it himself, but I thought I should. I mean, she was my wife—the biggest mistake of my life. Dad found a way into her emails and read messages between her and people in that demon-hunting church."

That explained why Jeffrey had acted so hostile and unwelcoming when I walked into the computer room and interrupted him, Jeffrey must've been hacking her files.

Cameron continued, "He found proof that she called them to come and set a trap. That's why they were here shooting at Dima and Charlotte. And why they set the trap that netted Henrietta's crane and Charlotte's jaguar." He stopped, took a deep breath. "I'm afraid it was Joy who stabbed Marko. If so, it's no wonder that Marko's wolf attacked her. The wolf knew what she'd done."

"But it attacked you, too," Roy said. He'd joined us right after Cameron began his tale.

"Only because I tried to protect Joy. It didn't kill me. If I'd let it have her without a fight, it wouldn't have hurt me. But I didn't know then what I know now. So, stupidly, I kept trying to get it off Joy. The more I tried, the more it hurt me. When I collapsed onto the floor it left me alone."

"Why didn't you send your boar out to deal with the wolf?" Grandfather asked.

I'd been wondering that, too.

"I tried. He wouldn't go. He would have if the

wolf were feral. He would have protected me. But he knew the wolf was Marko's, and he knew it acted to protect Marko. To protect all of us. From a woman who'd betrayed us. Who wanted us all dead."

I couldn't keep quiet any longer. "Look, this is fascinating, and we all want to hear it, but is this the time? Dima and Marko may be dying. You've convinced me we can take the wolf to Marko, since it isn't feral after all."

Grandfather gave me the saddest look I'd ever seen. I thought he was going to refuse again. But he nodded. "*Ja. Ja*, take it. Save Marko." He choked up, but he'd said enough.

"Where's the wolf?" Gene asked, heading for the door.

"I'll show you," Roy said, joining Gene. I followed, stifling my surprise at Roy's sudden willingness to help.

We'd just reached the stairs when a pounding on the door accompanied by the shouted demand, "Open up! Police! We have a warrant."

"Go!" Grandmother told us. "I'll stall them."

We ran up the stairs.

Roy led us down the main hallway to a door that opened onto a stairway leading up to an attic, cluttered with boxes, a trunk, old chairs, other junk. Behind that junk, partially hidden, a large cage with thick iron bars held a pacing wolf.

It growled and its fur bristled when Gene and I approached. A heavy-duty padlock secured the cage.

"I have the key," Roy said, stepping in front of us. He unlocked the cage, and stepped back to let us open the door.

The cage door swung outward. The wolf crouched, ready to leap.

"Marko's here," Gene told it quickly. "We'll take you to him."

The wolf growled and raced past us before we could stop it. We should have had a rope ready to slip around its neck. Would have, if the cops hadn't come before we were ready.

The wolf jumped down the steps to the second floor and sped down the long hallway. Gene and Roy and I dashed after it. As we started down the hallway from the attic stairs, the wolf whirled around and ran back toward us.

We heard the reason before we saw. Cops. Coming up the stairs. One yelled, "What was that? Get it!" as he reached the top of the stairway.

The wolf dashed past us. The cop drew his gun. If he fired he would more likely hit one of us. But would that make him hesitate?

I wanted to turn to see where the wolf had gone, but I was afraid to take my eyes off the cop with the gun. His furious glare told me he was ready to shoot us if he couldn't get the animal.

His partner joined him at the top of the stairs, huffing from the climb. While he caught his breath, the first cop yelled, "Halt. Don't anybody move. Get against that wall."

I guess the contradiction in those orders escaped him. We looked at each other, then Gene shuffled to the wall and I followed, hands raised, eyes on the gun pointed at us. Roy didn't move.

"Against the wall!" The cop walked toward us as he repeated the order.

From the room behind Roy came the sound of breaking glass.

"Wha — ?" The cop leveled his gun on Roy.

This time Roy raised his hands and moved to the wall.

The second cop went to the room where we'd heard the breaking glass. "Your wolf jumped out the window," he called to his partner, who'd stayed behind to keep his gun trained on us.

"Can you see it?" our cop called back, not taking his eyes off us.

"Yeah, it's running — "

"Shoot it!"

A gunshot sounded, followed by a curse. "Missed!"

Another shot.

"You get it that time?"

"Don't know. I can't see it with the trees in the way."

This time our cop cursed.

The second cop came out into the hall. "Even if I missed, he might be hurt. He couldn't have gone through that window without getting cut."

"I don't want it hurt. I want it dead."

"No!" Gene burst out. "The wolf isn't wild."

"Oh?" Our cop fixed Gene with a glare. "What do you know about it?"

"It's a pet. It's tame."

"Sure it is."

Gene's efforts weren't helping. Except for distracting the cops. Roy leaned back against the wall, his eyes closed, his body relaxed. He let out his fox while the cops' attention focused on Gene.

"Hey!" the second cop shouted.

Roy slid slowly down the wall to a sitting position. The fox darted into the room with the broken window. Another tinkling of glass. Could the smaller fox survive a jump from a second-story window? Through broken glass? But I'd learned that Roy had guts. He was taking an awful risk. And for what? What could the fox do?

Again the second cop, pistol drawn, ran into the room.

The first cop stood in front of Roy and barked, "Get up!"

"He can't," Gene said. "He's passed out."

The cop kicked Roy's legs. "What's wrong with him?"

"He, uh, he has seizures."

"Yeah? I think he's faking." He grabbed Roy's hair and yanked. That would hurt, and Roy could feel it. He wasn't unconscious, just unable to respond.

A brown shadow slipped from the room across the hall and dashed for the stairs. The fox had tricked the cops, let them think it had jumped, hid, and grabbed its chance to get downstairs the safe way. I grinned.

The cop raised his gun and slammed the butt against Roy's shoulder, yelling, "Get up!"

Roy groaned.

"You're awake all right. Stand up now!"

"He can't," Gene said. "Leave him alone."

His face livid, the cop swung around to face Gene. "Then you tell me what's going on here. What's with the animals? And why are there two unconscious guys in a car hidden in the woods out back?"

So they'd found the car. My heart sank. They'd have it guarded. They'd send for an ambulance for Dima and Marko. The afternoon's work would be for nothing. Worse than nothing. Marko couldn't survive much longer.

Unless his wolf reached him.

Gene hadn't answered the cop. I thought the cop was going to hit him. He might have if his radio hadn't crackled to life. A voice said, "Barr! We need you out here."

The cop kept his gun aimed at Gene as he answered. "Sorry," he said. "We've got a situation here, too. Aren't they sending another team out?"

"Yeah, but they're not here yet," came the tinny response. "And a big wolf came right toward us. I drew my gun and damned if some other critter, a dog or something, didn't bite my ankles, and I went after it, and the wolf disappeared. I can't leave to hunt it down. There's a guy here that looks about to croak. We're doing what we can to keep him alive till the paramedics arrive."

"If he dies, this'll be a homicide investigation. If it isn't already." The cop sure wasn't sparing any sympathy for a dying man. "Okay," he went on. "If it's that important, I guess Steve can go. I've gotta stay here. I've got three suspects to watch, and they're playing games with me."

He clicked off the radio and said to the second cop, who must be Steve, "You're needed out back by the car. The wolf—" He stopped, looked at us, and said, "Just go. Hurry. I'll hold the fort here."

Steve left.

I worried. If the wolf had reached Marko, it had to

be Dima who was "about to croak." Eying the gun the cop held on Gene, I measured my chances of grabbing it without getting Gene or me killed.

Not good.

There must be something I could do.

"Funny thing," the cop said, still looking at Gene. "We had a crime last night where the guys looked like victims of an animal attack. And now we see a wolf here. And earlier we shot a leopard. And this afternoon a patient is kidnapped from a hospital room. And we find a car with two unconscious guys and one looks like the kidnap victim. So I'm thinking there's gotta be a connection. Anything you want to tell me about that?"

Gene didn't answer.

Time for me to get into the act. "You charging us with a crime?"

"Should I be?"

"Guess not. You haven't read us our rights, so we're not under arrest. But you're holding that gun on us as if we were. And you've abused an unconscious man. That's not legal, is it?"

His eyes narrowed. "You wanna bring charges?" he said, daring me.

Dangerous, this guy. Especially with his partner gone and nobody to keep him in check. My jaguar wanted out. But this wasn't the time. "The leopard you shot. Was it killed?"

"Why do you care?"

"It's my boyfriend's pet," I said.

"Like the wolf, huh? And now another critter. Lotsa strange pets in this house."

A loud clomping up the stairs heralded the arrival

of another "strange pet." Bet the cop never expected to see an aurochs haul itself off the stairs and lumber down the hall toward us. He was just a little slow — from the shock, I'd guess — swinging his gun around and taking aim.

Gene and I both lunged at him. Gene tackled his legs while I grabbed the arm with the gun. I wrested the gun from his grip as he toppled to the floor, his legs jerked out from under him. The aurochs stopped just short of trampling him.

It lifted its head and bellowed. I took that as a summons. "We need to find something to tie the cop up with first," I told it. It poked its head into the room with the broken window, then turned and headed back for the stairs. I held the pistol on the cop while Gene hunted for something to use as a rope.

I laughed when I saw what he came up with: two pairs of pantyhose. They worked just fine. We took his radio and left the cop lying on the floor, mad as a whole nest of hornets, while we ran down the stairs after the aurochs. We followed it through the living room into a downstairs bedroom.

Grandfather sat in a chair there, and the aurochs faded into him. He blinked and nodded at us. "Good. We'll deal later with the policeman you left upstairs. Right now we have to save Dimitri and Marko."

"How?" Gene asked.

I was too busy staring at the snow leopard on the bed to say anything. It was breathing, I noted with great relief. A blood-soaked bandage wound around its midsection.

"He lives." Grandfather hadn't missed my concern. "If we can return him to Dimitri, he will be restored." He didn't need to add that if we couldn't, both Dimitri and the leopard would die.

"There were cops down here. Where'd they go?" I spoke softly, scarcely above a whisper.

Grandfather said, "When the police that were hunting outside found the car with Marko and Dima unconscious in it, they called the others out."

"Without leaving anybody on guard in here?"

"I believe they thought the two policemen who were upstairs with you might be sufficient."

"But they sent for one of them. They wouldn't just leave a single officer here," I objected.

"They did not. Two others remained downstairs here. Velma is keeping one entertained in the kitchen, and the other is at the front door watching for the ambulance they sent for. We have little time to do anything. I—"

The radio I'd taken from the cop upstairs crackled to life. "Officer Barr, you there? Come in."

Grandfather Blass put a finger to his lips and motioned to me to hand him the radio. I did.

"Here," Grandfather said. "Report."

Nervous that whoever was on the other end would recognize that the voice wasn't Officer Barr's, I leaned close to hear the voice on the other end. Seeing my effort, Grandfather held the set toward me.

"One of the men in the car just woke up. He's confused, can't get any sense out of him. He acts really scared—keeps screaming, 'Don't hurt me, don't hurt me.' And we lost the wolf. I don't know where it went."

A big smile came over my face, and a matching one peeked out under Grandfather's mustache. It had to be Marko who was awake and screaming, which could only mean that somehow Marko's wolf had returned to him.

"Bring the man here," Grandfather continued to imitate Officer Barr's voice. "I'll try to talk to him. Carry the unconscious one in, too, if you can. We can't leave him out where the wolf could get him."

"We've got an ambulance on the way," the voice answered, disapproval clear in the tone.

"The ambulance will come to the front of the house. Better to have him in here. Hurry."

Grandfather pulled it off! I could have hugged him. The bad sound quality of the radios helped disguise his voice, but the ploy was his, and it was brilliant. At that moment I wanted more than anything to become a part of Grandfather's "family," I was so proud of all of them.

And I desperately wanted this house to be the peaceable kingdom Grandfather called it.

"I will go to the back door to meet the men bringing Dima and Marko," Grandfather said. "I want to know why Marko is so frightened. That is not like him. Gene, come with me. I may need your help. Your father is at the front of the house watching for the arrival of more police and ambulances. Charlotte, you stay here with the leopard."

I didn't argue. I trusted Grandfather's judgment, though I wanted badly to see what happened when the cops, obeying an order from "Officer Barr," were met by Grandfather instead.

I was probably safer here with Dima's leopard. Alone with it, I stroked its fur, caressed its head, scratched its ears. I wished it would wake, though if it did, it would try to rise and get to Dima. And I didn't know how I'd stop it.

"You are worried about Dima. You care for him."

I spun around. Henrietta stood in the doorway. "Be careful. He's more fragile than he seems."

Fragile? Dima? Or was she referring to the present precarious state of his leopard?

"They're bringing Dima to the house right now," I told her.

"I know. I just saw Grandfather." Henrietta came to the bed and checked the leopard's breathing as she spoke. "If anyone can get Dima to his leopard, Grandfather can. And when the leopard returns to Dima, his injuries will heal. But Dima has hurts that go deeper than the leopard's. If you want him to love you, you must be patient and take it very slow."

"Like Ronnie does?" My anger erupted; I couldn't help it. "She's all over him all the time."

"Yes. He tolerates her because he knows what it's like to be an outsider, which she was when we all thought she lacked an animal spirit." She sat on the stool in front of the dressing table and leaned toward me with an earnest look. "Now that we know about her badger, that will change. So don't worry about Ronnie, and don't act jealous. Just have patience."

"Do we have time for patience?" I wondered aloud, not really addressing the question to Henrietta. "What's will happen when the police figure out what we are? When they connect us to the killings in the church? Will they believe it was self-defense and to save you—your crane, I mean? We have no proof."

"Grandfather will find a way to protect us," Henrietta declared with conviction.

I wished I could share her confidence.

How could we justify Gene's and my tying up the cop we'd overpowered and left bound and gagged in the upstairs hallway? Or Grandfather's use of that cop's radio to get them to bring Marko and Dima to the house?

We were screwed no matter what. I longed desperately to find a way to get us all out of this mess.

So what was I going to do?

I had no idea, but I resolved to do *something.*

But first I had to know about Marko and Dima.

17
A DARING PLOY

I left the leopard in Henrietta's care and went into the hall. I crept along it, listening for any sign of danger. Hearing nothing, I kept going to the living room, where I halted at the sound of voices in the foyer, ducked behind the sofa, and listened.

Grandfather was speaking: "I tell you, officers, he has these spells. We know how to deal with his condition. We are well equipped to care for him and bring him out of this fainting spell. If you will just permit my son and me to take him—"

"We can't do that," came a voice that must belong to a cop. "I'm sorry, sir, but we're finding too many suspicious things here. That man out there matches the description of a patient taken illegally and with violence from Community General Hospital earlier today, and—"

"But you said that patient was in a coma," Grandfather interrupted. "The man out there is not. If you'd only let me talk to him ..."

So the first man they were talking about was Dimitri, and the other was Marko.

"Doesn't matter. Both these men are going to the hospital. Here comes the ambulance now. Where's Officer Barr?"

"He went upstairs to check something up there,"

Grandfather said. "I gave him permission even though I've yet to be shown a search warrant."

"Odd that we can't raise him on the radio."

"I'll check upstairs," another cop said. I couldn't see how many were out there, but more than three or four, I judged by the voices.

Somebody had to do something fast. Dimitri *had* to be reunited with his leopard before they found the cop we'd tied up. I was ready to send my jaguar out when one of the cops let out a yell.

"What the hell?" another voice hollered. "What was that?"

"I don't know, but it bit me."

"That was the same critter that tripped me up and made me lose my hold on the crazy guy."

Crazy guy? He must mean Marko.

"That another of your weird pets?"

I guess that question was directed at Grandfather, but he didn't answer. I heard a shot, and another voice saying, "Save your ammunition. It's gone, whatever it was."

I didn't have to guess what it was. Roy's fox jumped through an open window and dashed past me and up the stairs. My opinion of Roy went up another notch.

A cop walked through the living room to the stairs. I held very still, but he didn't look my way, just stomped up the steps. I waited for a shout or something to tell me he'd found Officer Barr.

I didn't have long to wait.

"Jim, Buzz, get up here on the double," the cop yelled down. "The rest of you, don't let those people out of your sight."

Trouble!

I had to do something. Fast!

The sensible thing would be to find a place to hide so I wouldn't be picked up and hauled off to jail with the rest of the family. Not to save my own skin but to help them. I couldn't do that locked up with them.

But if I hid now, who would save Dimitri?

I couldn't save him. But maybe my jaguar could. In theory it was possible for the were animal to enter a person other than its host, though only briefly and only under desperate circumstances.

This circumstance couldn't be more desperate. Time to test the theory. But to do so, I'd have to put myself in danger and hope that Dimitri and I both came out alive.

I left my hiding place and walked right through the living room, out the front door, and into the midst of the police and the family members they'd gathered up and surrounded.

Two ambulances were parked in the driveway.

The paramedics had placed Dimitri on a gurney and all four were tending to Marko, who was fighting off their efforts to restrain him. Good! While they struggled with Marko, I ran to Dimitri.

I threw myself down on the ground beside the gurney and directed my jaguar to leave me and enter Dima. She did, so quickly that if anyone saw her, they'd probably think they'd hallucinated.

Thoughts. Memories. Jumbled. Confused.

Who am I?

You are Dimitri.

Charlotte? Sharl?

I'm here. You have to get up, get to your leopard. My jaguar will help you.

I stand. No, not I. Dima stands. I urge him forward.

We walk toward the cops. Two paramedics jump toward us. One grabs our arm. Marko breaks away from the other two. They go after him. The cops draw their guns but can't shoot because the paramedics are in the line of fire. The guy holding our arm lets go when Marko heads our way.

In the house, quick. I'll take you to your leopard.

Dima moves, but too slowly. He's confused. Sick. I prod him along.

Marko runs, veering away from us, leading the paramedics away too. Intentional? He might be irrational, but the wolf within him wasn't.

We walk faster now. Dima's getting stronger. We make it to the front door. A cop breaks away from the others and trots over to us. "Stop right there," he yells, drawing his gun.

"I—I'm sorry," Dima says in a weak voice. "I'm going to be sick."

"You shouldn't have gotten off that gurney." The cop says sternly. He's got a firm grip on Dima's arm.

Which he loosens when Dima leans forward and barfs. So he hadn't just told a tale for the cop's benefit. Splattered, the cop draws back, releasing his grip. Dima staggers inside. We turn and lock the door.

Then we head for the room where the leopard lies. Dima moves like a puppet with jerky steps. My jaguar and I are the puppet masters.

Cops come down the steps, Officer Barr among them. They're carrying Roy, who seems unconscious.

So the fox is still out. They shout when they spot us. We keep walking. Have to reach the leopard. The cops follow. "Where're you going?" one demands. Not Officer Barr.

"Bathroom," Dima says, not stopping. "I'm sick. Threw up once already."

"Wait one minute," Officer Barr says. He grabs Dima's arm and spins him around, and I hope for a repeat of Dima's well-timed barf, but Dima just stands there swaying, ready to keel over.

"Nope, this isn't one of 'em," Barr declares.

I'm glad he can't know I'm there in Dima.

"Why aren't the paramedics treating you?" one asks.

"They're seeing to somebody else," Dima speaks my answer, his own thoughts too muddled to respond. He's terribly shaky. I have to keep him on his feet just a little longer.

It's no wonder the cop believes him when he says he's sick. He follows but doesn't stop us. The others, including Barr, have gone on out the door. I figure they'll turn Roy over to the paramedics. Good, that'll keep 'em busy so maybe they won't come after us.

We stagger down the hall and into the room where the leopard is. Henrietta's eyes go wide when she sees Dimitri. "How ...?"

She gets no answer. Dimitri totters to the bed and collapses on it beside the leopard. The cop has followed us into the room, but Henrietta confronts him. "I'm a nurse," she says. "I know what to do for him. Please leave."

Amazingly, he does, probably because of her insistent shooing motions more than her words.

She closes the door. My thoughts wrench free of Dimitri's; my jaguar comes out of him. Henrietta's jaw drops; she stares. The jaguar nudges the leopard. The leopard stirs. The jaguar leaps off the bed. The leopard very slowly fades into Dimitri.

Dimitri lies still, his eyes closed. The jaguar watches him for a few moments. When his eyelids flutter and his eyes open, she turns toward the window. It's closed, but Henrietta hurries to open it. As soon as she steps away from it, the jaguar leaps through it to hurry back to me.

She slinks along the side of the house, rounds the front corner, and crouches down among the sheltering shrubs. Her person is strapped on a gurney, about to be loaded into an ambulance. Police still surround some of the family members. Others have been put in police cars.

She cannot let her person be taken away without her, even if it means exposing herself to them. The police have guns already drawn. If they see her, they'll shoot her. But their attention is on those they hold captive. And the paramedics do not have guns. They have wheeled the gurney to the ambulance. In another moment they'll place it inside.

No time to waste. In three mighty leaps she covers the distance between the corner of the house and the gurney being lifted into the ambulance. A paramedic screams. A policeman whips around, ready to shoot. Too late. She fades into her host.

18
ESCAPE

I woke in the hospital. My jaguar! Where—? Panic shook me until I felt her safely inside me.

My head ached; my mouth felt stuffed with sand. Had they given me something, or was it just from the effort of helping my jaguar control Dimitri? When had my jaguar returned? Probing her memories, I followed her dash from Dimitri back to me.

Dimitri. I shuddered. I hadn't expected the access to his mind that I'd had while my jaguar was in him. Not his memories, but his feelings. Emotions. He might be "Mr. Cool" on the outside, but inside one big tangled mix of anger, fear, longing, bitterness, and hope twisted and turned like the raging winds of a cyclone. I understood what Henrietta had warned me about Dima's fragility. How in the world did he manage to keep all that under control?

What caused it? I almost wished I'd had access to his memories. But could I bear that kind of burden? I had memories of my own that I hadn't worked through. They still haunt me at times. But Dima. What haunts him so?

A nurse came in and glared at me like I'd committed a terrible crime. "You're awake," she announced in a tone that implied that maybe I should have gone on sleeping.

I didn't answer.

She aimed a thermometer at my mouth. I kept my lips clamped together. "Open your mouth," she snapped. "Unless you want me to take your temperature rectally?"

I opened and she jabbed the thermometer under my tongue. "Ow!" I said around the thermometer.

She was too busy strapping the blood pressure cuff around my arm to offer an apology. "Ow," I said again as the cuff tightened unmercifully.

"Don't talk," she ordered.

The cuff released, she removed the thermometer, made notations on the chart, and left. Good.

I sat up and swung my legs down off the bed. All I had on was a skimpy hospital gown, open in the back. I spotted a door I figured must be a closet and stood. Had to grab the side of the bed to steady myself. After-effect of my encounter with Dima's mind.

My dizziness subsided. I went to the closet. No clothes.

I went back to the bed and opened the drawers in the bedside stand. They held the usual toiletries provided by the hospital, but no clothes.

I went into the bathroom. Not there either, but while there I used the facilities. When I came out, the nurse stood in the room, waiting, her arms crossed.

"You're to remain in bed," she said.

"I can't even use the bathroom?"

"You may, but only with a nurse present. Use your buzzer and wait for me or another nurse to come before you get up."

"Why? There's nothing wrong with me."

"I'm merely relaying the doctor's orders. You'll have to discuss your condition with him."

"I don't have a condition. When will I see the doctor?"

"He'll be in sometime tomorrow. I can't say when."

I didn't intend to stick around until the doctor wandered in, but I didn't tell her that.

"The police want to talk to you," she said. "I've let them know you're able to be interviewed."

She marched out with an air of having performed a valuable service.

I understood why they'd hidden my clothes. I had to find a way out, but I wouldn't get far in a hospital gown. I put on the slippers provided for the patient's use, took the top sheet off the bed, wrapped it around me, and headed for the door.

Peering out cautiously, I waited until a couple of visitors disappeared into a room, made sure no nurse was in sight, then darted out into the hall. I hurried along, peeking into rooms until I spotted one with a sleeping patient, no nurse, no visitors. I slipped inside and closed the door.

The patient was a man. I'd have preferred a woman, but I didn't have the luxury of being choosy. I tiptoed to the closet, eased open the door, and found a shirt and trousers hanging there. I carried them quietly into the bathroom and put them on right over the gown. The shirtsleeves hung below my hands; I rolled them up. A belt hung from the pants. I buckled it in the tightest hole, rolled up the pant legs so I wouldn't trip on them, and left the bathroom. A glance told me the owner of the clothes still slept.

I eased out the door, ducked back inside at the sight of the nurse leading a cop to my room. As soon as they went in, I dashed from the room and headed for the elevator, came to a stair first, took that, and hurried up it. They'd expect me to go down.

At the next floor I walked nonchalantly through the corridor. I drew a few curious looks, but no one tried to stop me. The alarm hadn't yet been raised, but it would be soon. I found the elevators, took one to the second floor, started to get off, saw a cop heading toward me, hit the door closed button. I wasn't sure he'd seen me, but if he had, he knew what I was wearing and the description would be sent all over the hospital. I punched the button for the third floor, the fourth, the fifth, all the way up to the top. I jumped off at the third, hurried to the emergency exit, where a big sign warned that opening the door would sound an alarm. I opened the door, then ducked into the nearest room as the alarm screeched.

I peeled off the ill-fitting shirt and trousers while from the bed the woman patient stared, eyes bugging out. "Don't be scared," I told her. "I'm not here to hurt you. Just be quiet, please. I'll explain in a few minutes."

After kicking the discarded clothes into a corner, I stepped out into the hall in my hospital gown. Cops rushed to the door. "What's happening?" I asked in a quavery voice. "Is there a fire?"

One slowed enough to say, "No, ma'am. Just stay in your room. Everything's okay."

"I can get back in bed?"

"Yes. Absolutely."

I retreated into the room, closing the door. The elderly woman huddled in the bed, trembling. I hoped I wasn't giving her a heart attack.

"I won't hurt you. I'm not a criminal," I told her. "I'm trying to get away from my abusive husband. I need to get out of here without being seen. May I borrow some clothes?"

She didn't answer. I went to her closet, found a dress, a jacket, and shoes. Not my size, but closer than the man's shirt and trousers had been. I put them on.

"You'll find underpants in the dresser drawer," the woman offered quietly.

"Thanks," I said. I took out a pair and slipped them on. I'd have to manage without a bra.

The room's single window looked out on a roof one story down. I raised the window and broke the screen, which of course didn't swing open like the ones in the were house. I climbed out onto the sill, braced myself, and jumped.

It was a rough landing, but I only scraped hands and knees—no broken bones. I went to the edge of the roof and looked around, spotted a fire escape ladder, and scrambled down it to its end, a few feet above the ground. After that small jump I was up and running. With no money I couldn't take a cab or a bus.

I ducked into alleys, crossed streets dodging cars, and, when I'd put a few blocks between me and the hospital, slowed down and did my best to blend in with the pedestrian traffic while watching for cops.

Where could I go? Not back to the were house. That would be watched. Not to the homeless shelter that I'd been headed to when all this started. It was too late in the day; the shelter would have filled by now. Night would fall in another hour.

If I could phone Dr. Horshaw or the professor, I could get help. But I had no cell phone and no money for a pay phone. I could go into a store, claim I'd been robbed, and ask to make a call. But they'd want that call to be to the police.

As the daylight faded, the weather grew chill. And me without a jacket. No point in wishing for one; it only made me feel colder.

My erratic wandering wasn't entirely aimless; I'd been heading in the general direction of the center of town. Stores beckoned. I couldn't buy anything, but I could get warm while I browsed, always keeping a lookout for cops. I strolled down aisles and along showcases of merchandise until I started getting suspicious looks from clerks. When that happened, I meandered to the door, left, walked a bit farther and entered another store. I became familiar with the merchandise in a drugstore, a department store, a secondhand furniture shop, a shoe store. I was tired, cold, and my feet hurt from wearing shoes that must be two sizes too small for me. I needed a place to rest.

A restaurant sent out welcoming odors that drew me toward it. It was a small place that claimed to specialize in "meals like your mom used to make." That gave me a chuckle. I had no fond memories of my mother's cooking. Her meals were mediocre at best. But the smell of food was irresistible. I'd had no lunch and only a light breakfast, and I'd had a busy day. And my jaguar had been out. We needed food. So I swallowed my pride and entered the restaurant.

Most tables were full, but I did spy a couple of

empty seats. There was no hostess; I waited to catch a server's eye.

A waitress finally ambled over. I asked to see the manager. She looked me up and down, shrugged, said, "She's in the kitchen. I'll see if she can come out. She's pretty busy."

She hurried away and returned in a few minutes with a heavy-set woman wearing a scowl and a food-stained dress. "What is it?" the woman demanded in a sharp tone.

"I'm sorry to bother you," I said as humbly as I could manage and speaking in a low voice. "I have no money, no home at the moment, and I haven't eaten all day. I was wondering if I could do some work — cleaning, washing dishes, whatever you need — in exchange for a meal."

"I don't run a charity," she snapped, not bothering to lower her voice, thereby earning me stares from nearby diners.

"I'm not asking for charity. I'll work for what I eat."

"Got more workers now than I can afford. If business doesn't pick up, I'll have to let someone go."

I glanced around the nearly full restaurant. "It looks to me like your business is doing okay." I headed for the door.

"An alley runs in back of the place." Her voice stopped me. "Come up it to the rear door and I'll hand you out a bite. Best I can do." She turned and headed back to the kitchen.

I slunk out the front door, went to the end of the block, turned, and found the alley — dark, smelling of garbage and worse. Again I hesitated, not out of fear but disgust. Again my empty stomach growled insistently, urging me on.

I found the restaurant's rear door just past a big, smelly garbage bin. I knocked, the door opened, and the manager handed me out a paper plate with a slice of meatloaf, a scoop of mashed potatoes drowning in gravy, and a plastic fork. "This'll have to do," she said. "It's all I can spare."

She shut the door on my "Thank you," and left me standing in the dark holding the plate, already getting soggy from the gravy.

The food was hot. I wasted no time digging in. It wasn't the best meatloaf I'd ever tasted — or the worst. It did actually rather resemble my mother's. But it appeased my stomach. The mashed potatoes had lumps — so had my mother's. The person who put the sign on the restaurant must have had a mother who cooked like mine.

I finished and dumped plate and fork into the bin. I was still cold but not so hungry. The food gave me a little more energy. I walked on, not doubling back but continuing down the alley to the next street. A couple of cops walked along the sidewalk not far past me. I stayed out of sight until they reached the end of the block, then I crossed and started down the alley on that side.

The light from the streetlights didn't reach far. Soon I could see only by the scant light shed from tall buildings. I stopped at the sound of a scuffle up ahead of me.

"Stop! No!" A woman's voice gasped the words.

A man cursed. "Bitch!" The sound of a blow accompanied the words.

No time to find a place to sit. I leaned against the wall and let out my jaguar.

The jaguar slinks toward the sounds, almost invisible in the spotty light. She sees two figures, male and female. The female is on the ground. The male bends over her, his hands around her throat. Her weak struggles are useless against the much larger male.

The jaguar prowls closer, her paws making no sound. She crouches, springs, landing on the man's back. Her claws dig deep into his flesh. He screams and topples onto the female. The jaguar can easily kill him, but her person opposes the desire. So instead of fastening her powerful jaws around the man's neck, she takes the collar of his jacket in her mouth and stands, dragging him up, off the woman.

She shakes him until he slips out of the jacket, leaving it in her mouth while he stumbles away. She leaps toward him. He runs.

She lets him go and sniffs the woman lying on the ground. The woman is alive and awake, trembling. The jaguar drops the jacket over her body and zips back to her person.

19
NEW FRIENDS

I pushed off from the wall I'd leaned against and hurried to the woman. She was sitting up. Without light I couldn't tell whether she was injured or even what she looked like. She clutched the jacket to her chest.

"Are you hurt?" I asked.

"Just bruised. My neck's sore." She sounded hoarse, but her voice held steady. "What was that … that animal? That guy would have killed me if it hadn't attacked him."

"Who was the guy? Do you know him?" I carefully avoided answering her question.

"No. I just got off work. I had to wait for a taxi because my car's in the shop. He came out of nowhere, grabbed me, and pulled me in here. I gave him my purse, but that wasn't all he wanted." She shuddered. "He dropped my purse. It should still be here."

"If it is, we'll find it," I said. "You'll need money for the taxi."

She looked around. "Where is it? Where'd it go?"

"The purse? I'll hunt for it if you're sure you're okay."

"No. The animal. Some kind of big cat, I think."

"I didn't see it." I moved away, looking for her

purse, mostly for an excuse not to say more. But I didn't have to look far. In the dark I tripped over the purse, which lay just a few feet away. Good thing the would-be thief had been too scared to grab it as he ran off. I picked it up and took it back to her. She tried to rise. I gave her a hand. She grasped it firmly and pulled herself to her feet.

"Here's the purse," I said, handing it to her.

"Oh, thank the Lord! And thank you!" As she took the purse, she handed me the jacket the guy had abandoned. "Looks like you need this."

I took it gratefully and put it on. It was fleece-lined and warm but smelled sour and probably hadn't been cleaned in a long time. I was too cold to care.

We walked out of the alley, and under the streetlight I got a good look at her—and she at me. She was a young woman, well dressed, though her clothes were mussed and dirty now. Her hair was in disarray and studded with bits of paper and other trash from being pressed down into the ground in the filthy alley.

She was recovering faster than I would have expected from the experience of nearly being raped and probably murdered. "I should report the attack to the police," she said, looking up and down the street. Then, gazing thoughtfully at me, no doubt taking in my ill-fitting clothes and lack of purse, she added, "Or maybe I shouldn't? Why were you in the alley?"

I sighed. "It's a long story. Edited version: I got tossed out of my apartment because I couldn't pay the rent, and I've been walking around all afternoon trying to figure out where to go and what to do."

That *very* edited version held enough of the truth to satisfy, I hoped, and avoided all the dangerous details.

I guessed she knew I'd left out more than I'd told her. At least she didn't ask difficult questions.

"I'm Julia Saunders," she said, extending her hand.

I grasped it and said, "Charlotte Ramirez. My friends call me Sharl."

"Then Sharl it is. Please, come home with me. I have room, and I can't leave you out on the street after all you've done to help me."

"I didn't do that much," I said. "Just helped you up and found your purse."

"That's a lot." She hesitated before adding, "But I think you did much more."

Could she suspect that the "big cat" came from me? I didn't see how, but something in her eyes and the upward curve of her lips told me she did. I shouldn't accept her offer, shouldn't go with her and face more questions. But I was tired and cold and had nowhere else to go.

"Do you really have room for me?" I asked. "I don't want to put you to any trouble."

"It won't be any trouble. I'll be glad of the company."

"You don't even know you can trust me," I protested.

"I think I can. I'm a pretty good judge of character."

So I went with her. We found a taxi, she gave her address, and in a short time we reached her home, a cozy apartment in a gated complex in the better part of town. She remained calm throughout the drive, but as soon as we got inside she started shaking and collapsed on the sofa. She must have held herself together by sheer force of will until she reached the safety of her home.

"I can't believe how close I came to being raped. And probably killed," she said, tears spilling from her eyes. "I'm sorry. I didn't mean to fall apart like this."

"You have every right to, after what you went through. Sit still. I'll get you something to drink."

The apartment was small. I found the kitchen, opened the fridge and then cabinets, hunting something stronger than water. Not finding anything else, I grabbed a glass, filled it from the tap, and took it to her. "Drink this," I ordered. "Or if you have anything stronger, tell me where it is."

She shook her head. "Water's fine."

She drank it slowly, managing not to spill it despite her shaking hands. "Thanks," she said. "Look, I need to just sit here awhile and get myself back together. The bathroom's in there, through the bedroom." She pointed. "The bathroom closet has clean towels and washcloths, and there's shampoo on the window sill. Go ahead and take your shower. I'll get up before you finish and find something you can put on to sleep in. But right now I just want to be quiet and calm myself."

"Sure," I said, eager to clean up. "I really appreciate your help, Julia."

She gave a little laugh. "I owe you big time, Sharl. Go take your shower."

I walked through the bedroom into the bath, found the linen closet, got out a towel and washcloth, located the shampoo and body wash, and took a wonderful, steamy shower, making liberal use of the items I'd found. I felt much better when I emerged, clean, warm, and undoubtedly smelling better. Julia had pajamas laid out for me along with a warm robe to wrap up in.

"I've opened the sofa bed and made it up for you," she said when I emerged into the living room. "Make yourself comfortable. I'll be taking a good long shower. I feel slimy."

She went into the bedroom and closed the door, leaving me to get into the sofa bed where, warm, snug, and wonderfully relaxed, I had time to consider my options.

In the morning I could call Professor DuChamps. He'd been at the university while the other were house residents were rounded up. No one would have mentioned him, and I hoped Grandfather had had time to contact him and let him know what was going on. I should be able to reach him at his university office.

If I couldn't, I could call Dr. Horshaw. Henrietta had probably found a way to let her mother in on what was happening. Either way, I'd learn where and how everyone was and let someone know I was trying to help.

That settled, I thought about the day's events.

Officer Barr was a sadist, but our treatment of him would not be easily forgiven. Gene and Roy would have a hard time of it if, as I assumed, they'd been taken into custody. Also, I was certain that Grandfather would be charged with obstruction of justice. What of Ronnie and Lisette? And Henrietta?

Could charges be brought against them? Might they be free?

And Marko. We had rescued him only to have him retaken and probably returned to the hospital, this time to the psych ward on the basis of his actions when he recovered consciousness. He'd been separated from his wolf for a few days. Had that caused his strange behavior, or was it something deeper and more sinister? What had happened to him during the two years he'd been missing and thought dead? I still needed to solve that mystery.

But the thing that haunted me most was what I'd experienced when I'd sent my jaguar into Dima. The confusion. The whirl of emotions, including *guilt*.

Guilt? For what?

Yet it had been there, strong and unmistakable.

It and the other emotions had come to me in waves as overpowering and disorienting sensations. Although I couldn't read the thoughts that lay behind them, I was left with the impression of a highly intelligent but deeply troubled mind—and a feeling of shame that I had invaded his privacy.

He'd never forgive me for it. I'd lost any chance I ever had with him. I'd done it to save his life; that ought to count for something. But would it? He'd worked hard and long to build up the image he presented to everyone. He wore that image like armor, and I'd broken through it. No, he wasn't likely to forgive that. Where was he now? In the hospital? In jail? Or still at the were house?

There was a phone on a stand not far from where I lay. I resisted the temptation to get up and call. That would be foolish.

In the first place, Julia might hear and grow suspicious. I didn't want to do anything to destroy her trust in me. And in the second place, even if anyone remained at the were house and could answer, the phone could be tapped and my call traced. I didn't want to put anyone at the house in greater danger than they already were, and I definitely did not want the police to find me.

So I tried instead to go to sleep. And, despite all my worries, sleep came.

I remembered no dreams when I finally woke, stretched, and sat up feeling greatly refreshed.

I smelled coffee. Maybe the aroma woke me, or the sound and smell of bacon sizzling in a pan. I got up, put on the robe Julia had lent me, and went to the kitchen. I halted just past the door.

Julia wasn't alone. A boy, a teenager, sat at the table drinking coffee, a piece of buttered toast on the plate in front of him.

I recalled Professor DuChamps saying there might be other weres in the area. I'd just discovered one. Within the kid I saw a large brown bird. Not a crane, like Henrietta. A bird of prey. Some kind of eagle.

He looked up at me, grinned, and waved.

Julia turned from the stove, a pan full of scrambled eggs in her hand. "Oh, Sharl, come in," she said. "I hope we didn't wake you. This is my cousin, Ryan. His mom's my aunt, my mother's sister. Ryan, say hello to Sharl."

"Hi, Sharl. You're just in time for breakfast. Have a seat."

I sat. My knees had started to buckle. Julia set a plate in front of me and filled it with scrambled eggs, followed by bacon and toast. And a cup of coffee. All of which I ignored to stare at Ryan. I saw the family relationship between him and Julia—the same light brown hair, same warm smile. Like Julia's, his cheeks dimpled when he smiled. But Julia wasn't were.

"Um, do I have butter on my nose or something?" Ryan asked, rubbing his nose and still grinning.

"No. I'm sorry. I guess I'm still half asleep. I didn't expect to see anyone here but Julia." *Does Julia know what he is? Is that why he's here?*

"Ryan lives just around the corner," Julia said. "He often drops in for breakfast on the weekends."

Weekend. Today was Saturday. I'd forgotten. Lost all track of time and days.

"Mom has to get up early to go to work, so I'm on my own for the day," Ryan explained.

It all sounded perfectly innocent. A coincidence. Maybe too much of one.

"Don't let your eggs get cold," Julia said, joining us at the table with a plate of her own.

I scarfed down the breakfast while trying to figure out how to get the kid alone to confront him about being were. Maybe Julia already knew, but if she didn't I shouldn't blow his cover.

By the time I finished eating I had a plan. "I need to make a couple of phone calls, but I don't want to use your phone, Julia. I need to call from a phone that can't be traced. Please don't ask why. I'm in trouble, but I swear I haven't done anything wrong. Do either of you know where I can find a pay phone or—"

"Use my cell phone!" Ryan interrupted, pulling the phone from his pocket. "Nobody'd know you used it. Will that work?"

I considered. I didn't want to get Ryan in trouble with the police, but I had to make at least one phone call. And why would the police check his phone? "Okay, that should work," I said. "But I have to get dressed first. I'll make the call outside so it can't be traced back here. I'll go all the way beyond the gate."

"I'll wait and walk out there with you," Ryan said, still excited.

Julia hadn't said anything, and now she was frowning. Obviously she didn't like the idea.

"Julia, you've been so kind to me, and I don't want to bring any trouble your way. Please trust me. It's safer if I call away from this building."

The frown didn't leave her face. "I don't want Ryan to get into any trouble. I'd rather you didn't involve him."

"Aw, Julia, I want to be involved."

"Without knowing what you're involved in? You've just met Charlotte."

So I wasn't Sharl anymore. Can't say I blamed Julia. But Ryan's enthusiastic willingness to help could mean he'd recognized me as a fellow were. The kid clearly wasn't stupid. He had no other reason to be so cooperative. He had to be bursting with curiosity, and he couldn't ask questions in front of Cousin Julia. That could mean she didn't know what he was or that he figured she didn't know what I was, and he didn't want to tell her without my okay.

"Look, Julia, I understand your concern. I don't want Ryan involved in anything, either. But I do desperately need to use the phone. It's very important—not just to me. To a lot of people. People who're depending on me for help. I promise you, I'll keep the calls brief and give Ryan back the phone in a matter of minutes. He can go home, and I'll get out of your lives."

I probably laid it on too thick. I certainly hadn't resolved her doubts. But Ryan took it out of her hands. "Get dressed," he told me. "Hurry. I'll wait and we'll go outside."

Fifteen minutes later Ryan and I were standing outside on the walkway to the gate. Julia stood in the front doorway, watching until we passed through the complex gate, at which point she slammed her front door. I'd obviously worn out my welcome.

Ryan handed me the cell phone.

I fumbled with it, not familiar with the way it was set up. "I need the number that'll give the directory for the university," I told him. "Gotta look up a prof's office number."

"Will he be in his office on a Saturday?"

Damn! I hadn't thought. But he might be there. He couldn't return to the were house, could he? "If I can find the number. I'll try it anyway."

"Let me find it for you," he offered, taking back the phone. He knew just how to go about it, found the university number, punched in the digits for the directory, and handed the phone back to me.

I found the extension number I needed, and dialed. It rang until it went to voice mail. I didn't leave a message.

I looked up Dr. Horshaw's number, called it, and got her answering machine. The message gave an emergency number. I called that and prayed it wouldn't go to voice mail.

Hooray! She answered. I identified myself.

"Oh, Charlotte, you're safe! We couldn't imagine what had happened to you!"

We? I was bursting with questions, but this wasn't the time to ask them. "I'm fine except that I'm kinda stuck. No money, borrowed clothes that make me look like a bag lady. Nowhere to go. And I don't want to stay on the phone any longer than I have to."

"Tell me where you are and I'll come and get you. We'll talk then."

I could have hugged her! I asked Ryan for the nearest cross streets and gave her that location. I'd wait for her on the corner, away from Julia's house and from Ryan's.

I gave the phone back to Ryan. "Now go right home with this. And if the police should somehow trace the call and question you, tell them you were just walking down the street, texting somebody, and a strange lady stopped you and asked to borrow your phone, and you let her. But you didn't ask her name, and you don't know who she called or why. Will you do that? Please?" As I spoke I walked to the corner Ryan had indicated, and he walked with me.

I understood why. I wasn't at all surprised when he said, "First I gotta ask you something. If you answer my question, I'll do whatever you say."

"Fair enough," I said, knowing what he was dying to ask. "But make it fast. I'll worry about you until I'm sure you're safe at home."

"Okay." He stuffed the phone into his pocket. "I, well, uh, I think—I mean, I—" Now that he could finally ask, he'd lost his nerve.

To save time I helped him out. "You want to know if I'm were."

"Were?"

Sounded like he'd never heard the word. "Okay, I'll make it simple. You have an eagle spirit within you that can come out in physical form. Like you, I have an animal spirit. So we're both weres."

His eyes widened; his face lit up.

"My animal isn't an eagle, though," I went on. "She's a jaguar."

"A jaguar! That's awesome." He stared at me, awe mingled with fear. "I guessed—felt—you were like me. My whole body had goose bumps when you walked into the kitchen. But I thought that meant you'd have an eagle, like me."

"No. A were can have any kind of animal spirit."

"But a jaguar! Does it come out? And hunt?"

"Yes, she's a predator, but I know how to control her. Your eagle's a predator, too. Can you control him?"

"I—No, I guess not. I mean, he comes out when I get mad or upset, so I try not to ever get mad. Or upset. I don't want anybody hurt."

"That's good, but it isn't enough. You need to learn to control him." I quoted something Pierre, my mentor, had so often said to me: "Let him be your guide but not your master."

"How can I learn?" He was so desperately eager, hanging on my every word. If only I could help him!

But now I had no time, nor would it be safe for either of us. "Listen, I know a lot of people like us, and they—we—can help you learn what you need to know. But not now. Now you need to keep what you are secret. Don't let your eagle out. Don't tell anybody about it."

"Why not?"

"Because some people are trying to kill us. And until we find them and deal with them, we're all in danger. You, too, if anybody knows about you. Does Julia know?"

"No, I haven't told her. I tried once, but I didn't get far. She just thinks I'm strange."

Hmm. I hoped he was right, but I suspected Julia knew more than he realized.

A car pulled up. I peered in, and Dr. Horshaw waved at me.

"That's my ride. I have to go. Give me your phone number. I'll get in touch when it's safe."

He told me, and I repeated it twice so I'd remember it until I could write it down.

"Okay. Bye, Ryan, and stay safe."

He nodded. I opened the car door and jumped in. I waved as we drove off.

20
JUDGED

"Who's the boy?" Dr. Horshaw asked right off. Her usually serene and kindly face wore a grim expression. Not good.

"Someone I just met. He's were," I said. "He needs training, but this isn't the time. Got to write down his phone number before I forget it. Do you have any paper and a pencil?"

She kept her eyes steady on the road ahead. "Look in the glove compartment."

I looked, found a notepad and a pen, wrote the number.

"Now, please," I begged, "tell me what you know about the family. What's happened to everybody?"

"Most of them have landed in jail," she said. "They even took my Henrietta, though they had no grounds to hold her. I got her out this morning. Grandfather Blass has contacted his lawyer, so most of the others should be out on bail soon if they aren't already, but the charges are serious. I don't know what will to happen to them."

"What about Dimitri? And Marko?"

Her face became even grimmer. "They've taken Marko back to the hospital. He's in the psych ward. They won't let me see him. Dimitri was taken to the hospital, checked over, and pronounced fit enough to be hauled off to jail with the others. How did you escape?"

"They took me to the hospital, but I found a way out, or I'd have been arrested, too." I went on to tell her briefly what I'd done, how I'd escaped from the hospital, and how I met Julia and, this morning, Ryan.

"So Julia doesn't know what you are?"

"No, but I think she suspects something. Probably suspects something about her cousin, too. And I don't think she trusts me anymore."

"That could be dangerous." She kept her gaze fixed on the road ahead of her and a too-tight grip on the steering wheel. I seemed to make everybody nervous lately.

"I hope not," I said. "She's a good person. She worries about Ryan."

"That could lead her to ask questions. And if the paper reports the raid on the were house and she reads about it, she may put two and two together and feel obligated to report you to the police."

"Even if she does, she won't know my location. By the way, where are we going?"

"Right now we're going to my condo. Henrietta is there. But you can't stay there, and you can't go back to the Blass's. The police have taken over the house and are giving it a thorough going over. That's very bad."

A huge understatement. They'd find evidence of the animals, and they'd probably find fingerprints matching ones Gene and Dimitri'd left at the church. They'd charge them with murder — they'd never accept a claim of self-defense.

I had to find that preacher, the only survivor, and persuade him to confess. Dangerous, yes. Foolhardy, absolutely! But it offered the only hope for Dima and the rest. People I'd come to regard as my family.

I told Dr. Horshaw what I needed to do. She pursed her lips. After an awkward silence she said, "You'll get yourself killed."

"Maybe," I acknowledged. "I have to try, though."

She continued to stare at the road ahead. "Ronnie blames you for everything that's happened."

"I know. I hope you don't agree with her."

"No. But I do think you've acted rashly at times."

She put it nicely, but I didn't miss the powerful undertone of disapproval.

"Believe me, I'm still grateful to you for saving Henrietta by rescuing her crane." She still hadn't looked at me.

"I didn't do any more than Dima and Gene. Without them the rescue wouldn't have happened."

"And look where they are now."

It sounded like she resented me for not sitting in jail along with them. That she thought I'd gotten off too easy.

Maybe I had. But at least I had a chance to help them that I wouldn't have if I'd been thrown into jail too. Dr. Horshaw must realize that, but she probably feared I'd involve Henrietta again. I wouldn't. Her crane didn't offer her the protection my jaguar gave me.

We reached Dr. Horshaw's condo, in a fancy building. When we entered the foyer, Henrietta rushed to hug me. It was a relief to know she didn't share her mother's unspoken but obvious bitterness toward me. Or maybe not toward me alone but toward the whole chain of events that I'd somehow precipitated and that had brought harm and danger to her daughter and others that she loved. I didn't blame Dr. Horshaw. I felt bitter, too.

"I'm so happy you escaped," Henrietta said, still hugging me.

"And I'm happy you're free and here," I answered, hugging her back. "Who else is free? And where are they?"

"Georges DuChamps hadn't left the university when the others were arrested," Dr. Horshaw said. "He's free and probably at the apartment he keeps near the campus."

That news brought me some relief. I'd assumed he lived at the were house.

"We're hoping some of the others can stay with him when he's released," Henrietta offered. "The police have barred entry to the were house while they examine it for evidence."

"And have any of the others been released?"

"I think Ronnie and Lisette were, after being questioned, but they haven't been in touch with us." As she spoke, Henrietta grasped my hand and pulled me into the living room to the sofa and sat down on it, pulling me down with her. All the while she continued to talk. "We don't know where they've gone. I called the nail salon where Lisette works, but she hasn't showed up. The manager is quite upset. Wherever Ronnie's hiding out, I'm sure she won't leave town while Roy's in jail."

"It's probably better that the group disperses rather than trying to stay together," Dr. Horshaw put in. taking a seat in a comfortable-looking armchair opposite the sofa. She didn't relax. Her hands gripped the edges of the chair arms and she sat forward, her posture stiff. "Safer, I'd think."

She was probably right, but I'd feel better knowing everyone's location and how to reach them.

"The family lawyer was working on getting Cameron released, but we haven't yet gotten word that they have been," Henrietta said. "I asked to be notified, but Mr. Harper, the lawyer, hasn't called. Fortunately, Helene and Jeffrey weren't home, so the police don't have them."

"I'd hoped you might have heard something while I was out picking up Charlotte," her mother said.

Henrietta shook her head.

"What about Roy? And Grandfather and Grandmother Blass?" I asked.

"The lawyer's working on their release, too, but they've been charged with obstruction of justice and resisting arrest without violence. Those charges shouldn't prevent them from getting bail, but the police have linked Dima and Gene to the killings in the church, and they're investigating whether others in the household were involved. Funny, you and I were there in the church in our animals, but the police have no way of knowing that, leaving us in the clear."

"But no one else was involved but you and me and Gene and Dima."

"Not directly, but Grandfather helped with the cover-up, hiding the car that got wrecked and providing alibis for Gene and Dima."

"But do the police know that? Besides, Gene and

Dima only defended themselves. They can plead self-defense."

"I'm not sure what the police know, but they police won't believe a self defense claim. They have no proof of it except for our word."

"I know. That's why I'm going to try to find that preacher and get him to tell the truth."

Henrietta gasped.

"I'm trying to make her see the danger in that foolhardy course," Dr. Horshaw put in. "It could get her killed or make matters worse for us all."

"It could," I agreed. "It's also the only way to keep Gene and Dima from being tried for murder."

The phone on the table beside Dr. Horshaw's chair rang, and she picked it up, said, "Hello, Dr. Emmaline Horshaw speaking," listened for a moment, then took the handset into another room to continue the call.

Henrietta shook her head. "That could be a patient calling, or the hospital," she said, "but I can't help feeling it's something about this mess. Mother's far more upset than she lets on."

Since I'd picked up on a lot of upset, I wondered how much worse it could be. "I know she's worried about you and she's afraid I'll involve you even more. I don't intend to do that, though. I do feel responsible for a lot of what's happened, and I feel an obligation to try to make it right, but I mean to do that on my own."

"I want to help," Henrietta insisted, placing a hand on mine.

"Your crane can't protect you the way my jaguar can protect me. But you can help by keeping me informed about what's going on with everybody. I won't stay here, but I'll find a way to check with you often."

Dr. Horshaw returned but didn't resume her seat. "That was Mr. Harper, the attorney," she said. "Grandfather and Grandmother Blass have been freed on bail. They are returning to the were house. The police have completed their search and have okayed their return. But Mr. Harper said that under no circumstance should any of the rest return there. Cameron has been released with no charges filed against him. He's gone to Helene and Jeffrey's gallery. They have an apartment above the gallery where they stay sometimes. They may take a trip out of town, ostensibly to purchase art. Cameron can't go with them; the police have told him not to leave town. He'll go back to the were house. The police are still looking for Joy and suspect foul play. They haven't said they suspect Cameron of hurting or killing his wife, but they are keeping him under surveillance. We can neither call the were house nor go there, so we have no way to contact the Blasses directly. I wish I knew how to find Ronnie and Lisette."

"Did he say anything about Dima and Gene? Or Roy?" I asked

"They've been refused bail, although he thinks bail will eventually be granted for Roy. They have nothing to link him to the deaths in the church."

"What have they charged him with then?"

"Battery on a police officer. Obstruction of justice. And Harper thinks they're trying to come up with more charges. Seems the arresting officer is out to get him."

"Officer Barr," I said, anger growing as I replayed the cop's cruel treatment of Roy. "He's a sadist. He's the one that ought to be charged with battery." I described what I'd witnessed.

"Would you be willing to testify against him?"

"Sure, but would anybody believe me? I mean, it would be my word against a cop's."

"Gene also witnessed his behavior."

"Yeah, and Gene's charged with murder."

"Point taken," Dr. Horshaw said. "But still, we can't foresee the future. I have to believe that the truth will come out and justice will triumph."

"I hope you're right," I said, "though I think justice will need a lot of help."

At least Dr. Horshaw seemed to have warmed to me a bit. "You can stay here long enough to have lunch with us," she said. "That will give us time to help you find a place to stay. You'll need better clothes. I can lend you money to buy a few things. Eventually we should be able to get your own things out of the were house."

I frowned. "I'll need money to rent a place or pay for a hotel room. That'll take a good bit. I can't borrow that much. I'd never be able to pay it back."

During my conversation with her mother, Henrietta had been sitting very still, cranelike, brow puckered. Now her head snapped up.

"I know a way to get in touch with Grandfather Blass," she announced. "We'll write a note telling him that Charlotte is here and what she plans to do. I'll let my crane out and, Mother, you can attach the note to her leg. Then the crane will fly to the were house, let herself in, find Grandfather, and make sure he sees the note. He'll read it and write an answer and attach it to her leg, and she'll return with it. It should be safe enough. And maybe Grandfather will know the whereabouts of Lisette and Ronnie. And what to do about Charlotte. And everything."

I had to smile at Henrietta's faith in Grandfather. She seemed to imbue him with near godlike abilities. But while I smiled, Dr. Horshaw frowned.

"That's dangerous," she said. "You promised me you wouldn't let your crane out until all this is worked out."

"Why is it dangerous?" Henrietta rose to her feet. "The crane will fly there, deliver the note, and come right back. We can't phone because the phones are probably tapped, and even if they aren't, the police could trace any calls. This is the only way to get the information we need and give Grandfather the information we have."

I nodded. "It could work," I said.

"I don't like it," Dr. Horshaw stated flatly.

"Well, I can't bear to just stay here and do nothing, and I don't know anything else we can do," Henrietta said, plunking her hands on her hips. "I know I made you a promise, but I have to break it. My crane wants to do it. It feels right to her. So I will do it, whether you approve or not."

Her mother's eyes filled with tears. She turned away, I guess to hide them from us. Henrietta went to her and put her arms around her. "I'm sorry, Mom. I love you, but I have a responsibility to do all I can for my fellow weres. And this is something—the only thing—that I can do. So please understand and don't withhold your blessing."

Dr. Horshaw sighed, rested her head on Henrietta's shoulder, and whispered something into her ear. She must have yielded. Henrietta hugged her and said, "All right, let's compose the note." She pulled her mother over to a desk in the corner of the room. I rose, followed, and stood behind them while Dr. Horshaw sat at the desk and Henrietta stood beside her, one hand on her mother's shoulder.

The writing of the note took some time and some discussion over the wording, but eventually we had an account that satisfied us all. We had to keep it short, so without going into the details of my escape from the hospital and omitting mention of my encounter with Julia, we stated that I'd come here but would not stay, that we didn't know where Lisette or Ronnie had gone, that Mr. Harper had called Dr. Horshaw and what instructions he'd given, and finally that to clear Gene and Dima we had to prove they acted in self-defense by tracking down the minister and persuading him to confess to what he and his followers had done. I'd insisted that we add that part. We concluded by asking him to tell us what he could about Marko.

Henrietta lay down on the couch, relaxed, and let the crane emerge. Dr. Horshaw threw an afghan over her daughter while I rolled up the note and taped it to the crane's leg. Dr. Horshaw inspected my taping, declared it secure, and opened the door. The crane stepped out, walked a short distance, flapped her wings, and soared into the distance, disappearing behind a cloud.

Dr. Horshaw and I settled in to wait. Time crawled. Lunchtime came and went. Neither of us felt like eating. Dr. Horshaw tried to work on some reports, but her eyes kept straying to the clock. I tried to read a news magazine but gave up after I'd read the same paragraph about four times and still had no idea what it said.

Both of us glanced frequently at Henrietta. Her eyes were open but unfocused. Once she gave a little jerk, but she didn't try to speak.

Only a little over two hours went by, but it seemed like a full day. A tap tap sounded on the front door. I jumped up and rushed to open it. So did Dr. Horshaw. We collided. She pushed me aside and threw open the door. The crane walked in. A thick roll of paper was taped to her leg. Dr. Horshaw removed it with expert care. As soon as it came off, the crane walked to the sofa and faded into Henrietta.

Henrietta sat up, rubbed her forehead, and let out a big, "Whew!"

Dr. Horshaw sat beside her, still holding the unrolled message in her lap. "Your plan worked splendidly, dear."

"Yes, we had no problem at the were house. Grandfather let in the crane, read the message, thought about it awhile, and then wrote his reply, and we started back. Then along the way somebody shot at us. Just missed. I think it clipped a couple of tail feathers."

"Oh, dear! Was it the police, do you think?"

"No, we'd flown well away from the house. I think some idiot just thought it would be fun to shoot a crane."

"But that's illegal!"

"Some people don't care."

"Oh, I'm so glad you're safe." Dr. Horshaw hugged her.

I was ready to grab the message out of the doctor's lap when she finally unrolled it. A newspaper clipping slipped out of it. She placed a hand over it and looked at the rather long note. I thought she'd read it aloud, but she didn't.

"Oh! Oh dear!" She raised a hand to her mouth. "Oh, Charlotte, this is terrible. Terrible." She picked up the newspaper clipping and scanned it. "Oh, no! We must get a message back to Grandfather Blass. But not by the crane. I won't risk you again, Henrietta, no matter what you say."

"Please, tell us what the note says," I begged.

"Yes, please," Henrietta seconded.

"I can't." She handed it to me. "Here, you read it."

I started reading aloud. "Dear Henrietta and Emmaline, I can't tell you what a relief it is to hear from you and know that you are safe and well. I feel deeply concerned for all our family and friends. Velma and I are fine now that we are home, but we spent a most unpleasant night in jail cells, and I worry greatly for Dima and my poor Gene, who must remain incarcerated. Stanley Harper has done all he can, but he has not succeeded at negotiating their release and under present circumstances is not likely to. He does believe he'll have Roy out soon, though the bail may be quite high."

"That Charlotte Ramirez is with you concerns me deeply. I am not … certain she …" I stopped reading aloud, unable to speak the words written in Grandfather's flowing script. I shook my head and read the rest silently.

I am not certain she can be trusted. She may mean well, I do not know, but she seems to draw trouble as a magnet draws iron filings.

I rejoiced when Marko and his wolf were reunited at last, but poor Marko is now in a locked psychiatric ward. I fear the way he was removed from the hospital caused serious, perhaps irreparable damage. He seems convinced that everyone is trying to hurt him, and fear consumes him. As they placed him in the ambulance, he called out to me, and his words haunt me. "Grandfather, save me, they're killing me." I'm told that when he is not sedated he still calls out for me and screams in terror. I have begged to be allowed to see him, but my plea has been refused.

We here have also not heard from Rhonda or Lisette, and like you, we are concerned about them. Only Cameron is here with us. It is possible Lisette has returned to Deland to her parents' home. It does seem odd that she would not have informed her employers in that case. We shall endeavor to discover if she has gone there. Georges will be able to make discreet inquiries.

Now, back to Charlotte. On the supposition that you may not have read the morning newspaper I have sent herewith an article that greatly troubles me. I read the paper carefully, fearing that news of our arrests and the charges against us would be blazoned on its pages, but apparently the police are being more circumspect in that regard than I would have anticipated. However, this news item caught my attention. The "large cat" it speaks of can only have been Charlotte's jaguar. Helene most certainly did not let her lynx out, and Dimitri could not have released his leopard if he wanted to. Velma insists that Charlotte would not have been so reckless, but I feel she has been consistently reckless and that this bears her trademark. How she could allow her jaguar to attack in the way described I cannot fathom. I can only say that I regret taking her into my home and so bringing conflict where peace and harmony had prevailed.

I will have her things gathered together and will try to find a way to get them to her. Beyond that I will do nothing more for her. I believe you will understand when you read the article. I cannot countenance such behavior. If I am wrong, and the animal described was not Charlotte's jaguar, I shall certainly apologize. However, I shall also be very surprised if that is the case.

Thank you again for finding a way to inform me of your situation and to learn ours. I assure you that I will not rest easy until all the family is once again reunited under my roof (sans Miss Ramirez, of course). Tell her most emphatically that she must not endanger herself and others by attempting further "assistance" that can only lead to greater disaster.

Yours truly,

Martin Blass.

For several moments I was too stunned to look at the newspaper article. I just sat holding the letter and staring into space, my eyes filling with unshed tears.

Henrietta placed her hand on mine. "Sharl, what is it?"

Without a word I handed her the letter.

How could Grandfather be so quick to judge me? He'd given me tough assignments, and I'd carried them out to the best of my ability. I'd saved Dima's life and probably Marko's as well. I'd helped rescue Henrietta. But none of that counted for anything, apparently. He'd put all the blame for everything that happened on me. I didn't deserve that.

Did I?

I looked at the article he had sent with the letter. It was an account of a guy by the name of Calvin Astinger, temporarily homeless, who had been walking along the street hoping to find a place to sleep, when a large cat attacked him, knocked him down, badly scratched and bit him, so that he barely avoided death. He'd been spared only because someone, whom he had not seen, called off the cat, allowing him to get up and stumble away. Police, investigating Astinger's strange account, found the bloody paw prints of a large feline. Police say there may be a connection with the homicides in the Christian Witness Church, where tracks of a large feline were also found. Zoos and wild animal refuges in the area have reported no missing animals, so police suspect that an unlicensed private owner allowed the animal's escape. There followed the usual plea for information and numbers to call to report any sighting of the animal. I dropped the clipping into my lap and stared off into space.

Grandfather just assumed that this creep was telling the truth? That my jaguar had jumped on him without provocation? That he was an innocent victim of some careless or deliberate action of mine that led me to turn the jaguar loose on him?

While I sat wallowing in self-pity and resentment toward Grandfather, Henrietta plucked the clipping from my lap. A few minutes later she broke through my black funk with the declaration, "Charlotte, you've got to go back to the woman you saved and get her to talk to Grandfather and tell him what really happened."

Somehow I mustered the energy to speak. "She doesn't know what really happened. It was pitch dark in the alley the man dragged her into, and he'd dropped down on top of her when my jaguar leapt onto his back. She saw it, but she didn't see it come back and fade into me. She didn't know where it came from or where it had gone."

"But you said she suspected something and also knew something was strange about her cousin," Dr. Horshaw said.

"I thought she might know about Ryan and therefore might suspect I was were, too. But Ryan swore he'd never told her, and I believe him."

"I don't see why that matters," Henrietta objected. "She knows the jaguar saved her from being raped and probably murdered. She can tell Grandfather that. He knows where the jaguar came from and went back to."

"And how am I supposed to get her and Grandfather together? She pretty much threw me out, afraid I might be in some trouble that Ryan could get involved in. After all, she didn't know what made me lurk in that dark alley."

"What did?"

"I'd seen couple of cops walking along the street and figured I should avoid them."

"So go tell her that."

"Then she'd be even more suspicious of me."

"Which is more important to you," Henrietta asked, "Julia's trust or Grandfather's?"

"I've already lost Grandfather's trust—if I ever had it," I almost choked on the words.

Dr. Horshaw patted my hand. "Then you must

gain it back. Henrietta is right; Grandfather's trust is vital. Julia is, after all, only a chance acquaintance, and not were."

"But I promised Julia she wouldn't see me again," I said, feeling my resolve weaken.

"But without Grandfather's good will, you may not be able to help Dima and Gene," Henrietta said.

That did it. "All right, all right. I'll go see Julia. But what do I tell her?"

"As much of the truth as you can without revealing that you're were," Dr. Horshaw advised.

I shook my head. "That's not much. Everything's bound up with my being were."

"Just see her and ask her to tell Grandfather exactly what happened from her point of view," Henrietta said. "You don't need to explain anything. Grandfather will get the true picture."

It sounded so easy. Somehow, I didn't think it would be.

21
SECRETS REVEALED

Dr. Horshaw decided that we should pay Julia a visit right away. I wanted to wait until tomorrow morning, but Henrietta agreed with her mother, overruling me.

I suggested calling her first, but they talked me out of that too. I didn't think Dr. Horshaw's phone would be tapped, but she refused to take the chance. "It could be," she said. "The police know of my connection to the Blass family, and they know that Henrietta is staying here temporarily."

"But Henrietta isn't involved in anything," I objected.

"Tell that to the police," Dr. Horshaw said with more than a trace of bitterness.

So I let Dr. Horshaw drive me back to the corner where she'd picked me up, and from there I directed her to Julia's apartment complex.

Her *gated* complex. I couldn't just walk up and ring her doorbell. Since I didn't know the gate code, The gate guard had to ring her apartment, tell her I was there, and ask if I had permission to visit.

Dr. Horshaw leaned out the car window to speak to the guard. "Please tell Miss Saunders that it is vitally important that we speak to her."

The guard, not smiling, ducked back into his post and phoned. He stepped out of the guard post wearing a big smile. "Miss Saunders said for you to go right up."

I stared, not taking it in at first. I'd expected to be turned away and have to find a way to sneak in. But luck favored us. Julia was willing to see me!

"Shall I come with you, or would you prefer to face her alone?" Dr. Horshaw asked.

I considered. "Come with me," I decided. "In case I need a character witness." I said it in a kidding way, but it really could come to that.

We reached the door to Julia's apartment, and I raised my hand to ring the bell but hesitated, still unsure of my welcome. And in that instant the door opened and Julia reached out to draw me inside and into her arms.

"Oh, Charlotte, I'm so glad you've come! I didn't know how to get in touch with you." She released me from her embrace. "This is an answer to my prayers. I hadn't read the morning paper until after you left. Did you see — ?"

"The article about the man who claimed to be just walking along the street when a big cat of some kind attacked him?" I interrupted. "Oh, yes, I saw it. That's why I've come."

"The nerve of the guy! He mugged me and would have raped me and maybe killed me. Oh, I'm so glad you've come back! We have to tell the police what really happened."

"Wait, Julia," I said. "Before we go any farther, I want you to meet Dr. Horshaw. She drove me here because I need your help."

"You need *my* help?" She sounded incredulous. "I need yours! But sit down, please. Dr. Horshaw, I'm pleased to know you. Thank you for bringing Charlotte here."

She indicated comfortable easy chairs, and we sat. She perched on the couch and continued. "As soon as I read the article, I called the police and told them what had really happened. And of course, they wanted to know why I hadn't gone to them right away. I should have, but you talked me out of it. Now I don't think they believe me. It's my word against his. I don't want the dirty creep to get away with it. He'll just do it to someone else. So I need you to corroborate my story. To be my witness."

This wasn't going to be easy. I took a deep breath. "And I need you to be mine, to tell someone what really happened," I said.

"So we can help each other. I'll call the police and tell them I have a witness." She stood and headed for the phone.

I looked at Dr. Horshaw. She shrugged, which I took to mean I was on my own. "No, wait!" I said. "Don't call."

She stopped and turned toward me, eyebrows raised over wide eyes. "Why not?"

"I … I can't go to the police. They're looking for me, and I can't let them find me."

"Why? What did you do?"

"That's a long story and I can't tell it. It involves a lot of other people who expect me to keep quiet."

"Charlotte's situation is similar to yours, Julia," Dr. Horshaw put in. "Someone told the police a false story, and without witnesses who can substantiate her story, Charlotte has no way of proving that the story is false."

"But then you need someone who can tell the police the truth."

"Yes, I do." How much did I dare tell her? I went on, but a bit falteringly. "Um, not about what happened last night in that alley. There's nothing you can tell the police that would help me. But there is someone who needs to know what really happened last night, someone who unfortunately believed what the article in the newspaper reported."

"And who is this mystery person?" Julia's tone had grown frosty. I understood. She resented the fact that I wouldn't help her but expected her to help me. And without an explanation.

"His name is Martin Blass," Dr. Horshaw stated while I hesitated, unsure of what I dared tell Julia. "He needs to know he can trust Charlotte because she may be his only hope of proving that his grandson is not a murderer."

Gene! She means Gene. Not Dima. She didn't mention him. But they're both innocent.

But of course Gene, being his grandson, would be Grandfather's main concern. And Julia didn't need to know—mustn't know—all the details.

"Who is he? Who is his grandson? Why is he being accused of murder?" Julia had so many questions. She'd never accept that I couldn't answer them.

I remained silent, and so did Dr. Horshaw.

Julia's eyes widened suddenly. She looked at me. "The murders in the church. The paper said the police had taken two suspects into custody."

Grandfather hadn't sent us that article. Guess he knew we already knew.

I still didn't answer in words, but Julia must have read the answer in my face. "It is, isn't it? That horrible massacre. And the police have the wrong people in custody?"

"Not exactly," I said slowly. "The whole thing isn't what it seemed."

I should have kept my mouth shut.

"Four men slaughtered? The pastor severely wounded? And it wasn't what it seemed? What was it then?" Her voice rose more with each question.

"Self-defense," I answered weakly.

"Self-defense! That's nonsense."

Dr. Horshaw came to my rescue. "Not nonsense at all. They were saving my daughter's life. And putting themselves in terrible danger by doing so."

"And you were there?" The question was directed at me, not at Dr. Horshaw.

"Not exactly." I didn't expect my evasive but truthful answer to satisfy her.

It didn't. "What in the world does that mean? You either were or you weren't." Scorn dripped from her voice. Her eyes flashed.

"I can't explain." We shouldn't have come here.

"Wait! The big cat. Or whatever it was. The animal that saved me. It was yours. Wasn't it?"

I nodded, hoping she wouldn't probe further.

She did. "Where did it go? I didn't see it after the attack. You didn't have it with you when I brought you back here. Did you just turn it loose?"

"Oh, no. She was ... well, she was safe."

"Safe? But we were right downtown. Where could she go?"

This wasn't getting any easier. I tried desperately

to think of some explanation that would make sense without really explaining anything.

Dr. Horshaw seemed equally at sea.

Until Julia said slowly, "Unless ... Ryan tried to tell me something once. About him. And about an eagle. I thought he was kidding. Then I thought he must be delusional. And I thought the delusion passed, because he never brought up the subject again. But when he met you, he got so excited, and I couldn't understand why. It seemed like he'd found a relative or something."

"Yes," I said and gave Dr. Horshaw a helpless shrug. "Yes, in a sense he did. He realized we were alike in one way. We each carry within us an animal spirit." Since Ryan had tried to tell her about it, I didn't feel I was betraying a confidence. I was, however, breaking an unstated rule of the were house.

"I carry a jaguar. Ryan carries a sea eagle. I was the first person he'd ever met who understood what he had. I know what that's like. But there are many like me. Like us. People who carry within them the spirit of an animal. A spirit that can come out and take physical form and then return to us in its spirit form.

"I let my jaguar out to save you, and then she came back to me, so when you saw me, you no longer saw her."

"I—I don't know whether to believe this or not. I saw the—what was it? A jaguar?—and then I didn't see it. But still ..."

"You've gone this far, Charlotte," Dr. Horshaw said. "You might as well let her see the jaguar."

Julia turned toward her. "And are you one of these people?"

"No, but my daughter Henrietta is. Her animal spirit is a crane. And 'these people' call themselves weres."

Julia shook her head. "It's too strange."

"I'll let my jaguar out for just a moment, and you can see for yourself. Don't worry. She won't hurt you. She's proud of having saved you yesterday." I relaxed, leaning my head against the back of the chair. To avoid Julia's intent gaze I closed my eyes. And sent the jaguar out.

Julia screamed as the big cat bounded toward her, reached her, and rubbed against her legs like a tame house cat, letting her feel her body to know that she had substance. Then she turned slowly and walked back to me. She sat in front of me for a moment, then rose and faded into me.

I sat up, opened my eyes, saw Julia trembling.

"I know it's incredible," I said. "And startling. But my jaguar would never hurt anyone unless I or someone else needed protection. Weres aren't killers. Our animal spirits are extensions of ourselves, not wild beasts."

"That's why it didn't kill the man who attacked me?"

"Yes. I didn't want any more killing."

"Any more? In addition to the killings in the church?"

"Yes." I saw no way to get around it. I looked at Dr. Horshaw. "I'm going to have to tell her the whole story. I guess I'll never get back in Grandfather's good graces."

"He's not that unreasonable, Charlotte," she said. "Think about it. I know about weres and am not one. And consider Velma. Julia may not be as closely related to weres as Velma and I are, but she is related to one. I think Grandfather will understand."

"I hope you're right," I said.

I launched into the long account of what really happened that night. Julia listened, wide-eyed. I concluded by declaring my resolve to somehow prove Dima and Gene innocent. "I need to find out more about the preacher who intended to sacrifice the crane. He survived being shot, but that's all I know. I need to find out whether he's still in the hospital, or, if he's been discharged, where he is. And why he wanted to kill us. I get that he thinks our animal spirits are demons, but how'd he even know about us? And why does he think that?"

"I may be able to help you there," Julia said excitedly. "I'm a church secretary—at the First Church of Christ. Our pastor is chairman of the United Council of Churches this year. I'm sure I could get the information through the council even if that church isn't a member."

"But you can't reveal any of what I've told you," I cautioned. "I just came here today to ask you to tell Grandfather Blass the truth about what happened last night."

"I'll do that for you," she said. "And I'll keep your secret. I know how to be discreet. I can get the information without anyone knowing why I want it."

"Well, if you're sure ..." I yielded despite a warning chill down my spine.

"I'm sure," she said firmly. "After all, I want to

keep Ryan safe. But I did give the police your description."

I guess my alarm showed in my face. And Dr. Horshaw looked horrified. But the police didn't know where to find me. And we still had to work out a way to get Julia to talk to Grandfather.

"Charlotte can't go to the Blass home," Dr. Horshaw told Julia. "And Grandfather shouldn't leave it. But I can go there. Suppose I pick you up tomorrow and take you there."

"Can't I just go on my own?"

"It wouldn't be wise," Dr. Horshaw said. "The police know my car. If they're watching the place, as I expect they are, they'd be curious about a car not known to them. They might ask awkward questions. They might even have you followed. If I take you there, we can get in, talk to Grandfather Blass, and get out before the police have time to get curious."

The police were already curious. But as I had no better plan to propose, I kept quiet while Dr. Horshaw arranged the time to return tomorrow to pick Julia up and take her to talk to Grandfather.

Lost in my own thoughts, I jerked back to attention when I heard Dr. Horshaw say, "Charlotte, while I'm at the Blass's, I'll pick up your clothes and anything else you need."

"You can stay here with me," Julia said. "I'm sorry I sent you away like I did."

I accepted, since Dr. Horshaw had never retracted her declaration that I couldn't stay at her place. I liked Julia, and I felt safe here. And if Julia really could get information about the preacher, I could set my plans in motion.

22
DECISION

Morning. I awoke and sat up in Julia's comfortable sofa bed. Remembering what this day could bring, I stretched, got out of bed, and headed for the kitchen, where I found Julia dressed and finishing her breakfast.

"I'm heading for church in a few minutes," she said. "I'll be back around noon, and grab a quick bit of lunch before Dr. Horshaw comes by. She's making her hospital rounds this morning so she'll have the afternoon free."

I'd forgotten this was Sunday. With all that happened yesterday it felt like a week must have passed since yesterday morning. I was grateful to Julia for letting me sleep in rather than waking me and trying to persuade me to go to church with her. I'm not much for church—even less so after church people tried to kill my jaguar and Henrietta's crane. Julia insisted that her church was very different from that, and I'm sure it is, but I don't know that I'll ever feel comfortable in a church again.

I spent the morning wandering around the house and worrying about Dima. And Gene. I tried to think of other things. Tried to read the paper. Tried to read a *National Geographic* Julia had on a table in the living room. I couldn't concentrate. I wanted action. Needed it. Yet I could do nothing but worry about Dima. And Gene.

The morning ended at last. Julia came in with Ryan, who joined us for lunch. To my surprise Julia explained that Ryan would go with her to her interview with Grandfather Blass. "Dr. Horshaw called me on my cell phone while I was still at church. She said Mr. Blass wanted to meet Ryan, and it would be safe for him to go with us this afternoon."

There must have been an exchange of messages again by means of Henrietta's crane. I wouldn't have thought Dr. Horshaw would have approved that after the crane was shot at yesterday. She must have considered it vitally important to get a message to Grandfather.

I wondered what else was in the message.

Dr. Horshaw arrived shortly after one o'clock and collected Julia and Ryan, leaving me to wait and stew. I'd have gone out for a walk, but I didn't feel like parading around in borrowed clothes that didn't fit right.

I decided to phone Dr. Horshaw's apartment and see if Henrietta was there. Her mother wouldn't be, and it would give us a chance to talk. It ought to be safe enough. I doubted that Dr. Horshaw's phone would be tapped, and Julia's certainly wasn't.

The phone rang and rang, and just as I was about to hang up, Henrietta answered. I said, "Hello, Henrietta. It's Sharl."

"Oh, Sharl! What a surprise! I thought it was surely one of Mother's patients, and I waited for the answering machine to pick up, and when it didn't, I thought maybe I should answer it, and I'm so glad I did! Is something wrong? Mother got there all right, didn't she?"

"Oh, yes. Nothing's wrong. I'm just here alone and bored, and I thought I'd call and see if there have been any new developments. I figured you must have sent Grandfather another message with your crane to let him know your mother and Julia were coming. I wondered if he sent any news in his return message."

"Yes, I did send my crane. And he sent a message back saying it was fine for them to come and that he wanted to meet Ryan. We'd told him about Ryan in our message. Oh, and Roy is out on bail now. He's gone back to work, and I think he's staying there at the shop." She stopped, hesitated.

I wanted to ask her where Roy worked, what she meant by "the shop," but something held me back. I could tell she had more she wanted to say but wasn't sure how to say it. More bad news, I guessed, but I needed to hear it, regardless.

She continued, "I was told you weren't to know this. I shouldn't … but I think you ought to know. It's about Marko. Grandfather hasn't been allowed to visit him. They have him in a locked psychiatric ward. But Grandfather talked to his doctors. He's learned that Marko's body bears signs of torture. Prolonged torture. Over a considerable period of time. That's what has affected his mind. He can't accept that he's free. He keeps yelling, 'Don't hurt me. Leave me alone.' Grandfather is furious about it. That's probably why he was so unkind to you in his note yesterday. I doubt that he meant it. He's terribly upset about Marko and about not being allowed to see him."

"Why didn't Grandfather want me to know?"

"Because of what you'd said about going after the preacher and persuading him to tell the truth about what was happening when Gene and Dima shot those men and why they had to do it. Grandfather figured you'd be even more determined if you knew about the torture. I think he's worried about you—about what you might do."

"That I might make matters worse, you mean."

"Well, that, too, but also that you might get yourself killed. We know how dangerous that preacher and his followers are."

"Yes, we do. I plan to take great care. But I haven't changed my mind. And, yes, I guess the news about Marko does make me more determined."

"You won't do anything about it before Mother and Julia return, will you?"

"Of course not. I want to hear how their visit to Grandfather went."

"Yes, so do I. But, please, Charlotte, don't do anything rash."

"I won't."

We said our goodbyes. The conversation had left me with much to think about.

I thought back to when I'd first seen Marko. He'd passed me on the street, walking fast, but not running. Not in a panic. And then he'd gotten stabbed. I'd seen his wolf in him at that time. Then they took him away in an ambulance and hospitalized him. When could he have let out his wolf? It had to have come out between the time he was stabbed and when he was taken into the hospital It must have gone out on its own to hunt down the stabber. Could it be the wolf's long absence rather than the torture that propelled him into madness? Or perhaps that, when added to the torture, had proved too much to bear?

I understood why Grandfather was so anxious to see Marko. I wanted to see him, too, but there was no chance of that. But maybe Dr. Horshaw could help me find out what I wanted to know. I had several things to ask her when she returned. They'd been gone about three hours, and I started to worry.

Could Grandfather have had so much to say? Or had the police interfered with their visit? I became more and more uneasy, thinking about the fact that Julia had talked to the police about being mugged and being saved by a cat that chased off the mugger and potential rapist and killer. If they saw her visiting a house where strange animals had been seen, what would they think? They might take her in for questioning.

I'd just decided to call Henrietta back to find out whether they'd contacted her, when I heard footsteps outside, and a key turned in the lock. And in walked Julia and Ryan and Dr. Horshaw. I sank down on the sofa, weak with relief.

Ryan came and stood in front of me, eyes bright. So excited he could hardly stand still, he said, "Sharl, that man is awesome! You know what animal he has? He showed it to me! It's huge! It's a—some kind of ox or something. He said I'd never see one any place else. They're extinct. But he has the spirit of one! How could that be?"

He didn't stop to let me respond. Just as well, since I didn't know the answer. He continued his animated account, scarcely pausing to breathe. "He wants to help me learn to control my eagle. But he can't now. But as soon as it's safe, I'm invited back to his house for training. And I said, 'Why do I need training?' and he told me there're ways I could use my eagle and things I must never do, and I had to meet other weres and know how we protect each other and not do things that put other weres in danger, like, uh, like …"

He wound down and gazed at his shoes.

"Like I did?" I asked with some bitterness.

Dr. Horshaw came up beside Ryan and put her hand on his shoulder. "I'm sorry, Charlotte," she said. "It brought Grandfather great relief to hear Julia's story and know that your jaguar came out only long enough to save her life. We convinced him that it never left your control. But he still feels that you have acted rashly, and that the difficulties with the police can all be traced to your decision to let your jaguar out when it wasn't safe to do so."

What could I say? It was true.

If I hadn't let my jaguar out after being shot, Henrietta wouldn't have sent her crane out after it, the jaguar and the crane wouldn't have been captured, and the massacre in the church wouldn't have happened. But we'd still have had to get Marko's wolf back to him somehow. And we'd still have faced the threat of attack by the people who'd shot at Dima and me and who'd set the net that captured my jaguar and Henrietta's crane. They'd have kept after us and gotten to us some other way.

Julia had hovered in the background but now came up and sat beside me. "I did convince him that you were brave to come to my defense, and that you probably saved my life. His attitude toward you softened considerably after that. His wife came in and served us cookies and lemonade. She's so sweet! And she told us to tell you to be patient. She said they're both terribly worried about their grandsons, and that's why Mr. Blass is so edgy right now."

Dr. Horshaw nodded. "Grandmother Blass sent your things." She handed me a shopping bag filled with my purse, clothes, shoes, and personal items. "Grandfather is worried that you'll do something to try to help Gene and Dima, and you'll make matters worse instead." She didn't need to tell me she agreed—I could read it in her eyes.

It didn't make me change my plan, but I kept quiet about that.

"I want you to know, Charlotte," Julia said, "that you're welcome to stay here as long as you want. And I still mean to find out all I can about that preacher that got shot."

I hugged her to let her know how grateful I was for her help on both counts.

"Whatever you do, Charlotte, let me help," Ryan begged.

Julia frowned.

I said, "No. Absolutely not, Ryan. You are not to get involved in this. I'm already involved up to my ears. But you aren't, and you need to do nothing until you can get the training Grandfather Blass wants you to have."

"He's not your real grandfather, is he?" Ryan asked.

"No. But all the other weres call him Grandfather,

so I got into the habit. Guess I shouldn't do it anymore. He's more or less disowned me."

"I don't think he has, really," Dr. Horshaw said. "He just wants you out of this for now."

For now. How long would that be? Until Dima and Gene were freed? How would they ever get free unless the preacher confessed?

I kept my thoughts to myself. To change the subject. I told Dr. Horshaw about trying to figure out when and how Marko's wolf had gotten out. I knew the wolf was in him when he was stabbed, and it couldn't have left him before they loaded him into the ambulance or people would have seen it. "From all I've been told, Marko was unconscious from the time he reached the hospital until we brought him out and the wolf got back to him. But maybe he did come to briefly and for some reason sent out his wolf. How would it have gotten out of the hospital without being seen? It doesn't make sense. Maybe it doesn't matter, but I'm curious."

"You know I don't have privileges in that hospital, but I do have friends there," Dr. Horshaw said. "I can make discreet inquiries and see what I can find out."

"I'd appreciate it. Knowing how the wolf got out might tell us something, maybe give some clue as to why Marko's crazy. He didn't act crazy when I passed him on the street just before he was stabbed."

"As I understand it, he lost a lot of blood. That could partially explain his mental confusion," Dr. Horshaw said. "I don't think he's 'crazy.' I suspect he's suffering from post-traumatic stress disorder. And you couldn't possibly know what went on in his mind just from that brief encounter."

"No, but ... well, I still want to know when he let out his wolf. And something else I want to know. Grandfather said that someone in his household witnessed the stabbing, or at least its aftermath, after the police and ambulance arrived. But Grandfather didn't say who. Why? Who was it? Supposedly the person couldn't get close enough to get a good look at Marko and didn't recognize him. I didn't see another were, though I'll grant you, my attention was on Marko. Plus I was being questioned by a policeman. So I could easily have missed seeing a were in that crowd."

"I think you're grasping at straws," Dr. Horshaw said, "but I'll see what I can find out. I don't mind satisfying your curiosity, so long as you follow Grandfather's advice and don't try to take any action on your own against that preacher."

Again I made no promise. Her frown told me she knew just what my silence meant.

She turned to Julia. "I must get home," she said. "I want to thank you again for letting me take you to meet with Grandfather Blass. And Ryan," she turned to him, "I'm pleased that you could go with us. I hope you'll be able to meet with Mr. Blass again in a happier time."

Julia and Ryan both answered something polite, I'm sure, but I didn't listen, too busy re-creating my view of the stabbing to pay attention. I tried to envision again the crowd surrounding the stabbing victim. Was there someone there that I later met at the were house?

No, that was going about it backwards. Had there been anyone at the were house who looked vaguely familiar to me when I first met them? Because whoever it was, the person had to have been in the crowd around the ambulance and close enough to have recognized the injured man as were. So I should have seen him but without picking up a were signal.

I leaned back and closed my eyes to try to recreate that day's scene. There'd been so much confusion. How could I see now what I hadn't seen then?

But the scene had fixed itself in my mind. I could still visualize the victim, blood pooling beneath him, could see the gathering crowd, cell phones pulled out to call 911, the cop appearing in only seconds, the ambulance arriving, its siren screaming. The paramedics jumping out and hurrying to the bleeding man. Police holding the crowd back, while the first cop questioned me and other witnesses.

A man edging away from the cops. To avoid being questioned? He'd been standing in the street near the curb, but turned away as the cops called for witnesses. Pushed his way through the crowd. Did I see him taking out a cell phone as he hurried away? Or was I imagining more than I actually saw? Imagining the cell phone because the witness from the were house had to have lost no time in calling Grandfather to report what he'd seen.

And what *had* he seen? Not the actual stabbing. He hadn't have arrived until after the ambulance got there. By then the cops had taken charge of the scene and were keeping everybody well back, away from the victim. Yet this mysterious witness who hadn't seen the victim's face nevertheless had been close enough to recognize that the victim was were. Was that possible?

Other weres couldn't actually see the animal spirit inside another person, as I can. They only sense wereness. It's a strong sense, that's true. But how close does one were have to be to another to sense it?

I opened my eyes and found Ryan staring at me kind of funny, like he thought I might be going to let my jaguar out. I smiled at him, and he relaxed.

"Ryan, tell me something. This is important, so think carefully before you answer, okay?"

"Sure." A puzzled expression crossed his face.

"Yesterday morning when you came here and sat at the table ready to have breakfast with Julia, I came into the kitchen. Just my presence there surprised you. But when, exactly, did you realize I was were? Was it right away? Or as I came to the table? Or after I sat down opposite you and we started to talk? Think, now. When was it?"

He furrowed his brow. "Gosh, Sharl, I'm not sure. I think I got kind of a funny feeling right before you sat down at the table. Prickles ran all up and down my arms. Then when we talked and you were eating your breakfast I started to suspect you might be like me. I thought first that my imagination had gone into overtime, but then I reacted physically with kind of an itchy-all-over feeling."

I grinned. "Yeah, that's a good way of putting it." Ryan wasn't really a good test subject, given that I was the first were he'd ever met. Naturally he was slow to recognize what caused the "itch."

Okay, when had *I* realized what *Ryan* was?

I'd come into the kitchen, not knowing anyone was there with Julia. So I'd been startled to find Ryan there. But as I crossed the kitchen, before I reached the table, before I spotted the eagle within him, I'd known.

I knew, as Ryan didn't, about the existence of lots of other weres, and I'd had a lot of practice in recognizing the meaning of what Ryan referred to as an "itchy-all-over feeling." Plus I had my special ability. So neither of us served as a good gauge of how long it took for one were to recognize another.

It might be more difficult with a crowd of people around. But on the other hand, everyone's attention had centered on the victim. Those who couldn't see him had been trying to. The cops had kept pushing people back. So the crowd kept shifting, people changing places, those with a front-row view being shoved to the back. Cops had rerouted traffic, making the street empty of cars, except for the ambulance, but full of gawkers. Only a few pedestrians kept on walking past, slowing a bit but not curious enough to stop and push through the crowd to discover what was happening. The mystery witness must have been someone who did stop and push through. If I'd seen him, I should remember something. Something like
...

A heavy-set woman shoving back at a stocky man, not tall enough to see over the crowd. He could only peer around her. Face just barely visible. Just enough to let me see gold-rimmed glasses perched on a long nose.

Professor Georges DuChamps!

Why hadn't Grandfather told me who made the report? I'd noticed that Grandfather and the professor seemed to be close friends. Did that explain it? Or was it simpler than that? At the time of my first meeting with Grandfather, I didn't meet Professor DuChamps. He'd worked late at the university that evening rather than join the rest for dinner. So maybe Grandfather didn't mention him because I didn't yet know the professor. That was the simplest explanation.

Still, I very much wanted to have a talk with Professor DuChamps. Tomorrow, Monday, he'd be at the university. I could go there safely enough, if I took care. I doubted that the police would have Professor DuChamps under any sort of surveillance. Maybe I could get Julia to take me.

No. She'd be at work. And Ryan would be in school. So rather than worry them, I wouldn't mention my plan. Now that I had my own clothes, I wouldn't need to borrow anything of Julia's. And while my purse held little money, I had enough change to let me take the bus to the university and return here afterward. I could talk to the professor and be back by the time Julia got home from work. She'd never know I'd been away.

Julia left for work at 8:30 the next morning. Her workday started at 9:00, but she explained over breakfast that she liked to arrive early and get things set up before the pastor arrived. He often had morning appointments, and she liked to have coffee brewing and cookies or other sweets set out, ready to offer to people who came for counseling or on other business.

She promised to find out about the preacher who'd been shot. The Reverend Hanley Carlisle. I hadn't told her that when I knew his condition and his location, I intended to find a way to see him. I knew what Grandfather thought about that plan, so I wouldn't mention it to anyone.

But today I'd pay a visit to Professor Georges DuChamps.

23
AN UNFORTUNATE REUNION

I spent an uneventful bus ride to the university gazing out the window, not looking at the other passengers. I figured that would keep them from looking at me.

At the university, I headed for the Humanities Building, where I spotted a directory by the stairwell and found the room number of Professor DuChamps' office.

I went upstairs and looked for the room, prepared to wait if he taught a class at this hour. But when I found the door and knocked, a voice within called out, "Enter."

I did.

"Charlotte!" He rose and leaned over his desk toward me, extending his hand. "What are you doing here? Is it safe for you to be out and about like this?"

"I needed to see you. To ask you something."

He sank back into his chair and waved me to another chair to the side of the small room, in front of the bookcases that lined the walls. "What was so important that you risked coming here to ask it?"

Suddenly my reason for coming here sounded lame to me, a poor excuse for endangering myself and possibly the professor as well. But here I was, and I might as well satisfy my curiosity. I pulled my chair around to the front of his desk so that I faced him directly.

"Professor," I began, "I've been thinking back to the day I saw Marko get stabbed. Of course I didn't know his identity then. I only recognized him as were. You knew Marko, didn't you?"

"Yes, of course. Poor boy. Such terrible things have befallen him."

"Yes. But something puzzles me. Why didn't you recognize him when you saw him after he was stabbed?"

I expected some kind of reaction to my knowing he'd seen him. I saw none. He probably just assumed Grandfather had told me. He took off his glasses and wiped them with a lens paper from a box on his desk. "Nothing puzzling about that," he said calmly. "I'm very near-sighted." He held his glasses up, letting me see the thick lenses. "I couldn't get more than a glance at the fellow lying on the gurney. The crowd and the paramedics blocked my view of his face."

"But you knew he was were."

"I sensed it, yes. I didn't need to see his face for that. I got a strong sense of the animal spirit within him, though of course I couldn't see it as you do. I couldn't tell the kind of animal, but I knew enough to extract myself from the crowd and locate a spot quiet enough to allow me to call Martin and tell him that a were had been stabbed and possibly killed. I wanted assurance that it hadn't been one of our were family. It puzzled everyone to have you identify him as Marko. Even before his identity was confirmed, we all felt great relief to learn that, although seriously injured, he survived!"

His sincerity came through strongly. I'd satisfied my curiosity, but I'd come no closer to learning who'd stabbed Marko or why or anything else that would help me find a way to free Dima and Gene.

One other thing I wanted to know. "I've wondered how Grandfather Blass knew that the witness to the stabbing—that I—was were. He sent Dima to get me. How'd he find out where I lived?"

"Er, I believe, ah, that he has an informant with access to police records. He must have called that person."

"You don't know who that person is?"

"You'd have to ask Grandfather Blass directly about that."

Why couldn't he, or wouldn't he tell me? This revived my suspicions. I saw, though, that I had all the information I'd get from him. I thanked Professor DuChamps, rose, and turned to leave.

The office door burst open. Ronnie stepped inside, saw me, and stopped short. "What's she doing here?" she demanded, pointing at me.

"Now, Ronnie," the professor began soothingly.

She launched herself at me, fingers curled, ready to choke or claw me. I grabbed her wrists and pushed her back. She kicked me, hard.

"It's all your fault. All of it!" Ronnie screeched, breaking free of my grasp.

"Ladies, please, desist," the professor begged.

I would have stopped, but Ronnie's fresh attack forced me to defend myself.

She got me by the neck and squeezed hard. I grabbed her hair and jerked her head back with a force that had to hurt, but it didn't make her loosen her chokehold. The professor by this time had come around his desk and was trying to separate us. We were both yelling, or at least she was. I had to stop when she started choking the life out of me.

I got in some good kicks, but they didn't break her hold, either. My hands around her head, my fingers poking into her eyes had more effect. Her fingers loosened enough to let me keep breathing.

And then strong hands yanked me from her. Two cops came between us. My arms were pinned to my sides.

"Now look what you've done!" I whispered, knowing but too mad to care that the cops could hear me. My throat hurt, or I would have shouted at her.

"Good! I hope you rot in jail!" she screamed at me, her eyes red where I'd poked them. Luckily the other cop held her just as tightly as mine held me.

"All right, you two. What's this about?" my cop demanded.

I spoke quickly. "I was talking to Professor DuChamps and she barged in and attacked me for no reason."

"That right, Professor?" the other cop asked.

The professor was leaning against his desk, breathing heavily, one hand on his chest.

"She didn't really barge in," the professor said, earning a glare from me. "She had an appointment. She didn't expect anyone else to be here."

"She sure didn't knock first," I countered, as though it mattered. "I stood up to leave, and she came in and jumped me."

"She's a troublemaker," Ronnie screeched. "She's ruined everything for everybody."

"All right, ladies. Let's have your names and then we'll hear your stories, one at a time."

So they hadn't recognized me. They weren't city police. The university hired its own campus cops. But when they had my name, it wouldn't be long before they discovered that the city police wanted me. And if I gave a fake name, Ronnie'd be quick to correct the lie.

"I don't think I've seen you on campus before," the other cop said. "Are you students here?"

The professor sagged against his desk, his hand clutching his chest. "My heart!" he gasped.

The cop holding me released me to go for his cell phone. "I'll call 911."

"No. Medicine. In desk. Need water."

"I'll get you some," I offered when the cop holding me released me to go behind the professor's desk for the medicine.

His horse spirit did not act troubled by the "attack." He was faking. Clever. And he'd given me a look when I said I'd go for water that I'm sure I interpreted correctly as meaning I should run. I headed for the door.

"Stop her!" Ronnie yelled.

The other cop still had Ronnie in a tight grasp. He couldn't grab me without letting her go. My cop, busy rooting through the professor's desk for pills, couldn't stop me either.

I left the room and ran—for the exit. I hit the stairs, took the steps two at a time to ground floor, earning curious looks from a few students out in the halls. I reached the ground floor and headed for the way out.

This NBA type stepped in front of me, arms outstretched like he was blocking a shot. "Hey, what's wrong? Need help?"

"Just need to get by," I panted. "Gotta catch a bus."

"I heard about something weird going on upstairs."

"Don't know. Just let me past, please."

I didn't think he was going to move, but he did, grudgingly, oozing suspicion.

"Thanks," I said, and hurried from the building.

Outside, I stopped to get my bearings. From the building entrance, walkways wound away in several directions, and I couldn't remember which one led to the exit gate.

The basketball star came up behind me. "You lost? You aren't a student here, are you?"

"Just a visitor," I acknowledged, heading in what I hoped was the right direction.

"And you don't know anything about all the yelling and screaming that the campus cops went to see about? Sounded like women yelling."

"No, sorry. I mind my own business. Like I said, I have to catch a bus." I kept walking, and he walked right with me. I had to ditch him.

I turned toward him and thus toward the building we'd left. One of the cops from the professor's office and another, different cop were coming out of the building, heading my way. Fortunately my companion had his back to them.

"You know," I said, "I've always had a thing for tall guys." I threw my arms around his neck, stood on tiptoe, and planted my lips firmly against his.

I can't say he returned the kiss, but he didn't draw away. His arms closed around me, probably just by reflex. I held the position as long as I could, peeking to see where the cops went.

They headed in a different direction. I drew away and wiped my lips. Tall Guy looked at me with a bemused expression.

"Thanks," I said. "That was awesome. Really."

"Uh, yeah. Sorry for bothering you." He turned and walked back toward the Humanities Building as fast as his long legs could carry him.

As I walked more slowly in the other direction, still trying to get my bearings, it occurred to me that the cops would probably watch the main entrance, figuring I'd go that way. I had to find another way out. I picked a walkway at random and wound up at the library. I went in. As I'd guessed, the library was huge, an easy place to hide in.

I wandered around a bit, saw no sign of campus police, found an interesting book, and sat down in a secluded nook on the third floor to read. My thoughts, though, wouldn't let me concentrate. I'd done it again! I'd called attention to myself and thus to weres. I'd endangered Professor DuChamps. Ronnie hadn't run, so she was in trouble now. I didn't feel sorry for her. She'd brought it on herself. She'd attacked me, after all. But Grandfather Blass would blame me, even if I told him Ronnie had started it and the professor verified it. I shouldn't have come here, shouldn't have gone to the professor's office.

Neither should Ronnie, but that wouldn't take blame away from me. I'd probably burned all the bridges leading back to the were house.

And Julia would be frantic when she got home from work and didn't find me there. If I only had a cell phone. The library must have a phone I could use just to call and leave a message on her voice mail. But I didn't dare move around much. The more I wandered around, the more likely a campus cop would spot me.

A large map of the campus stood just inside the doors of the first-floor lobby, and I'd have liked to study it, but its prominent position guaranteed I'd be spotted easily.

I could call the professor's office, but if the cops hadn't left there, they'd know where to find me.

I even considered letting my jaguar out to reconnoiter, but that would be foolhardy. I couldn't think of anything to do other than to stay put.

Minutes, hours turtled by. Students came and went. No sign of cops, campus or otherwise. Was it safe to leave?

I got up and stretched, stiff from sitting so long. I took the stairs down to the second floor, walked around a bit on that floor, looking out windows, checking for cops.

All seemed quiet and safe. I headed for the ground floor, walked to the lobby and planted myself in front of the campus map, studying the layout, figuring out the best route to take to get out safely. A hand fell heavily on my shoulder. I whirled around.

One of the cops from the professor's office grinned at me. "Thought you might turn up here," he said. "Now we can have the little talk you ran out on."

24
BANISHED

I guessed the campus cops hadn't yet found out that the city cops wanted me. I'd have thought this one would have checked with them, but I was very glad he hadn't. I guess the campus cops are jealous of their authority and don't like the city cops barging in. Worked well for me.

"Let's just sit down over there." He pointed to a bench against the foyer wall, close to the restrooms.

He had me by the arm, leading me there, so I had no choice but to take his suggestion. We sat, and he got out pad and pen.

"First, I want to see some identification. " He nodded toward the purse I carried.

"I don't have any with me. You can see for yourself." I handed him the purse.

He looked through it, frowning. It held a change purse with coins for the bus, a compact and lipstick, a comb, some tissues. No ID. I'd taken that out before I made the trip here. "No driver's license? No credit cards?"

"No car. No credit." That was true enough.

"No form of ID?"

I shrugged. "I have a birth certificate but I don't carry it with me."

"Okay. What's your name?"

"Mary Louise Shaldinger," I said with no hesitation.

"Spell the last name."

"S-h-a-l-d-i-n-g-e-r." When I was a kid, we had an elderly neighbor by that name. She died several years ago, so she couldn't object to my appropriating it.

"Age?"

"Twenty-two."

"Occupation?"

"Unemployed at present. That's what I came here about. I'd heard Professor DuChamps was looking for a secretary."

"That's your usual occupation?"

"Well, file clerk, mostly." I'd never done that in my life. My latest employment was working as a clerk in Macy's lingerie department, but I didn't want him nosing around, asking questions there.

After busily writing down my answers in a small notebook, he looked up to ask, "Where'd you hear that Professor DuChamps was looking for a secretary? Most of the profs use students as their aides."

"Yeah, I found that out. I had to try, though. I think I almost had him persuaded when that nasty girl burst in."

"I thought you said you were leaving when Miss Ashford arrived."

Oops! Forgot to keep my stories straight. "Well, I let the prof think I was leaving. I thought he might call me back, see, and tell me he'd give me a try. But she came and spoiled any chance I might have had."

"You and Miss Ashford know each other, right?"

Gotta be careful here. Who knows what Ronnie told

him? "Yeah, we know each other. We've never been friends, but I never imagined she'd attack me like she did."

"And what did you say your name is?"

"Mary Louise Shaldinger. You wrote it in your notebook."

"So I did. But that isn't the name Miss Ashford called you by."

"Oh? Well, she calls me a lot of things. Plus, she's always been a liar."

"So your name isn't Charlotte Ramirez?"

"No, it's not. Look, it's getting late, and my folks will be worried about me. I was the one attacked. How about letting me leave now?"

"Doesn't seem you were in much of a hurry to leave before. Why've you been hanging around here?"

"I was hoping for another chance to talk further with the professor after you guys cleared out."

"So you were avoiding us? Why is that, if you're innocent?"

"In my experience, the innocent ones are usually the ones that suffer. Did you arrest Miss Ashford?"

"The campus police don't arrest. We call in the city force for that."

Wish I'd known that. "Well, I don't see that you have any cause to have me arrested, so how about letting me go? I promise, I won't come back onto the campus. It's for sure Professor DuChamps won't give me a job now, so I've got no reason to come here."

"Yet you've spent the afternoon here. I think before I let you go, I'll call the city department and see if they have any reason to want you."

If he makes that call, I'm sunk. I shrugged, trying to appear nonchalant. He took out his cell phone. I thought fast.

"Look, I'll level with you," I said. "Ronnie and I, well, we're after the same guy. Lately he's been paying more attention to me than to her. She's jealous. That's what the fight was about."

"And your name really *is* Charlotte Ramirez?"

"Hell, no! I told you my name. Don't know why she'd say I was Charlotte Ramirez. Except that's another friend she'd like to see get in trouble, because she's on my side in this boyfriend business." I'd probably regret that lie even if it got Ronnie into more trouble. With my luck, it would probably just get me into more.

He made a notation in his notebook, always holding his hand over the page so I couldn't see anything he wrote. I don't know how much of my story he bought, but at last he said, "All right, Miss Shaldinger. I guess you can go. Just keep your promise and stay off the campus in the future."

"I will, Officer. Definitely."

And he let me go! Probably because it was past the end of his shift and close to his suppertime.

I found my way to a bus stop and after a couple of transfers got off the bus about thirty-five minutes after I'd left the university. Night had fallen by then, and streetlights lit my way as I walked the last couple of blocks into the complex and to Julia's apartment.

The moment I opened the front door, Julia came rushing to me. "Charlotte, thank the Lord! Where have you been? No one knew where you'd gone, and we've been so worried!"

We. That meant she'd contacted Dr. Horshaw, and possibly Grandfather as well.

"I went to the university to talk to Professor DuChamps. He's, uh, a friend of Grandfather's." I decided the fewer of us she knew as were, the better.

"Now I'm worried about Ryan," she said, her brow creased.

"What about Ryan?"

"It was getting late and you weren't here, and Ryan insisted on sending his eagle out to look for you. And the eagle hasn't returned."

"Where's Ryan?" Alarm flooded my mind.

"Here. He didn't want to worry his mom or grandmother. He's lying on my bed."

"I'll go see him, let him know I'm safe."

Without waiting for permission, I marched into the bedroom. Ryan lay on the bed, eyes closed but not sleeping, I knew. I went to the bed and took his hand. "Ryan, it's Charlotte. I'm back. I'm fine. Call your eagle back."

His eyes opened. He looked at me, smiled. I checked to be sure the window was open. The screen had been pushed out. Julia had followed me into the bedroom. "Is he okay?"

"Yeah, he's fine. The eagle should be back soon."

About ten minutes passed before we heard a screech and saw the eagle swoop down and through the window. It flew straight to the bed and faded into Ryan. He sat up. "Gosh, where've you been, Sharl? We've been looking all over for you."

He meant him and his eagle, I guess. "You shouldn't have sent out your eagle. I've told you how dangerous that is right now."

"I told him, too," Julia put in. "He wouldn't listen. He insisted it would be okay. Nobody would bother an eagle."

"Don't count on that," I told him. "That's not a bald eagle. It's a European bird. Seeing one flying free here in America could attract a lot of attention if someone spots it and recognizes what it is."

"Oh, dear. I hadn't even thought of that," Julia said.

"But nothing did happen. And the eagle found the church where the pastor tried to sacrifice the crane. And the house next to it where the pastor lives."

"You let it go there?" I asked, my voice rising in horror.

"Well, I thought that's where you might have gone. And they might have caught you or something." Despite his apologetic tone, his eyes sparkled. He'd enjoyed his adventure. He didn't comprehend the danger, the little fool.

"You were told, warned not ever to let your eagle out," Julia scolded. "And you let it go there! What if it had been killed? What would happen to you then?"

"But he didn't get killed. He's got awesome eyesight. He could see without landing or even getting close to the ground."

Julia turned to me. "What does happen if a were's animal gets killed?"

I shouldn't tell her. I bit my lower lip. Julia already knew too much, but Ryan needed to know and probably didn't.

"They go into a coma and never wake up," I said, talking too fast as if that would make it easier. Of course, it didn't.

"Oh, Lord! I'm glad I didn't know that while the eagle was out. I'd've been even more frantic than I was."

"Well, it's all right now," I said. "We're all safe. No harm done."

The phone rang. Julia hurried to answer, while Ryan got off the bed and he and I trooped into the living room.

"Yes, Dr. Horshaw. She's back," Julia was saying.

I sank down onto the sofa, afraid of what might be coming. Julia handed me the phone.

"Hi," I said brightly.

"Charlotte, whatever were you thinking of," she said, "going haring off on your own and bringing poor Georges DuChamps to the attention of the police and getting Ronnie Ashford into terrible trouble?"

Getting Ronnie into trouble? I was getting blamed for getting Ronnie into trouble? "Me? Ronnie was the one—"

"Ronnie couldn't have done anything if you hadn't been where you had no right to be."

"But if Ronnie hadn't attacked me—"

"Ronnie was taken by surprise. She'd been invited by Professor DuChamps and didn't expect to see anyone else there. Certainly not you."

"That doesn't excuse her for starting a fight."

"Charlotte, you're a loose cannon. We simply cannot allow this to continue. The next thing we know, you'll go off and try to deal with the Reverend Carlisle on your own. We can't risk that. You've endangered us all already."

"I'm sorry, Dr. Horshaw, but I don't think—" I wanted to say I didn't think everything was my fault.

She didn't give me the chance. "No, that's just it. You don't think. I'm coming to get you. You can't stay there and endanger Julia and Ryan further. You need someone to guard you and see that you don't leave and don't let your jaguar out."

"And you volunteered for that?"

"No, I only volunteered to pick you up and drive you to a safe place—safe for you and for all of us who've been placed in danger by your actions."

"And where is this place?" I was boiling mad but trying to control my temper.

"I won't say over the phone. And it's best if Julia and Ryan don't know where you are."

I stood and paced in the living room while I talked. "And if I refuse to go?"

"You'd continue to impose on Julia after all the trouble you've caused? You must know you've now put her and Ryan in danger."

"I don't see how I've put them in danger. Ryan could have been in danger, but his eagle's back safely. Why am I not safe here?"

"Because the police aren't stupid. They're hunting for you. They know now that there's a connection between you and Julia. If Julia hadn't gone to them as a result of the article in the paper, they might never have discovered that connection, but they can figure out that the description she gave of the woman who helped her matches your description. I'm surprised the police haven't already paid her a visit. They may be waiting to get a warrant. No, you can't stay there any longer. I'm already on my way. I'll be there in a matter of minutes. Be ready. And tell Julia to have the guard ready to let me in."

What choice did I have? The police would track me down if I stayed here, and Julia would be involved. Probably Ryan, too.

I passed on her message to Julia. "I'll leave when she gets here," I said, getting my things together as we talked. "Tell me, did you find out anything about that preacher today?"

"Oh, yes! I'd forgotten in all the excitement. He's been released from the hospital to continue recuperating at home. He lives in the house next to the church. He isn't married, no family, but his parishioners are looking after him."

That made Ryan's eagle's excursion this afternoon even more unsafe, but I refrained from pointing that out and emphasizing even more all the trouble I'd caused.

I thanked her for the information.

"Ryan, you need to get home," Julia said. "Your mother knows you're here, but you know she doesn't like you to be late for supper."

"Ah, Julia, let me stay until Charlotte leaves."

"That'll be in just a couple of minutes, so okay, but you leave as soon as she's gone."

"Where are you going? To stay with Dr. Horshaw?" Ryan asked me.

"No. I don't know where she's taking me, but it won't be to her place. She says it's better if no one knows where I am. And, listen, Ryan, you see all the trouble I'm in for going off on my own. Don't you try it. Don't let your eagle out again until you hear from Grandfather Blass that it's safe. Promise?"

He looked unhappy about the restriction, but he promised.

A car horn blasted outside. "That's the doctor," I said.

Julia gave me a hug, and so did Ryan. I hurried out to the car, Ryan following. He waved at Dr. Horshaw, behind the wheel. I climbed into the car, waved to Ryan, and we drove away.

To where?

25
LOCKUP

Dr. Horshaw told me to buckle my seatbelt when I got in and hadn't said a word since. Probably figured she'd said all that needed to be said on the phone.

We headed toward town, and I got a terrible feeling we were going to the police station, where she'd force me to turn myself in. Whatever the charges were against me, they'd include my part in subduing and binding Officer Barr. They had no evidence that would put me at the scene of the church massacre. Well, except they knew I had some connection with the jaguar, and they'd probably connected the jaguar to the cat tracks at the scene of the church massacre. They'd have plenty of questions about that!

Grandfather Blass had hired lawyers to get him and Velma released, and they'd gotten Roy out on bail. They were also defending Dima and Gene. But I doubted Grandfather would pay them to defend me, and I didn't have any money. In fact after paying for the bus ride to and from the university, I'd be lucky to have enough left to put in a vending machine for a candy bar. And I hadn't eaten since breakfast.

As we neared the center of town, Dr. Horshaw began making sudden turns, doubling back, taking side roads, even swerving into an alley once. I looked behind, didn't see any car following. But would she need to take these measures if she was going to the police station?

We did draw close to the station. But then she doubled back, took a cross street to a residential section, and headed for a road that took us in the direction of the beach. I had the crazy thought that maybe she planned to drown me.

We turned on to a street just a block from the waterfront, lined with high-class shops: exclusive dresses, fine antiques, small and pricey bistros, gifts from around the world. The bistros were open; the shops were closed. We pulled into a space in front of an art gallery with lights on inside but a Closed sign in the front window.

"What's this?" I asked.

"This is where you're going," she said unhelpfully.

"An art gallery? Or are you taking me to that bistro a couple of doors down?" I added hopefully, "I'd love a meal."

She ignored that. "The gallery belongs to Jeffrey and Helene. They're art dealers. Didn't you know?"

"Yes, but I thought they'd gone out of town, supposedly to buy art but really just to get away from the trouble."

"They were planning to take a trip but decided they were safe enough remaining here and staying in their apartment. They were too worried about Cameron and Gene to leave town."

"Oh. Nobody bothered to tell me that, and I didn't think to ask."

"They only occasionally use the apartment above

the gallery, but it's really quite lovely. Not at all a bad place to stay," she said, getting out of the car. "Come on. They're expecting us."

So Jeffrey and Helene were assigned to be my wardens. I'd never really gotten to know them. I guess now I would.

Dr. Horshaw accompanied me to the gallery door and rapped on it. Jeffrey opened the door.

"Here she is," Dr. Horshaw said, practically shoving me inside. She didn't come in with me. It hurt that she was so eager to be rid of me.

"Come in, Charlotte," Jeffrey said, though I was already in. While he closed and locked the door, I gazed around at walls hung with paintings of many different styles, all in elegant frames.

"Helene has dinner ready upstairs," he said. "Let me carry your bag."

I handed him the shopping bag filled with all my possessions and followed him through the gallery into a short hallway that led to restrooms on one side and a stairway with a chain across it on the other. He unhooked the chain. "Go on up. I'll follow as soon as I've turned out the lights down here and set the security code."

I climbed the stairs, and Helene met me at the top, looking stylish as always. "Charlotte, I'm so glad you've come. Dinner's on the table. I'm not the cook Mother Velma is, but I've done my best." I followed through a small, beautifully appointed living room and to an equally elegant dining room, where wonderful odors rose from serving dishes on a table set for three.

"If you want to wash before you eat, the

bathroom's right through that door." She pointed, and I went and washed and used the facilities and tried to pat my mussed hair into some sort of order. I felt too dirty and lower class for this fancy place.

I hadn't expected such a warm welcome. Both Jeffrey and Helene were treating me like a friend, not a criminal. I returned to the dining room and found them standing at two of the three places, waiting. Jeffrey pulled out the chair at the third place and seated me. "I put your bag in the bedroom, Charlotte."

"Thanks." I sat carefully, hoping the dirt I'd accumulated during the day's adventures didn't soil the chair's brocaded seat and back.

The delicate china and sterling silverware all made me feel out of place but at the same time special, a valued guest rather than a prisoner. Helene had been too modest in saying she wasn't the cook her mother-in-law was. The thin slices of beef au jus and the potatoes au gratin tasted marvelous, not to mention the green salad and the still slightly crisp green beans with slivered almonds. I ate every bite and decided that maybe this house arrest wouldn't be so bad, after all.

When Helene brought out the dessert and I saw that it was chocolate mousse, I thought I'd gone to heaven. But I'd only taken a single bite when I fell back to earth with a hard landing on my rump when Helene said, "My father-in-law didn't ask us to keep you here, Charlotte. He wanted to take, well, sterner measures. But Jeffrey and I had been allowed to visit Gene yesterday, and he's worried about you. As if he doesn't have enough to worry about with another

murder accusation hanging over him. He begged his
father and me to make sure you were safe and not
wanting for anything. He's very fond of you."

Jeffrey nodded. "He went through a terrible time
after Marko disappeared off Gene's boat and Gene
was suspected of killing him. Now Marko's been
found alive, but he's apparently not capable of telling
anyone what really happened out on the boat that
night. And Gene's accused of another murder. He
needs something positive in his life."

"Some*one*," Helene amended. "We've hoped Gene
would find a nice girl who was also were. All too
often marriages between weres and nonweres just
don't work out, though they don't usually end in
tragedy like Cameron and Joy's did. Jeffrey's parents
are the rare exception. But Mother Velma obviously
carries the gene for wereness, even though she has no
animal spirit. If she didn't, Jeffrey and our sons
wouldn't be were."

I'd set my spoon down in the parfait flute when
this conversation started and not taken another bite of
mousse. I picked it up and ate a bit just to keep from
having to say anything, but what had been so
delicious had lost its taste. How could I say that I
wanted Dima, not Gene?

I couldn't. Not now, especially when they were
being so nice to me. I had to find a way to discourage
the matchmaking. I put down the spoon. "How is
Gene holding up?" I asked, mostly for politeness'
sake.

"Not well," Helene answered. "He's very
depressed. I wish you could see him. But of course
that's impossible. At least we can relay messages

from you to him and him to you. Your staying here with us will make that so much easier."

Great! How was I going to get out of this? I didn't want to hurt Gene. Not at all. But I didn't want to give him false hopes, either. "I want to do more to help than just send messages to Gene and Dima," I said, including Dima to indicate that my concern extended beyond Gene's welfare but didn't exclude it. "I'd hoped to visit the preacher who really caused what the papers call 'the massacre in the church' and persuade him to tell the truth about what happened that night and that Gene and Dima only acted in self-defense. I've learned the preacher's out of the hospital and back home. Grandfather Blass said I mustn't go there, but how else can we get Gene and Dima free?"

"Dad's working on it, Charlotte," Jeffrey said. "He's afraid you'll make matters worse, not better. He's hired a top law firm to defend them, and they'll depose the preacher and force him to testify at the preliminary hearing and—"

"And he'll lie about everything and blame it all on Dima and Gene, and his minions will back him up, and things will be worse, not better." The delicious dinner now felt like lead in my stomach.

"We can't know that. These lawyers are clever. They're very good about ferreting out the truth," Jeffrey insisted.

"Do they know about weres? Do they know Gene and Dima are were?"

"It isn't necessary for them to know that," Helene put in. "We've said nothing about it and have instructed Gene to say nothing about it. His defense will be built on other factors."

She did not mention Dima.

"So you agree that I shouldn't—that no one should—confront the preacher? Try to force him to tell the truth?"

"A genuine confession can't be forced," Jeffrey said. "Any such attempt would only lead to more charges against us."

I gave up. If they couldn't see that the only hope Gene and Dima had was in proving they'd acted in self-defense, I had to act on my own. But first I had to get out of here. And that wouldn't be easy.

I helped Helene clear the table, rinse the dishes, and put them in the dishwasher. That gave me plenty of time to scope out the kitchen, finding out how hard it would be to escape. I spotted a back door, and by casually wandering over and looking out the small window in the door, I discovered that it led to a fire escape. Good to know.

Helene hadn't missed my check of the door. "Be careful, Charlotte. If you try to open that, it'll set off an alarm."

Not what I wanted to hear!

After the kitchen work was done, Helene asked if I wanted to watch TV with them. I said, truthfully enough, that I was tired and just wanted to go to bed. The apartment had only one bedroom, but the living room couch opened up into a queen-sized bed. I figured I'd be sleeping there and could sneak out during the night while they slept. I'd have to figure out how to get out without triggering the alarm, but there had to be a way.

"You'll sleep in the bedroom, Charlotte," Helene told me, dashing that hope. "Jeffrey and I will take the sofa bed while you're here." When the sofa opened out, it left little space to get from the bedroom to the front door. In the dark I'd be sure to bump into something and wake them if I tried to escape that way.

I protested that as the guest, I should have the sofa bed, but Helene wouldn't hear of it. So I was shunted off into the bedroom, and it didn't take me long to realize why. The bedroom windows were not only closed and screened, they were protected with iron grillwork. All the windows in the apartment were. I could see no way to get out or send my jaguar out.

The place looked more like a prison all the time.

I did the only thing I could do. I went to bed. After the long day and all its trauma, I fell asleep promptly and slept soundly until morning.

Maybe during the day, with the gallery open and Jeffrey and Helene tending it, I could find a way to get out. After breakfast they let me come down with them while they readied the gallery for opening. While I wandered around admiring the art (and noting the exits and plotting an escape), Helene pointed out paintings illustrating various art styles, some by modern painters, some reproductions of old masters. She prattled on, and I only pretended to listen until she mentioned the painting of *The Peaceable Kingdom*, explaining that she and Jeffrey had acquired the piece of art that graced the were house mantel at considerable expense and had presented it to Grandfather and Grandmother Blass on the occasion of their fiftieth wedding anniversary.

"That was such a fitting piece of art for them," Helene burbled. "It represented everything the were house was — or should be. Everything it has been until, well, recently."

Until I arrived, she meant. And I didn't believe it. I hadn't created the underlying currents of anger, jealousy, and suspicion. Stirred them up, maybe, but not created them.

Jeffrey found us and pointed to the clock on the desk. "Time to open," he said.

Apparently that was the signal for me to be taken upstairs, because Helene said, "I'll see you in a while," and guided me to the stairs. "You need to stay out of sight in case someone comes in and recognizes you."

How likely was that? But I toddled to the stairway like a good little girl, and she followed me up. It seemed I was to be watched at all times. Helene provided me with reading material, but I wasn't in the mood to read. She invited me to use her toiletries and gave me a manicure. She let me help her in the kitchen. We ate lunch around noon, and she set Jeffrey's lunch on the table, then went downstairs and took over in the gallery while he came up and ate. Later they switched places again.

And so that day went, and the next, and the next, and the one after that. Helene did her best to make my stay pleasant, I'll say that for her. She insisted on arranging my hair to make it "more stylish" than the ponytail I usually wore. "You have lovely hair, Charlotte," she said. "So glossy and black. You need to show it off to best advantage." So I let her trim it a bit — wouldn't let her cut it short — and shape it around my face, and I had to admit it improved my looks.

Jeffrey, too, was unfailingly courteous. They talked often about Gene and a little about Cameron. One day Helene got out a couple of photo albums, and we sat on the sofa and looked at the photos. Of Gene as a baby. Gene and Cameron as young boys. As teenagers. Gene on a sailboat, looking sexy in T-shirt, bell-bottoms, and sandals. Gene on a speedboat, standing at the helm, waving. One of Gene in a captain's get-up at the wheel of a big boat. The one from which Marko had disappeared, Helene told me, choking up a bit. "Gene was so proud of that boat," she said. "He called it his baby. It was a 32-foot Sea Ray Sundancer, a gorgeous boat. He took his dad and me out on it—such a smooth ride! And he was a good captain. But after the accident he never went out on it again. He sold it as soon as he could." Without elaborating further she turned the album page.

I had questions I'd have liked to ask, but she seemed too near tears, so I merely tried to look interested in the rest of the photos, many of which were taken, Helene told me, by Cameron, who was now a professional photographer, having developed an interest in photography while still in grade school.

There were pictures of Cameron with Joy and one of their wedding, which Helene removed from the album. "It was a lovely wedding," she said, regarding the removed photos sadly, "but I felt uneasy about their marriage almost from the beginning. And Jeffrey never liked Joy, though he tolerated her for Cameron's sake. He certainly turned out to be right about her. I don't want Gene to make a similar mistake. I want him to find someone with whom he has a lot in common. Someone who is were."

Yeah, I got that the first time she said it. But I heard it at least once a day as the week dragged on.

About the fiftieth time I'd heard it, I couldn't stop myself. I said, "He's not going to find anybody while he sits in jail, and I can't see that your high-powered lawyers are having much success getting him out."

Helene's face turned stony. "They are working on it, Charlotte," she said. That let me know I'd hit a nerve, because she'd taken to calling me Sharl. "These things take time."

She turned away and busied herself in another part of the apartment, leaving me sitting on the sofa twiddling my thumbs. Until the phone rang.

It was on the table next to the sofa. I couldn't resist. I picked up the receiver and said hello.

"Helene, is that you?" I recognized Dr. Horshaw's voice.

"No, it's Charlotte. What's happening?"

"Oh, Charlotte, something terrible. Ryan's disappeared. He may have been kidnapped."

Helene came into the room and snatched the phone from my hand. I jumped to my feet and snatched it back. "When? How?" I managed to get out while I fought for possession of the phone.

I couldn't hear her answer.

"Helene, I have to talk to her. It's Dr. Horshaw. It's an emergency." I clutched the phone and turned away from her, and we did a little dance around the sofa as I said, "Repeat that, please."

"Ryan didn't come home from school today. His mother called the school to see if they knew where he was, and he hadn't been in school all day. His mother swears that he'd never have skipped school. She went out in her car looking for him, and she called a few of his friends. Nobody had seen him. Then Julia came home and heard about it and went out walking around the neighborhood. She found his book bag lying in the gutter not far from the bus stop. She and her aunt are frantic. Julia called me to ask if I thought his disappearance might have something to do with his being were. I said I didn't see how it could, but I'm not so sure."

"Neither am I," I said. "I've got to get out of here and help find him."

Helene wrested the phone away from me, but I'd heard the story. While she listened to Dr. Horshaw, who must be telling her just what she'd told me, I tried to think what to do. Helene was making soothing noises. "Teenage boys do run away," she said. "Has she contacted the police? ... Then they need to let the police take care of it."

Helene placed too much confidence in police and lawyers, damn it! None of their training showed them how to deal with us weres. They didn't even know about us.

Ryan wouldn't have run away. Whatever had happened to him was because he was were. I'd stake my life on it.

I demanded to leave. Helene refused.

I lost my temper. "Somebody's got to do something," I shouted. "Everybody thinks I'll make matters worse. What do you think sitting around doing nothing does? I've got to try to help Ryan. Maybe I will make matters worse. But at least I'll know I tried."

Jeffrey came bounding up the stairs. "What's

going on up here?" he asked as he came off the landing. "It's a good thing there aren't any customers in the gallery right now."

"Charlotte thinks she can solve everything if we let her go."

"I never said that! I said I had to try to find Ryan. The boy's missing, Jeffrey. I think he's caught up somehow in this mess with the were haters."

"You don't know that," Helene snapped.

"No, but I aim to find out." I headed for the stairs.

Jeffrey blocked my path. "My father expects you to stay right here with us."

"Your father doesn't own me. Nor do you. I appreciate your hospitality, but I won't be a prisoner any longer."

Jeffrey just stood there, arms stretched out to each side to stop me if I tried to go around him. Recalling the injuries Dima's leopard had inflicted on Jeffrey's bear, I was tempted to loose my jaguar and see what she could do. But I wasn't sure she could cope with a bear and a lynx together, and anyway, I had another trump card.

"You've been talking to me all week about Gene. How do you think he'd feel if he knew you were keeping me prisoner? He'd understand what I want to do. Hell, he'd be eager to help."

"And maybe get himself killed," Helene stated with bitterness, though not disagreeing with me.

"Or just maybe he might be a hero. Look, I know how dangerous these people are, but I feel responsible for Ryan. I have to try to help him. I can't just stay here and do nothing, knowing what they did to Marko, and what they might be doing to Ryan."

Jeffrey shook his head and stepped aside.

"Jeffrey! What are you doing?" Helene screeched.

"Might as well let her go. She'll find a way sooner or later. And maybe she's right. Somebody does need to do something."

"But your father will be furious with us."

"Only with me. I'll take full responsibility."

They may have gone on arguing, but I didn't stay to listen. I grabbed my purse, dodged around Jeffrey, and pounded down the stairs and through the gallery to the door, which fortunately Jeffrey hadn't locked. I stood on the street, blinking in the bright afternoon sunlight. It was near enough to rush hour that traffic was heavy.

Even though I'd thought to grab my purse, my wallet held little money, only a bit of change, enough for a short bus ride but not enough to get to Julia's apartment. But I'd get there somehow.

26
AN UNEXPECTED ALLY

I couldn't get far on foot. If Jeffrey or Helene came after me, they'd catch up to me in no time. As I hurried away from the gallery, I watched for the free tourist bus that ran along the waterfront every fifteen minutes. I was in luck; it came as I reached the corner. I boarded and rode to the end of the line. From there I'd have to take a city bus. I counted my change. Thirty cents. Not enough for a transfer that would take me to Julia's place. Without a cell phone, I had to make do with what I had — thirty cents and my wits.

I got on a bus headed in the general direction I needed to go and rode until the bus came to a major north-south artery, where I got off and started walking north. After several blocks I reached a row of car dealers. I took careful note of the cars parked along the street before entering a Ford dealership. Finding a salesman, I let him give me a sales pitch. When I expressed interest in a particular model, he wanted to know what kind of car I was driving now.

I pointed to a parked car I'd scoped out. "That one."

He shook his head. "That car belongs to one of our salesmen."

"No, not the black Ford. The Toyota Camry next to it."

But I'd aroused his suspicions. I broke off the meeting and walked on to the next dealer, where I went through the same routine and got far enough to ask for a test drive. "Sure," he said. "Let me check out the car, and we'll take it for a spin."

We? Nope. While he was in the showroom getting the keys, I headed for the next dealer.

It was a dealer in fine used cars—Porsches, Ferraris, Mercedes Benz, all looking like new. A pain stabbed my heart when I spotted a Lamborghini just like the one Dima had driven the day I met him.

No point even stopping here. I walked on past, heading for the Toyota dealership, my last chance. But as I passed the showroom, I looked through the window. A man standing by a Porsche, talking to a woman, drew my attention. He looked familiar.

He turned and met my gaze. Roy! He worked *here*? As I stood there staring, he said something to the woman he'd been talking to and headed toward the door. I needed to get away. With the heavy traffic I had no chance of getting across the street here in the middle of the block. I headed on to the next dealership.

"Charlotte. Wait!" Roy called behind me. I looked back over my shoulder to see him running toward me. "Wait!" he called again.

I waited. Might as well. He'd caught me.

He reached me and grabbed my arm. "What are you doing here? You know Dima's still in jail."

"Yes, of course." Why did he ask me that? "I'd heard they bailed you out."

"Thanks to Grandfather's lawyers. So you were looking for me?"

Why would he think that? "No. I didn't expect to see you."

He looked puzzled. "You didn't know I worked for Dima?"

I shook my head, trying to make sense of the conversation. "I was actually heading to the Toyota place next door. Looking for a car."

"Why would you look there? You do know this is Dima's dealership, don't you?"

I guess my open-mouthed astonishment gave him all the answer he needed. Now it all made sense. The fancy cars in Grandfather's garage. Dima's Lamborghini that wasn't his. No wonder the Lamborghini in the showroom looked like his. It was the same car.

"So Grandfather didn't send you here?" Roy was still trying to figure out why I was here.

"Grandfather isn't happy with me right now," I said. "I've been staying with Jeffrey and Helene in the apartment over their gallery."

"I'm staying with Georges DuChamps for the time being. He told me about your tangle with Ronnie. He's been worried about you."

Roy knew about the fight I'd had with Ronnie and wasn't angry with me? Not that he had any reason to be, but I'd been told he always stood up for his sister.

Roy still had questions for me. "How were you going to get a car?"

"I was going to ask to take one out for a test drive and just keep it for a little while. I'd bring it back eventually, of course. I just have to get somewhere, and I've got no money for the bus, much less for a cab."

"You'd get into a lot more trouble, and you're in enough already."

Yeah, tell me something I don't already know.

I saw no recourse than to explain about Ryan's disappearance and my escape from Jeffrey and Helene's apartment. He hadn't heard of Ryan, so I had to backtrack and tell him the whole story about how I met Julia and then through her met her cousin, Ryan. And about Ryan's sea eagle and his lack of knowledge about weres even though he was one. And that I very much feared he'd blundered into trouble. I told him Ryan knew of my plan to confront the preacher and force him, somehow, to tell the truth about what happened that night at the church, that Dima and Gene had only defended themselves when the preacher's goons attacked them.

Roy stroked his chin, a habit he'd probably picked up from Grandfather. "It's a mess, isn't it?"

That was such an understatement I didn't bother to answer.

"Charlotte, I'm trying to keep Dima's business open. I don't want him to lose it. But I'm a mechanic, not a salesman. I'm going to close up and drive you where you need to go. I want to help. You'll need backup when you go to see the preacher, and with Dima and Gene in jail, nobody else will provide it."

That was unexpected! I couldn't believe it! I could have hugged Roy right there in the middle of the sidewalk.

"Let me go shut the place down. It'll take about twenty minutes. You can come wait inside."

I did, and I watched to be sure Roy didn't go near a phone, because I kept thinking he'd double-cross me and have Jeffrey come and pick me up. Or even call the cops on me. But after a little over twenty minutes, time spent locking doors, setting alarms, sending an employee, apparently the only other one there now, out to secure the cars in the lot and lock the lot gate, he came to me, car keys in hand. "Let's go," he said.

He took one of the older, less valuable cars. I didn't care. I just wanted to get to Julia's. Impatient as I was, I understood why Roy kept right to the speed limit. Neither of us could afford to get stopped by the cops.

I had a thought. "What if we get to Julia's and find cops all over the place?"

"Do you know her number? You can call her." Roy pulled a Blackberry out of his jacket pocket and handed it to me. "This is Dima's, but he won't mind if we use it."

I had to think a minute, but I did remember the number. I punched it in. Julia answered almost immediately. "Julia, it's Charlotte. Has Ryan turned up?"

"Charlotte, where are you? No! We're frantic! We don't know what to do!"

"Is it safe for me to come there?" I hoped she'd know what I meant.

"No. Not now. Aunt Mary, Ryan's mother, is here with me, and we've been talking to the police, trying to convince them that he wouldn't have just run away."

I relayed that message to Roy.

"What now?" he asked.

"Let's go talk to the preacher."

"Okay." Just like that. Again I could have hugged him.

"Julia," I spoke into the phone, "I hope Ryan's disappearance doesn't have anything to do with that church and its preacher, but I'm going to go check it out. I'm not alone. Roy, another were, is with me."

"Please be careful."

"We will." I meant to keep that promise, but I knew it probably would not be easy.

I didn't know the exact location of the church, since I'd been there only through my jaguar. But I had a general idea of where it was, and I didn't think it would be hard to find.

It wasn't. When I saw it, a shiver climbed up my spine. "That's it," I told Roy.

"Do we just park in the church lot? And walk up to the preacher's front door?"

"Why not? He doesn't know either of us. We can scope things out, then retreat and come back later if we see we need to sneak in."

He pulled into the parking lot, and we got out and trekked to the parsonage next to the church. I rang the doorbell. A gray-haired woman opened the door. She looked too old to be the preacher's wife, and I remembered that Julia had said the preacher wasn't married, but the church people were taking care of him. So this woman must be one of his parishioners.

"Good afternoon," I said. "We're here as representatives of the United Council of Churches. We want to offer the Rev. Carlisle our sympathy for the terrible things that happened in his church and to assure him of our concern and our prayers. Is he able to have visitors?"

"Oh, yes, he's doing quite well. But our church is not a member of the United Council of Churches." She said it in a disdainful sort of way, like she didn't approve of the Council.

"We understand that. We still regard you as brothers in the Lord." Fortunately, I remembered the vocabulary from a time in my teens when my mother had dragged me to a church in an attempt to "straighten me out." I didn't dare glance at Roy, afraid neither of us could keep a straight face. I had nothing against religion, but what had gone on in the church next door didn't resemble any religion I was familiar with.

"I'll tell the pastor you've come to see him." She bustled off, closing behind her the door to the next room.

"Well, we're in at least," I whispered to Roy, who merely nodded, apparently too busy gazing around the room to speak.

I looked, too, and saw what had caught his eye. The living room was small, its furniture well worn; the carpet had seen better days. Nothing remarkable there. But the wall was covered with framed Bible verses, some embroidered on what looked like burlap, others written, calligraphy style, in various colors of ink on fancy paper.

The verses all had a single theme: "In thy name we have cast out devils." "Heal the sick, raise the dead, cast out devils." "I cast out devils by the spirit of God." "He suffered not the devils to speak." "Lord, even the devils are subject unto us through thy name." And in a big fancy frame inscribed in bright red calligraphy, "Babylon the great is fallen, is fallen, and is become the habitation of devils, and the hold of every foul spirit."

On a chair lay what was evidently an embroidery in progress, probably what the woman had been working on when we arrived. The words were complete; leaves and flowers were in the process of being embroidered around them. I walked to the chair and read the message. "Your adversary the devil, as a roaring lion, walketh about, seeking whom he may devour."

"Not hard to see what's on their minds, is it?"

Roy joined me and read the freshly embroidered words. He shook his head. "I'd say they have a serious fixation."

"Call it rather a dedication to the clear command of our Lord," came a booming voice.

Startled, I looked up to see the Reverend Carlisle standing in the now open doorway, looking perfectly healthy. I'd expected to see a man confined to his bed or maybe using a wheelchair. How had his severe wounds healed so quickly? I had not the slightest doubt he'd been nearly dead when we'd left the church.

He strode toward us. "As my housekeeper told you, my church is not a member of the United Council of Churches, nor do I welcome its concern. Those member churches need to be concerned for their own neglect of their Christian duty to cast out demons and to keep the bride of Christ pure."

Huh? Bride of Christ? What was he talking about?

I couldn't ask. Couldn't speak. Because by now he was standing directly in front of us, and I saw it! Something. Inside him.

Not an animal. He wasn't were. A blackness filled him. Moving like smoke, it twisted and flowed in one direction and then in another.

As it shifted about, it formed what looked like faces. Distorted, mouths open as if in a scream.

Was I hallucinating? The faces drifted about within him, fragmenting and reforming. One face looked vaguely familiar. I must be hallucinating.

"Something wrong, Miss?" Carlisle asked, not in a tone of concern but one of triumph. "Does talk of demons frighten you?"

I couldn't stop myself. "No, but the sight of them does." I grabbed Roy's arm to steady myself.

Because suddenly I knew why that one face seemed familiar. I'd seen it on a dead woman—what was left of her. Cameron's wife, Joy!

And then I recognized another. One of the men my jaguar had killed. The face dissolved almost as quickly as it had formed, so how could I be so certain? My jaguar recognized it too. She stirred, wanting out. I held her back with some effort.

What was that quote I'd read on the unfinished piece of embroidery? The devil "seeking whom he may devour"? This supposed preacher might not be the devil incarnate, but he sure was one of his henchmen.

"Is something wrong, Miss?" the preacher asked. Like he cared.

"Are you okay?" Roy's worried question told me he couldn't see what I did.

I wanted to say, *No. Let's get out of here.* But I knew more than ever how urgent it was to find Ryan. I hadn't seen his face in that swirling black smoke.

Yet.

"I'm sorry," I managed. "I just felt faint for a moment."

"You should sit down. Please." The preacher took my arm and led me to a chair. It was all I could do endure his touch. Even through my jacket and long-sleeved shirt I felt his fingers like bands of red-hot metal burning my skin.

I sat in the chair. "I'll get you a glass of water," he said and left the room but returned in seconds, giving me no chance to tell Roy what I'd seen. "Lacy will bring water," he said. "She's one of my flock. The dear sisters have taken such good care of me since my return home after the terrible accident."

I was still too shaky to speak. Thank God, Roy responded, "You're fortunate to have such loyal followers, Reverend."

"My flock is faithful to God, and their service to me is done to honor Him. I am but his humble servant in our crusade against demons."

Yeah, right! There was nothing of God in this place. Couldn't his followers sense the evil that flowed from this man? Even though they couldn't see what I saw inside him, they should have sensed the wrongness in every word he spoke.

The woman, Lacy, came in with a tray holding two glasses of water and offered one to me and one to Roy. I took the glass and raised it to my lips but didn't drink. I didn't trust anything in this house.

Roy took his glass, got it up to his mouth, and gave me a quizzical look over the rim. I shook my head very slightly and was relieved to see he hadn't taken a drink either.

Lacy turned to our host. "Will you be needing anything else, Brother Carlisle?"

"No, Sister. You may go. As always, I'm grateful for your selfless care."

"Pastor, it's an honor to be able to serve you." Her eyes were filled with adoration.

I wanted to throw up.

"God preserve you from the demons that surround us," he said by way of goodbye.

She paused long enough at the door to say, "And you, dear pastor."

I did gag. Carlisle turned toward me. "Are you all right?"

"Yes, thank you. I just choked on the water." I hoped he couldn't tell that I hadn't drunk any.

I couldn't look at him directly; I couldn't bear seeing that smoky blackness etched with dead faces.

"We should go," I said, all too aware that he was regarding me with suspicion. "We've taken up enough of your time, and we have delivered the message of good will and concern from the United Council."

I started toward the door.

"Please extend my thanks to the Council. It was a kind action to send you, although they know well that I do not agree with their theology."

"We'll do that." I reached the door, opened it, not waiting for the preacher to open it for us. I couldn't get out of his presence fast enough.

As soon as we were outside and the door closed behind us, Roy said, "What the heck was going on with you in—"

"Not now," I cut in. "Wait till we're in the car."

We reached the car and got in. "Now," Roy said. "What did we accomplish in there? Do we know anymore that we did before we went? I thought we were going to look for the missing kid."

He was peeved, and I didn't blame him. He hadn't seen what I had. "Oh, yes, we'll look for Ryan. We have to be sneaky about it. We couldn't just ask the preacher, "Oh, by the way, do you happen to have a teenaged boy tied up around here somewhere?""

"Hardly. But I thought you had some plan."

"My plan was just to get in and see something of the layout of the house."

"We didn't see anything but the living room and those framed mottos or whatever they were."

"Bible verses, I think. Come on, start the car. We'll drive away then double back and park someplace where the car can't be seen and then walk back. If Ryan's there, I'd guess he'd be in the garage. That's were they put my jaguar and Henrietta's crane."

"The garage will be locked," he pointed out.

"We'll have to break in."

"Not easy in daylight. If he hears us …"

He didn't need to finish. I shuddered, thinking of the black smoke. Should I tell Roy about it? I'd better. He needed to know what we were up against.

"Roy, I have to tell you what I saw inside that man."

"Inside him? He's a were?" He stared, openmouthed.

"No. I saw something like black smoke that twisted around through him, and faces took shape in the smoke and then vanished. But, Roy, the faces— they were of dead people."

"Dead people! How do you know?"

"I recognized some of them. A man my jaguar killed. And the men killed by Marko's wolf. And Cameron's wife. It's like he's captured their spirits. All looking like they were in terrible pain."

He drove the car over the curb and nearly hit a mailbox. I braced my hands against the dashboard and stifled a scream.

"Sorry," he said, getting the car back in its lane. "But that's a shocker."

"Yeah. Guess I should have waited and told you after we parked."

"Now that we have an idea what we're dealing with, you think we should go back there alone?"

I considered. "I think we have to. I think he might have gotten suspicious of us there at the end, and that could put Ryan in greater danger."

"I have my cell phone. We could call for backup."

"Who would you call? Grandfather flat out told me not to do this. I doubt that either Cameron or Jeffrey would go against Grandfather's wishes."

Roy swung the car around after winding through side streets. I was lost, but he seemed to know where he was and where he was heading. He took us back to about a block from the church and parsonage and parked, not on the street the church faced but on an intersecting street shaded with big trees on either side, and with other cars parked along the curb, making ours less noticeable.

"I could call Ronnie," he said.

"Are you kidding? She hates my guts."

He didn't deny it or try to defend her, just said, "Maybe so, but she'd come if I asked her."

I got out of the car, so did Roy, and we headed back toward the parsonage.

"Look, Roy, if you don't want to do this, just say so. I'll find a way to do it on my own. I know Ronnie would back you up, but I don't think she'd lift a finger to help me. I'm sorry, but I'd be afraid to trust her."

"How about Georges?" He didn't comment on what I'd just said, though I could tell he didn't like it.

"The professor? Hmm. Maybe." I didn't want to sound totally negative. Could I trust Professor DuChamps?

Roy was probably right in thinking that someone at least needed to know where we were. In case we didn't turn up again, someone ought to know where to look for us.

Julia knew. She'd get the word out. She was frantic about Ryan, so she wouldn't wait long before notifying Grandfather. And the police.

Was that enough of a safety net? What I wanted, what I knew we needed, was Dima and Gene. If they could be with us, I'd have a lot more confidence. But they were locked up in jail, and the point of this expedition was to free them as well as to find Ryan, so we had to do it without their help. And while I was thinking all that, Roy had keyed a number into his cell phone and I heard him tell Georges DuChamps where we were and what we were doing.

It was a short conversation. Roy clicked off his cell and said, "He isn't happy. He actually swore. I'd never heard him curse before. He'll probably tell Grandfather what we're doing. But at least he knows."

At least! I grew uneasier by the second, very much fearing that Roy had just doomed our expedition to failure.

But I still meant to make the attempt.

27
DEMON HUNTERS

Roy proved a useful ally when we reached the door to the parsonage garage. His lock-picking skill amazed me. He needed less than a minute to open the lock.

We eased the door open, letting the outside light spill into the dark interior. I stepped inside; Roy followed. A an older model car filled the central part of the garage. Along one side I saw the boxes my jaguar had sheltered behind. I walked closer and regarded them curiously, impressed that the jaguar had climbed the unstable-looking stack.

"Sharl!"

Roy's urgent whisper drew me away from the boxes and around the back of the car to the other side of the garage.

Ryan lay near the steps into the kitchen, bound and gagged. Even by the dim light I could see the bloody welts on his face, the swollen purple hands, the ripped and bloody remnants of his clothes.

"The bastards!" I whispered what I wanted to shout out. "They've tortured the poor kid."

Roy whipped out his cell phone and snapped a photo. "For evidence," he said, putting the phone back into his pocket and taking out a jackknife. He went to work on the ropes wrapped tightly around the boy's ankles and wrists. I removed his gag. "Ryan?" I whispered. "We've come to get you out of here."

His eyes remained closed. Kneeling beside him, I checked the pulse in his neck. He was alive but unconscious. How badly they'd hurt him I couldn't tell. Nor did I know how Roy and I would get him to the car.

Roy got the bindings off, stretched out Ryan's limbs, and massaged them to get the circulation going. I appreciated what he was doing, but we needed to get him away fast. I got my arm beneath his shoulders and raised his head and shoulders, supporting him against my body.

The door from the kitchen burst open. Light flooded the garage. The Reverend Carlisle stood framed in the doorway, staring down at us, the black spirit-smoke writhing and swirling within him. He held a handgun pointed at us as he stepped down into the garage.

"Well, well. My kind visitors. Not from the United Council of Churches at all, I'll warrant. I thought it odd that they'd be so concerned about my welfare."

I eased Ryan off me. "You've tortured this poor boy," I accused, anger overcoming my fear. "Why? He's done nothing to deserve this."

"What we do is a kindness. He has a demon that must be exorcised. When the demon comes out of him, we will do him no more harm." He walked closer, loomed over me.

"You're the one with the demon," I said, rising to my feet to face him. "I can see it inside you, it and the souls it's devoured."

"Liar! Blasphemer!" he struck my face with the pistol.

The blow staggered me. Roy grabbed me, kept me from falling. "Stop!" he yelled.

"Are you like him? Demon-possessed?" the preacher asked, holding the gun ready to strike at Roy.

"The only person here possessed of a demon is you," I said, earning another blow that sent pain stabbing through my head. My cheek felt like it was on fire.

"By what right do you hold this boy captive?" Roy demanded, distracting the preacher.

"By the command of my God, who orders his followers to cast out demons in his name."

The smugness of the man! The self-righteous ass! Could he possibly be ignorant of the evil curling through him?

Ryan groaned. He was regaining consciousness. Not at a good time.

Carlisle kicked Ryan in the side. He stirred, got his eyes open, groaned again.

"Let out your demon, boy. Let your friends see what's inside you."

Ryan blinked, stared up at Roy and me. He seemed to have trouble focusing. I don't think he could see who I was. "Please don't hurt me," he begged. "I don't have a demon."

"That thing that takes the form of an eagle, maligning our national bird, is no eagle but a demon from deepest hell. Let it out, I say!" He aimed another kick at Ryan, who squirmed in an attempt to avoid it.

Roy lunged for the arm holding the gun, grabbed

it, twisted. I reached across Ryan and yanked the gun from his hand.

I leveled it at him. "Now let's see who has the demon."

But the preacher only smiled. "Yes, let's," he said. "Brothers, come in and see what we've caught."

I aimed the gun at the man who stepped through the kitchen door, only to hear from behind me the order, "Give the gun back to Reverend Carlisle."

I turned. Five men had come quietly into the garage from the front, and all had weapons pointed at Roy and me. Two other men and a woman came through the kitchen door, also armed and looking eager to shoot. Those men and the woman held handguns. Two of the men behind us had assault rifles. They must be some of the guys that shot up our car. With a sick feeling I handed the gun back to the preacher. The men closed in on us. The woman walked around the car and returned with lengths of rope.

"You see how we've disciplined the boy to persuade him to send forth his demon. Release yours and you can avoid that treatment. Be stubborn like him, and we will have no choice but to force you to release your demons."

"What makes you so certain we have demons?" I was stalling for time.

"Your defense of the boy implies it. And why else would God have led you to us but so that we could rid you of your demons?"

While he spoke, two of the men took the ropes from the woman. One grabbed my arms, twisted them behind my back, and tied the rope around my wrists, pulling it so tight it cut into them. He drew a length of the rope down from my wrists and bound my ankles the same way, laughing when I lost my balance and fell forward, landing on Ryan, who let out a scream.

Roy was soon trussed up just as I was, though he managed to remain standing.

I'd hurt Ryan when I fell on him. I tried to roll off and earned a kick from the preacher for my efforts.

"Release your demons and be set free," the preacher roared. "I command you, demons, come forth in the name of the Lord. Leave these poor, deluded sinners and suffer the fate ordained for you and all demons."

"Amen," chorused his followers.

I'd have liked nothing better than to release my jaguar and let her take down the preacher. But they'd kill her before she could get more than one or two of them, if she even managed that. And when she died, I'd be as good as dead, never regaining consciousness.

That was what they wanted: to lure our animal spirits out in physical form so they could put them to death. I was so thankful I'd told Ryan what would happen to him if his eagle died. He'd resisted their torture to protect his eagle and to save himself. But how much longer would he be able to hold out? How long would I? Or Roy? These people were determined to break us no matter what it took.

This must be what they'd done to Marko. And he'd resisted. For two long years!

Roy hunched over, groaning. My throat ached from

screaming. I begged for water, and they threw a bucketful of icy water in my face, laughing when I licked my lips to get the few drops that clung to them. I was soaked in blood from being beaten with the prong end of an electric cord, cut with knives, scratched with a thin board studded with nails. My face ached; my eyes were swollen nearly shut from all the blows to my face. I almost certainly had broken ribs from all the kicks.

The worst thing was that my jaguar *wanted* out. She longed to tear into these torturers. But two or three men stood ready, rifles drawn, not taking part in the torture but waiting for it to have its effect. They intended to kill my "demon" the second it emerged.

The preacher came to stand beside me. He looked down at me and spoke softly. "Come now, put an end to this. Let the demon out so we can rid you of it. You'll thank us for the freedom you'll have then."

The smoke within him thickened and filled him entirely, so that its motion was only visible in the way the faces in it came and faded and reformed.

I looked up into his face and wished I could spit that far.

"I don't know why you people are so stubborn." He shook his head and put on a sad face. "I'd think you'd want to rid yourself of demons, but of course the demons within you are strong, and it's by their influence that you resist so. I regret that we have to use such drastic measures to try to persuade you, but we've learned that nothing else helps. We tried kindness and earnest persuasion for many weeks on one of your number, but it did not move him. We prayed over him and read Bible passages that describe the horror of demon possession. Nothing helped. Finally we resorted to sterner methods. Yet he held back, and even after months of our efforts he had the strength and the cleverness to escape."

He was talking about Marko! And he had the nerve to chuckle before adding, "Not that he got far. We tracked him and called on a confederate to intercept him and take the final measure for dealing with a demon. A measure we'll have to use on you if we can't persuade you in any other way. We destroy the demon by killing its host."

Suddenly it all became clear to me. His confederate must have been Joy. He didn't know that Marko hadn't died. Or that Joy had.

"You don't want that, now do you?" he wheedled, bending over me. "Haven't you suffered enough? Hasn't your companion? And the boy you profess to care about? If you really care about him, really want him freed, tell him to free his eagle. And you free your demon, whatever it is."

He didn't know. Of course he didn't. How could he? He couldn't see my jaguar as I could see whatever the smoke thing was inside him. And that gave me an idea. I couldn't let my jaguar loose, but I remembered how I'd sent her into Dima.

"You'll free me if I do?" I asked in a plaintive voice. "You'll stop hurting me?"

Roy groaned. "Charlotte, no! You know what—"

"I know what will happen, Roy. But I have to stop this." Would he get the hidden message? That I wasn't giving in; I had something planned?

Would it work? I had to find out, or we were all as good as dead.

"You swear that I'll be set free? That the pain will end?" I made my voice very weak, so, as I'd hoped, he had to bend closer to hear.

"I do swear it. You have my word."

I sent my jaguar leaping from me into him in her spirit form. And watched as, within him, my jaguar fought and clawed at the smoke that twined around her.

The preacher stood up and backed away, a horrified look on his face. "What have you done?" he demanded.

He backed farther. "Thing of evil!" he screamed.

His followers stared at him. "What happened?" one asked.

Another kicked me. "What'd you do to him?"

I couldn't answer. Gasping for breath from the kick, dizzy and weak from the abuse and from the absence of my jaguar, I tried to watch what was happening inside the preacher. But I lost sight of my jaguar as the smoke enclosed her.

Would she survive or had I sent her to her death?

She wants to be outside, clawing and tearing at the man, crunching his neck in her powerful jaws. Instead, in obedience to her person, she's inside grappling with this black beast that smells of death and decay. Carrion!

She tears at it, but it flows through her claws. She opens her mouth to bite, but her teeth meet no resistance. But she is spirit here within the man, not flesh. The black creature can no more grasp her than she can grasp it. When it wraps around her, trying to smother her, it flows through her.

That causes her great pain, but she sees that it weakens her foe, so she twists and writhes, forcing it to coil around her, letting it course through her. She'd felt her human host's agony; now she suffers her own. Her human had endured it; so can she.

Through the black smoke I watched for glimpses of my jaguar, glints of red, the flash of white teeth. For a time I saw nothing and despaired. The black smoke had absorbed her.

But she must still live. I was conscious, though only barely. The preacher would have collapsed had his people not caught and supported him. They begged him to tell them what was wrong. He could only shake his head and mutter, "Evil. Evil."

They threatened to shoot me if I didn't tell them what I'd done. I had no strength for speaking.

"She didn't do anything. Leave her alone," Roy begged. I didn't know whether he really thought I'd done nothing, or if he'd seen the quick jump of my jaguar into the preacher. Could he even see the jaguar in her spirit form? None of the preacher's people had seen her. They had no idea what was wrong with their leader. Or what to do about it.

Something banged against the garage door. Loud. The sound reverberated through my aching head so that I'd have screamed if I could.

More bangs. Something was pounding on the metal door.

Then a loud crash. My stomach clenched. I fought to hold on to the thread of consciousness.

"Get it!" someone shouted. "Shoot it."

A shot rang out, sending shudders through me.

Loud squeal. A Thud. Screams. If only I could see what was going on. I didn't know what was happening to my jaguar, either. I couldn't see the preacher anymore; they'd moved him out of my line of sight.

More shots. A horse whinnied. The professor's! Had they shot it?

Unable to see or speak, I could only lie still and try to hold myself together.

28
SMOKE AND BLOOD

The black smoke fills the jaguar, choking her. She doesn't need to breathe in her spirit state, but she feels smothered nonetheless. She feels trapped, bound as she'd been when caught in the net. She snarls, bites at the bindings, but there are no bindings, nothing her teeth can feel.

Pain is everywhere, blinding her, deafening her. Yet she fights. And the black monster fights back, weakening her even as she weakens it.

She hears the screams and curses of the man she's in, rending sounds, as though her struggles with the black monster are tearing him apart. He is not her person, and she will not spare him. She understands that her life and her person's life depend on her winning this battle.

She fights on, drawing the blackness inside her, letting it pass through her and out again and then back through again. And each time it seems a bit weaker, thinner. She is weaker and thinner, too. But she must keep up the fight.

She has no sense of time. She does not know what is happening outside. Pain fills her and a terrible weariness. She has been fighting for so long!

She stretches. If she goes out of the man she will be in greater danger. So will her person. She cannot stop fighting. One more time she twists and turns so that the monster turns and twists and they entwine, and the monster passes through her, increasing her pain.

Does it feel pain?

She rests. It also seems to rest, gathering itself together into a tight ball in the center of the man. Seeing her chance, she summons her little remaining strength and pounces on the ball, opening her mouth, drawing it into her.

It is as if she has swallowed a flow of lava. She is on fire. Dying.

She senses more than sees that the black monster is also dying.

She feels it shrinking inside her all the while it is burning her, killing her. She claws at her stomach. Opens her mouth. Gags. Disgorges the tatters of black.

They flutter around her like flies. They are fading, gray now more than black. She spits out more. Gradually the tattered bits gather together. Is the fight to begin again?

No. They flow from her. Up. Out through the man's mouth. She has won!

She licks her wounds. She must return to her person, but she needs to rest first. She is too weak now to make the transfer.

I'd been asleep. When had I fallen asleep? So weak!

There had been noise. Now I heard only low muttering. I had to get my eyes open, see what was going on. My eyelids didn't want to cooperate. The lids felt glued together.

Brain wasn't functioning well, either. My jaguar! Where was she? I needed her. I sent out a tentative probe and located her—still in the preacher. Lying still. Not dead, she can't be!

No. There! A slight movement. And then I saw it. The black smoke. Gray now. Thinner. Faces breaking apart immediately on forming. The smoke swirled upward, into the preacher's head. And out of his mouth!

Someone screamed. Men shouted. They saw it, too!

"Look! There's your demon. Coming out of your preacher! He's the one who's demon-possessed. We aren't." Roy's voice. "Untie us and let us go."

I turned my head to look at him. Despite his tied wrists, he had propped himself up on one elbow. I tried to get into a similar position, but my arm wouldn't support me.

Hadn't I heard a horse? And something else? Had I dreamed that? Could the professor and another were have sent their animals in here? I had to see what was going on. The awkward position in which I was tied allowed me to see only a small portion of the garage.

That portion did include Ryan. He lay as still as he had before my little nap. Regarding him closely, I was relieved to see the rise and fall of his chest. Not dead. But how badly injured, I couldn't tell.

At present no one was beating or kicking or shocking us with an electric cord. And no one was shooting at us or at anything else. The preacher's condition seemed to be his flock's sole concern at the moment.

My concern was how to get my jaguar back from the preacher. She could come out in bodily form, of course, but if she did, she'd almost certainly be shot. Yet staying in the preacher was torment for her and for me. Somehow I needed to get someone to untie me.

A bit of black smoke slowly drifted past me. Was someone smoking? No, cigarette smoke wouldn't be so black. The black smoke thing in the preacher—this must be a remnant of it. I twisted my head to follow it as it floated upward, toward the ceiling. And there I saw several more black wisps coming together. Spiraling slowly as they joined and reformed.

That evil thing wasn't dead! It would return to the preacher or find another host. How could I stop it? Even if I were free, I wouldn't know how to kill it.

Motion behind me—someone walking softly. Hurrying to Roy. Ronnie! She bent over Roy with a knife in her hand, sliced through the ropes binding his wrists.

"Hey! Stop her!"

She'd been spotted. She put the knife into Roy's hands and stood, her hands raised. "Don't shoot," she called. "I'm not armed."

The little fool! Didn't she know what she was getting herself into?

But while she drew the attention of the preacher's followers, Roy sliced through the ropes on his ankles.

I thought he'd free me next, but he sat there massaging his legs and arms, ignoring my "Hsst!"

Then I forgot my own plight. The black smoke I'd watched gathering at the ceiling swooped down and around and into Ronnie.

She screamed and dropped her arms to her side. She leaned against the side of the car that occupied the center of the garage. I'd heard of people foaming at the mouth but I'd never actually seen it happen until now. Her head thrown back, spittle pouring from her mouth, she let out an inhuman howl. Then she slowly slid down the side of the car to sit on the floor.

Within her I saw the black smoke with its horror gallery of faces, but I also saw her badger awaken. It shook itself and tore into the smoke thing. Weakened by its battle with my jaguar, shredded by the badger's claws, the smoke creature tried to regroup, but the badger's continued attack drove it out of Ronnie.

Toward the one person on this side of the car who didn't have her animal spirit within her.

Me.

I tried to duck, but it curled around my head, and when I had to breathe it followed my breath in through my nose, and I thought I would choke. Not that it had real substance. It wasn't anything I could taste or smell or feel as you would feel food that you were swallowing. Rather it was like a rising tide of fear and rage and hate flooding through me and reminding me of every hurt I'd ever suffered, every cruel thing ever said to me, every slight, every failure, every foolish and embarrassing thing I'd ever done. I wanted to strike out, to hurt someone. Anyone.

Ronnie. My mind reviewed all her accusations, all her jealousy. I'd get her! She wouldn't get away this time. I'd make her pay for what she did. Turning Grandfather against me. That was her fault. Her fault that Dima was rotting in jail. Her fault that we were caught here. She'd put Roy up to it, no doubt about it. Just let me get my hands around that lily-white throat.

But my hands were still tied. My ankles, too. I'd have to call my jaguar, get her to attack Ronnie. And Roy. Roy should have set me free. Selfish son of a bitch, leaving me like this while he cut himself free. I'll get them both, him and his slutty sister.

I summoned my jaguar.

She didn't respond. I couldn't reach her, couldn't see her. Not just because the preacher was out of my sight, the car blocking my view. It was as though the bond between us had been cut.

My jaguar! Was she dead? No, I wouldn't be conscious if she were dead. Unless ... unless the smoke thing had taken her place. It had filled her absence in me. Its spirit was supplanting hers.

No! I couldn't lose her. She was all I had left. Everyone else had turned against me, but not her. She never would. She was the one good thing in my life. I had to get her back.

That thought consumed me, driving out the anger, the hatred, the self-pity. Everything left me but my need for my jaguar. I called her again.

This time she answered my call.

"Look!" someone shouted. "A demon. Coming from the pastor."

"Kill it!"

"No!" I screamed.

A shot rang out. I screamed again.

Another shot.

Tears filled my eyes. If they'd killed her ...

My jaguar bounded toward me. Leaped. Faded

into me. And black smoke poured from my nostrils and my open mouth. And the world righted itself. The anger, the hatred, and the self-pity all left with the smoke. Despite our still desperate situation, I felt joy.

"Ronnie, no!" Roy's voice.

I blinked away the tears and looked over where Ronnie had been standing. She'd fallen, blood pouring from a wound in her shoulder. A small handgun hung limp in her hand.

She must have smuggled in a gun and shot the person who was ready to fire on my jaguar. And someone else had shot her. She'd saved my jaguar and thus saved me. She must not die!

I had never felt so helpless, tied hand and foot, unable to do anything but lie still.

Someone came toward me. A woman. She bent over me. "Brother Carlisle wants to see you." She held a carving knife, probably taken from a kitchen drawer, and used it to saw through the ropes around my ankles. "Don't try anything," she warned, brandishing the knife. "Get up onto your feet."

"I can't unless you untie my wrists, too." I was too stiff and sore to sit up, and I thought my left arm might be broken.

Using one hand while the other kept a firm grip on her knife, she grabbed me under shoulder and yanked me to a sitting position. "I can't lift you," she said. "And I don't trust you. So stand up."

I tried, but without the use of my arms I didn't have the strength. She stood over me, glaring down at me, knife at the ready. I considered letting my jaguar out, certain that the jaguar could topple her before she could use the knife to defend herself. But my jaguar's battle with the smoke demon had left her weak. I couldn't risk her life.

The woman looked at Roy, who was trying desperately to stanch the flow of blood from Ronnie's shoulder. "You," she said. "You've got yourself free. Get over here and help your friend onto her feet."

Why didn't she call one of her people?

Reluctantly Roy tore himself away from his sister and came to us. He bent down, placed a hand under each of my shoulders, and lifted me straight up onto my feet. I cried out in pain.

"She's hurt," Roy said, still holding me up. "After the kicks and the beatings, how do you expect her to walk?"

"You're walking," the woman said, as though that meant I should be able to as well.

"Those kicks to her side probably broke some ribs."

I nodded agreement, too busy holding back screams of pain to speak. My jaguar was doing all she could to hasten healing, but it would take some time for her efforts to have much effect, especially as weak as she was. She needed to heal herself.

"Jim, get over here," the woman yelled.

A tall, skinny man answered her call, and Roy was allowed to return to Ronnie. "Want I should tie him up again?" Jim asked, nodding toward Roy.

"Yes, but first help me get this woman to Brother Carlisle."

He wasn't as careful as Roy had been. I screamed when he grabbed me and jerked me forward. He backhanded me across the face.

He forced me to keep walking, though every step was agony. It was really only several steps, but it seemed like several miles before we rounded the front of the car and stood before the preacher. The guy holding me up, Jim, looked around to see who he could hand me off to. In a hurry, I suppose, to get back to Roy and tie him up again. I sagged against him, determined to keep him from returning to Roy as long as I could.

The preacher was seated on the ground, leaning against one of the men, while his followers were gathered around him looking dazed, lost. There weren't as many of them as I'd seen before. One man was lying on the ground, bleeding heavily, not dead but surely dying. He must be the guy Ronnie shot.

The Reverend Carlisle's followers all glared at me as though everything was my fault. Nothing new there.

Carlisle's eyes were closed until the woman who'd come to get me said, "Here she is, Brother."

He opened his eyes, raised a hand, and feebly beckoned me closer. "What did you do to me?" he rasped, his voice a harsh whisper.

Jim was forced to move forward with me.

I decided to be truthful, hoping that by telling the truth I might avoid more slaps, punches, and kicks. Besides, I lacked the energy or the wit to lie. "I sent my animal spirit into you. She's not a demon. She fought the thing in you that looked like black smoke. It was quite a battle, but she won and drove it out of you. I let her rest a bit and then called her back to me. One of your followers shot at her, and my friend shot him to save her. And got shot doing it."

He waved a hand as if to dismiss all that as of no concern. "You sent your demon into me. You dared."

"I could see that horrible smoke thing inside you. I saw faces form in the smoke. Faces of people who are dead." I shuddered. "You talk about casting out demons, but if that thing inside you wasn't a demon, I don't know what it was."

"Where is it now?"

"I don't know. Gone, I hope." I glanced up to the ceiling, remembering how the fragments had drifted there before. I saw nothing. I hoped that didn't mean it had found another host. At least it hadn't returned to Preacher Carlisle.

But when an animal spirit died, its host was left in a coma from which he never awakens. Yet the preacher, though weak, was awake, his mind functioning. Somehow that didn't seem fair. But then, little in life is fair.

"I feel empty. Drained."

Well, of course he did. He should.

He hesitated, staring at the floor for a few awkward minutes before looking up at me and saying, "When your, ah, animal spirit was fighting this thing you said was inside me, it was a terrible experience. I didn't know what was happening, but I felt like I was being torn apart. It made me feel physically sick, but far worse was the mental torment. I heard voices shouting in my brain. Saying terrible things. Or pleading, begging to be set free. They— they sounded like the voices of people I've known. But that's impossible."

Impossible? Not if, as I suspected, that thing within him had swallowed the souls of those who'd died serving its host, like the men my jaguar had killed. And I'd seen Cameron's wife Joy's face there. She must have been part of his flock. Cameron had said she'd betrayed us to them.

I kept silent, and he continued. "Then I felt something leave me, but I was not empty. I felt at ease. At peace. Until you called your animal spirit back to you. That was when the empty feeling began. The feeling of abandonment. Of desolation. I can't bear it. Tell me what to do."

Almost I felt pity for this man. Perhaps it had been the thing within him more than he himself that did the cruel and heartless acts.

Almost. Then I thought of Henrietta's crane, hurt and terrified, lying on the altar, ready to be sacrificed. I thought of Dima and Gene in jail because of the actions of this man and his followers. I thought of Ryan, lying unconscious and who knew how badly hurt. And I thought of Ronnie, her life bleeding away.

I shook my head. "I can't tell you anything. I don't know how that black smoke creature got in you. I know it was evil, and it drove you to evil. You are well rid of it. Be satisfied that it's gone."

"But I need something to take its place. Something to fill the emptiness."

"Something like my animal spirit?" I asked, barely controlling my anger. "Something like what you've tried to kill? Wanted to sacrifice? Because you were so certain that it was a demon? You'll never have an animal spirit. That I can tell you. You'll have to live with that emptiness."

My anger kindled his. "You're as bad as the first one we found. Wouldn't let his demon out no matter what we did. Saw it once, but no more. He got away from us. You won't."

Talking about Marko again. They'd tortured him to force him to release his "demon," his wolf. Just as they tortured us. How had he held out not for hours, but for two years?

I turned away in disgust, and so he wouldn't see the tears that filled my eyes. Not for myself but for Marko. For what he'd suffered at the hands of these people.

When I turned away I saw the boar. It lay off to the opposite side of the car from the side I'd lain on. They'd shot it. It lay in a pool of its own blood.

Cameron! The poor man! After being injured by Marko's wolf, he'd come here in hopes of rescuing us. And now …

The boar twitched. Not dead. If we could get it to Cameron, or get Cameron to it, maybe it could be saved.

We didn't have time. I had no idea where Cameron might be. And we were still prisoners.

A low murmur came from over beside the car. "Hey," Jim, my captor, shouted. "What's going on?" He shoved me into the arms of a nearby man, who, startled, nearly dropped me, and hurried back to Roy.

"I was just talking to my sister, trying to rouse her," Roy said.

"She's your sister?" Jim sounded skeptical.

The man onto whom I'd been thrust lowered me to the ground while giving me a disgusted look. Guess he thought I was contaminating him.

I gave a loud groan when he dropped me onto the concrete floor — not faked; it felt like getting kicked by an elephant. And maybe I did black out for just a few seconds. But I pretended to remain unconscious.

"Damn her!" Preacher Carlisle cursed, then apparently decided that wasn't preacherly and added, "And I mean that literally. She and all those like her who harbor demons and refuse to give them up will be damned for all eternity."

I wouldn't have thought he had the strength for such a speech. He seemed to have recovered from his weakness. I wondered whether the smoke thing had found its way back to him, but I didn't dare open my eyes to look. Letting them know I was conscious would just earn me more torture.

"I've got the man tied up so he won't get loose again. I checked the girl. No need to tie her. I removed the bandage he'd rigged out of his shirt. At the rate she's losing blood, she won't last much longer." That was Jim, reporting on Roy.

"The girl" had to be Ronnie. I hoped he was wrong, but I was very afraid he wasn't. Her badger would do what it could, but she needed medical attention. Fast.

"If I let my eagle out, will you let these people go?" Ryan! He'd come to.

"We'll consider it." The preacher's lying offer was meaningless. But I was afraid Ryan might act on it.

I couldn't let him make that sacrifice. I opened my eyes. "No, Ryan!" I shouted. "He won't let us go no matter what."

"I have to take the chance," the boy called back.

"No," I said. "I'll let the preacher have my jaguar. You hear that, preacher? I'll send my jaguar back into you, if you'll just let the boy go."

"You'd let her send your demon into you?" the woman who'd brought me to the preacher demanded, disbelief and horror registering in her voice and on her face.

"No, no, Louella. I intend to vanquish the demon," he told her, then turned to me. "This is really quite touching." His unctuous voice sent rage racing through me. "I thank you for your offers. Young man, I accept your offer. Release your demon. And you, girl, will release yours as well, but not into me. Surrender it for sacrifice and be blessed. Otherwise we'll beat it out of you."

"Ryan, be strong. Don't—"

"Police," came a call from outside the garage. "Open up!"

So! When they'd heard Roy speaking, he hadn't been talking to Ronnie; he'd been talking on his cell phone, calling the cops. And Ryan heard him; he'd been stalling for time, never intending to release his eagle. Smart kid. Even after what he'd been through, he'd kept his head.

"We're doing the Lord's work here," the preacher called back. "You have no right to interfere."

"Sir, I'm sorry, but it sounds a bit more than that to us. Come out with your hands raised. You'll be released if we find we've been called in error."

The cop's response brought the Reverend Carlisle to his feet. "Someone called?" he asked, looking at the group around him. "Do we have a traitor here, or— Check these people for cell phones."

"Be careful," Roy shouted. "They're armed. They've already shot my sister. She needs medical help right away."

"Check him first," Carlisle said.

The men who'd tied Roy went to him. It didn't take them long to find the phone. They gave him a few more kicks while they were about it, and he hollered at each one, letting the police know what was going on.

"The phone was turned on," one of the men reported. "They've heard all that's gone on."

Livid at that bit of news, the preacher walked to me and reached down and hauled me to my feet, drawing screams from me that the cops outside could hear without benefit of a phone.

"We have hostages," the preacher called. "If you come in, we'll kill them."

"They plan to kill us anyway," I yelled before Carlisle clamped his hand over my mouth. I bit his fingers. He swore and slammed his fist into my mouth.

"You can't get away," the cop shouted. "It'll go much easier for you if you release your hostages and surrender."

"We're prepared to die for our faith," the preacher called back. The hypocrite! "These people are demon-possessed. We only want to defeat their demons. We have no desire to hurt or kill them."

"They shot my sister," Roy shouted.

"In self-defense," Carlisle called. "She shot first."

"Then you should be willing to surrender." The speaker could be heard clearly. Probably using a bullhorn. "Come out with your hands raised. Let us verify what you're saying." The cops were still being more polite than I liked. I know that's part of their training, but ...

"We've shot one of the demons. You can see it for yourself," the preacher shouted "Send one man in unarmed. I guarantee his safety. Let him see that I speak truth."

Uh-oh. He meant to show them the boar. That wouldn't convince the cops, but it would endanger us. And make it impossible to get the boar back to Cameron. If it wasn't already too late for that.

"Send out one of the hostages as proof of your good faith, and we'll send in an unarmed officer, as you've requested."

"Don't—" Roy's shout was cut off. Someone must have stuffed a gag into his mouth.

"Don't trust them," Ryan finished for him. The kid had spunk. I heard him gag, guessed they'd stuffed a rag into his mouth as well.

Sirens screamed, brakes squealed. Ambulance? The police hadn't used sirens when they'd arrived.

Maybe Carlisle had the same thought. "Are there paramedics there? You may send in two to remove the wounded woman. We'll keep the other hostages. They can see the demon and swear to its presence here."

They didn't answer immediately. I guess they had to confer.

Finally they called out, "Place the wounded woman by the door, and then have everyone else remain in the rear of the room. The paramedics will come in and remove the wounded woman. When they are safely out, we'll send in a negotiator, and you can show him what you want him to see."

"How do we know we can trust you?" Carlisle called back.

"You have hostages," the spokesman responded. We won't endanger them, so we'll do as you ask."

"All right," Carlisle yelled. "Send in the paramedics when I tell you."

Preacher Carlisle ordered a couple of his followers to pick up Ronnie and carry her near the door. My hope that the cops would break in then was dashed. The men laid Ronnie down none too gently and returned to the area behind the car, so that it partially shielded them. Ryan and Roy were hauled back there, too, and pulled upright to shield the group of one woman and three men, all that remained of the more numerous followers who had captured us. I wasn't sure where the rest had gone, but I suspected that they had eased away, not wanting to be involved with the torture that had gone on. I hoped I was right, and they weren't just lurking in the house somewhere, ready to join in an attack on the cops.

I was Carlisle's shield. With my ankles and wrists bound and a gag in my mouth, I couldn't do much. But there was one thing I could do.

The preacher was gripping my arms with both hands. That meant that he wasn't holding a gun. He was counting on his goons to defend him and themselves. We were standing near the front of the car, a little off to the side, I suppose so that the preacher could see what was happening at the front of the garage. I wasn't tall enough to see over the car, but the preacher was a lot taller.

"All right," he shouted, "send in the paramedics." And softly to his four followers, "Just stay perfectly still. Let them take the woman out. As long as no police come in, we will cooperate."

I could see that the door had been kicked partially open. The professor's horse must have done that when the horse and the boar had come. So where was the professor, and where was Cameron?

I had to take a big chance. Roy had taken one, and so had Ryan. It was my turn to be brave.

I leaned back against Carlisle so he bore most of my weight, and while our captors' attention was on the paramedics I sent out my jaguar. She flowed from me to the car and became solid only as she squirmed beneath it. So quick and quiet she was that I don't think anyone saw her.

Now I could see through her eyes the action blocked from my own vision by the car.

With my jaguar I watched and waited for the right moment, the opportunity to act. What I planned was risky — foolhardy, Grandfather would say. Or stupid. Possibly impossible.

It was also our only chance.

29
ACT OF DESPERATION

The jaguar crouches beneath the car, belly to the ground. She keeps to the shadow of a tire. The garage door is bent inward leaving a big gap on both sides of the door and a strip at the bottom wide enough for her to scoot under. But she cannot do that yet. Although it is night, outside the garage the men have set up bright lights, so the area in front of the garage is like a sunny day. She cannot leave her hiding place without being seen. Yet her errand demands that she leave.

She bides her time, watching. Men load the girl Ronnie into an ambulance. The ambulance leaves, its siren screaming. A police car pulls into the place where the ambulance had been, parking lengthwise across the front of the garage. Two other police cars pull in facing the garage, one on either side of the first car, boxing in the garage door. She cannot see the front of the house, but she knows from comments she hears that men and cars surround the house to which the garage is attached.

The police gather in a group, listening to someone giving instructions. She grabs the chance, crawls to the end of the car she's under, and dashes across the narrow space separating it from the police car. She dives beneath the police car and huddles there.

They are ready to send someone inside the garage. She must make her move soon. They are gathering in front of the garage door, between it and the police car under which she waits. Their attention will be on the garage and what is happening inside it.

Soon …

With my jaguar out it was hard to move, hard to sever my connection to her. But time was short. I had to act. To move. Fortunately, at the present moment my jaguar lay beneath the car, waiting quietly, allowing me to act.

The preacher was supporting me. He probably thought I'd fainted. Good. I gathered all the strength I could summon, steeled myself against the pain I knew would come, and jerked my head up hard beneath his chin. It startled more than hurt him, but it made him relax his grip on me for a moment. That moment was all I needed. I stepped away from him and elbowed him in the stomach.

He cried out. Teeth clenched against the pain of movement, I ran to the boar and threw myself down on it just in time to escape a bullet. I prayed that my weight wouldn't kill the boar. Prayed that it would understand.

"Don't shoot," Preacher Carlisle shouted.

But that single shot delayed the hostage negotiator from entering. The preacher called out that it was safe, but the police weren't fools.

"No one's been shot or hurt," Carlisle called out again. "That shot was fired by accident. The hostages are alive. If you want them to stay that way, send in one person to verify the truth of what I've told you."

I had my arms around the bleeding boar. *Come into me,* I thought to it. *Come in and I'll get you to Cameron. Hurry, so you and he can live.* The boar was so near death. Would it hear? Would it understand?

"All right. We have a negotiator set to come in," came the shout from outside. "He isn't armed, but we have a SWAT team out here ready to act if he's fired on."

"I give you my word," the preacher called back. "He won't be harmed. But if anyone outside fires, the hostages will die."

Now or never, I sent to the boar. *Fade into me. I'll get you to Cameron.* I think I put every ounce of strength into that sending.

The boar heard. Slowly it faded into me, as though the effort hurt it even more than it did me.

And hurt it did! The boar's suffering became mine, adding to the pain of broken ribs and bruised limbs the agony left by a bullet tearing through my gut. I fought to stay conscious.

I heard the preacher greet the man who'd come in. "Come this way," he said, directing the negotiator around the side of the car on which I lay, no longer cushioned by the boar's body but face down on the hard cement, wet and sticky with the boar's blood.

"You'll see the demon here," I could imagine Preacher Carlisle pointing to where the boar had fallen. The man looking and seeing only me.

I heard the preacher gasp. "It's gone!" he said. "It must have gone into her."

Smart man. And the negotiator's footsteps came near me. "What's this? You've shot her?"

"No! No, it's a trick!" the preacher yelled.

And was heard and misunderstood by the men outside. The garage door banged. The police stormed in.

I drifted into blackness hoping that Roy and Ryan wouldn't be hurt in the wild confusion.

It is time to move. But the jaguar feels the sudden severing of the bond between her and her person. It confuses her. She feels empty. Abandoned.

She must reunite with her host. Yet she dares not enter the garage. She remembers what she must do. She does not know how, and now her person cannot guide her. She must act alone.

She peers out from beneath the car. There are still a few men outside, but most have stormed into the garage. She hears shots from within. That draws the attention of those outside. They all look toward the garage.

She emerges from beneath the car and streaks down the driveway and across the street and under a bush. She crouches there, looking back to the garage and the house beside it. Had she been seen? She does not think so. No one is coming her way.

Staying in the camouflaging shadows, she moves away from the bush and creeps along the side of the street. A man steps out of the shadow of a large tree that overhangs the road.

He is not a policeman. He sees her and walks toward her. She tenses, ready to spring.

"Easy," the man says. "You know me."

And she does. She recognizes the one called the professor.

"Charlotte has sent you out?" he asks.

She nods. Of course she was sent out. She would not leave her host otherwise.

"To find Cameron?"

Again she nods. He is wise, this man. He understands.

"I'll lead you to him," he says. "Follow me."

There is no traffic in the street. The police have blocked it off. They cross in the shadows cast by overhanging trees. They wind their way carefully through a yard and in back of houses, toward the small woods behind the church and the house where the preacher lives. They see police, but the police do not see them. The police watch the garage and the attached house. They do not look toward the woods.

Cameron lies beneath a tree. He is shuddering violently. The jaguar wonders whether he is cold. The night is cool, but she does not think it is cold enough to make someone shiver so.

She goes to him, noses him gently. He does not open his eyes. She knows what she must do, but she does not want to do it. This man is not her host. To be within him will be painful. It will hurt in many ways. Yet she knows this is what her person wishes.

She braces herself. The professor watches her. "Go ahead," he says.

She fades into Cameron. He shakes even more, trying to throw out what to him is a foreign thing, a violation.

The professor speaks to him, calming him. Explaining. The professor helps him rise. Cameron stumbles. He is still shaking. He can walk only by leaning heavily on the professor. They head slowly toward the house.

The jaguar lends Cameron her strength. But it is not like being inside her host. It feels strange, awkward. She cannot communicate with him as she could with her host. He does not try to communicate with her. He stumbles along almost without conscious thought. The one thing that fills his mind is his desire to be reunited with his boar. That single goal is all that keeps him moving.

They reach the garage and are confronted by police. The ambulance is back. The jaguar sees her person being placed on a gurney.

The professor speaks to a policeman. "Let this man see her before you take her away. Please. She needs to know that he's alive, and he needs to know that she is. Please. just for a moment."

The policeman says, "I'm sorry, sir. He'll have to see her at the hospital when she's can have visitors."

"Please, only for a few seconds. I think it would be of great benefit for her frame of mind."

"As far as I know she isn't conscious. I doubt she'd know he was there. And for that matter, this fellow looks like he needs medical attention himself. I notice you're doing all the talking."

"He's upset, that's all. Please, let him see her."

"She his wife? Or girlfriend?"

"A member of his family. A close member."

"Well, you can ask the paramedics, I guess."

The jaguar has difficulty getting Cameron moving again. Already the gurney has been loaded into the ambulance. It will move out soon. She urges Cameron forward. The professor does, too. They approach the back of the ambulance. Another policeman stops them.

"Sir," the professor says, "this man needs medical attention. Before the ambulance leaves, perhaps the paramedics could take a quick look at him?"

"They need to get their patient to the hospital stat," the policeman says. "I'll see if they can transport him, too."

He goes to the ambulance and speaks to the paramedic. The paramedic comes out and looks at Cameron. He shines a small light into Cameron's eyes. "Yeah, he should be looked at. Were the two of you involved in this?"

The policeman has come up. "You didn't come out of the garage with the others. Where were you?"

"Hiding in back, in the woods," the professor says. "We got away from the sect members before they could take us prisoner."

"From what I saw of the other hostages before they took them away, you were lucky."

"Indeed we were. They shot at us, but fortunately the shots missed. But I think my friend here is in shock."

"All right," the paramedic says, "we'll get your friend into the ambulance, but he'll have to sit in it."

"That will be fine. Right, Cameron?"

The jaguar gives Cameron a nudge inside, and he mumbles, "Righ'."

They help him into the ambulance, where the jaguar's person lies strapped on a gurney. The paramedic is putting a needle in her arm and attaching a tube through which liquid drips. The jaguar doesn't understand this. She needs to reach her person.

The ambulance moves. Its siren blares. The

paramedic bends over the gurney. The jaguar comes out of Cameron. He falls forward. The paramedic whirls, catches him before he falls onto the floor. The jaguar leaps and fades into her person, displacing the boar. The paramedic pushes Cameron back into his seat and holds him while she straps him in. She lets out a small cry. Probably she has seen nothing but a dark blur as the boar fades into Cameron.

With that transfer complete, the jaguar can rest. She has done what she was sent to do, is back with her host, and the injured boar is back with his. Both boar and host can become whole again.

30
PEACEABLE KINGDOM

I lay comfortably in my hospital bed, having had a good night's sleep after being given something to relieve the pain of my broken ribs. By good fortune or maybe at someone's direction, I'd been taken to Howell Memorial Hospital, where Dr. Horshaw had privileges, rather than to Community General from which we'd rescued Marko. It was a welcoming place, and I was quite content to lie in bed and let my jaguar help me heal. She'd been through a lot, too, so the healing might take longer for both of us. But I had no sense of urgency about leaving the hospital.

The fact that none of the blood I'd been lying in when I was found in the garage seemed to be mine still puzzled the doctors, and I professed not to know where it had come from. In trying to get away from the preacher, I'd just slipped in it and fallen, I explained. And they accepted that explanation, having no better one.

Having been in Cameron had been much less traumatic for my jaguar than her brief time in Dimitri had been. She, and therefore I, had shared nothing of Cameron's thoughts other than his need to be reunited with his boar. Oh, and a vague sense of shame that Joy had been a part of the preacher's flock. I didn't know how he had discovered that or when. I guessed it was through what his dad had found on Joy's laptop.

But I wasn't worried about that now. I was too comfortable to think about such things. I suppose the pain medicine was responsible for some of my euphoria. Who cares?

A nurse popped in and said, "You have a visitor if you're up to it."

"Sure," I said.

And wished I hadn't.

Grandfather walked in, a scowl on his face. He came to my bedside and looked down at me, shaking his head. "Charlotte, Charlotte, you simply cannot follow instructions, can you?"

"Guess not," I said.

"I made myself clear that you were not to take it upon yourself to visit the Reverend Carlisle and place yourself and everyone else in danger, *ja*?"

"You did, but..."

"Ah, and yet there you headed as soon as you could get away from Jeffrey and Helene, who treated you as an honored guest, did they not?"

"They did, and I was grateful. But when I heard Ryan had been kidnapped, I—"

"You did just what I warned you against doing. You went to visit the Reverend Carlisle on your own."

"Roy went with me. I didn't go alone."

"Ah, *ja*, and it is a good thing he did. What more might you have done?"

"Probably would have got myself killed," I admitted. "Roy was great. Very brave and smart."

"Yes, indeed. The photos he took with his camera

phone will prove the case against the reverend and his followers. Although the police have plenty of evidence even without them. They could see that you and Roy and the boy had been tortured. And two of the reverend's followers have agreed to testify against him and the others.

"The only problem is that his lawyers have a good basis for an insanity defense. He swears still that they had shot a demon in the form of a large boar, and that it was there on the garage floor until you fell upon it. And it disappeared within you."

"Imagine that," I said, unable to suppress a grin.

And to my great surprise, Grandfather burst out with loud guffaws. Smiling now, his eyes twinkling, he said, "Charlotte, you are truly amazing. I know of no other were who could have done what you did. Indeed, I did not know it was even possible—to take into yourself another were's animal spirit. To place your animal spirit into another host. It is incredible. You are richly talented. I shall be proud to call you my honorary granddaughter."

I didn't know what to say. I wanted to thank him, but words refused to come. I couldn't express my feelings, tell him how thrilled I was. I guess the tears welling in my eyes and spilling onto my cheeks told him something.

"Ah, Charlotte, you were right and I was wrong." He grabbed a tissue from the box by my bed and gently wiped my cheeks. "That is something I have rarely had to admit. I did not know how special you are." He kissed me on each cheek. "I hope you can forgive me for my unkind words. They were spoken only out of concern for my children. Including you."

I grabbed his hands and squeezed. "I know, Grandfather," I finally managed to say. "Thank you for taking me into your family."

"It is my pleasure. And now I must go. Others are waiting to see you, and I must visit my dear Marko. He is still at Community General, but is no longer in a locked ward. He should be released soon. Velma is already planning a feast to celebrate your homecoming and his. He is much changed, but is once more in his right mind. Imagine, for almost two years he endured torture at the hands of those heartless ones because he would not send out his wolf so they could kill it."

"I don't know how he survived."

"Almost he did not. He told me about his escape and of trying to get to Dima at his dealership but being too confused to find his way. He doesn't remember the stabbing, only of more pain and of being treated by paramedics. He was certain he was dying. He slipped in and out of consciousness while they worked on him. When the ambulance arrived at the hospital, he grabbed the chance during a moment of consciousness to let out his wolf when they left him very briefly before taking him out of the ambulance. He hoped his wolf could reach us and somehow get help. Or, barring that, perhaps it could find another host and live on after his own death. The wolf seemed more bent on revenge for all his suffering than on trying to get help to him. Had it not been for your efforts, both Marko and his wolf would have died. I have told him all that you did. He will thank you himself when he is able."

"It wasn't just me," I said.

"I know, I know. But you provided the inspiration and guidance. And now I must leave and let your other visitors come in."

He bent and kissed me on the forehead and hurried to the door.

"Wait," I called.

He paused and turned back to me.

"How's Ronnie?"

"Ah, Ronnie. *Ja*. She is very weak, but the doctors now say she will recover. They did not at first expect her to, but then, they do not know of her animal spirit, her badger. It gives her healing power, *ja*?"

"*Ja*—I mean, yes. She saved my life. And was nearly killed doing it. I need to thank her for that and will as soon as I can see her.

"I will tell her when I next see her that you asked about her." With that promise he left.

And seconds later Dima walked in. As he approached my bed, Gene followed him.

Both were smiling and looked to be in good health despite their stay in jail. Dima took my hand. Gene smoothed my brow and ran his fingers through my hair, which I hadn't had a chance to comb. And I had no makeup on and my face was bruised and I looked a mess.

"Sharl, you're looking beautiful," Gene lied.

"Thank you for not abandoning us," Dima said. "You have such courage." And then he bent and kissed me on the lips, and I wanted the moment to last forever.

"Hey!" Gene elbowed him aside. "My turn." And he kissed me, also on the lips, and placed in my hand a heart-shaped box of chocolates.

Dima had come in empty-handed, but a nurse bustled in with a vase of beautiful roses and handed it to Dima. "Here you are, sir. I found a vase for your roses."

Dima accepted the vase and put it on my bedside table. "Not my roses but hers," he said. "We decided we'd each bring you a token of our affection and gratitude. When you're out of the hospital, back home, and feeling up to it, we have a party planned."

"We're out on bail after a preliminary hearing," Gene said. "But it's just a formality. There's no question we'll be completely exonerated now that the Reverend Carlisle's people are spilling their guts to save their own necks. And it's all thanks to you."

"Tell her about Marko," Dima urged before I could make any response.

"Grandfather told me he was better and no longer in the locked ward. He didn't give me any details, though."

"He wouldn't. It was thanks to Grandfather that they moved him to a room where he can have visitors. They'd finally agreed to let Grandfather in to see Marko. He'd calmed down enough, they said, but I think it was really because they'd learned about what happened to him. Anyway, Grandfather went in and spoke to him very calmly and told him that the people who'd tortured him were either dead or in jail, and he was safe, and he'd be coming home soon. And Marko made him tell him that over and over, and then asked him to tell him what had happened."

"A sanitized version," Dima put in. "Grandfather didn't mention the torture you and Roy and that poor kid suffered or how they almost killed Ronnie."

"No, he didn't want to upset Marko," Gene said. "But he did ask how Marko was captured by the demon hunters. And Marko told him. Starting with how he fell overboard off my boat. We'd both had too much beer, and I put the boat on autopilot, going at five knots, and went to use the head. While I was doing that, he, well, he had to relieve himself, too, and I don't know why, but he went and stood on the swim platform behind the boat. I guess he thought that would be the easiest place to piss into the water. It's just a few inches above the waves. The boat hit a swell or something, and he wasn't all that steady, and over he went. So it was an accident, just as I'd tried to tell everyone. The boat drifted off out of sight while he was trying to stay afloat, and by the time I came up on deck and realized he was gone, I didn't know where to look for him." shook his head.

Gene paused and I jumped in with the question I'd been wanting to ask. "But why did they think you'd killed him? Why didn't they believe you?"

Gene hung his head. "We'd been quarreling a lot," he murmured.

"Two male wolves in the same household," Dima supplied. "It happens."

"Shouldn't have, though," Gene said. "I wanted to talk out our differences. That's why I invited him to go out on the boat. I figured a long ride into the Gulf would give us a chance to resolve our disagreements. And it did. We each spoke our minds, got over our beefs, and celebrated with the beer. That turned out to be our big mistake."

"When you realized he'd gone overboard, you tried to find him, didn't you?" I asked.

"Sure I tried—drove the boat all around. But the Gulf's so big, and we were out pretty far. I couldn't spot him. I thought for sure he'd drowned." He choked up, unable to continue.

Dima finished for him. "He said he would have drowned, but his wolf came out and towed him ashore. Then went back into him while he was lying on the beach, unconscious. Unfortunately, somebody saw the wolf drag him up onto the beach and then fade into him. And that person was a member of the Rev. Carlisle's flock. And instead of calling an ambulance, he called Rev. Carlisle. He must've told him what he saw. I guess you can figure out the rest. They kept him a prisoner in the parsonage. They didn't torture him at first, but they wouldn't let him go. They kept trying to convert him. He'll tell us about it when he's stronger. The torture, when it did start, was really awful. But you don't need to hear about that now."

I shuddered, thinking about the pain I'd suffered and trying to imagine what it must have been like to endure it as long as Marko had.

"Don't think about it, Sharl," Gene said. "It's over now. For Marko, and for you. Just think about getting better so you can come home." He bent and kissed me again.

Then Dima said, "Okay, Gene, my turn," and kissed me, just on the cheek, so Gene didn't object. And I certainly didn't. I felt relief that Dima had apparently forgiven me for invading his mind. I guess he realized I only did it to save his life.

I couldn't believe he and Gene were both being so sweet to me and so civil to each other. This was

Grandfather's Peaceable Kingdom in action. But were they both just grateful to me for making it possible for them to get out of jail and free of a murder charge? Did either of them have any deeper motives?

Right now it didn't matter. I determined to enjoy this delightful, if temporary, truce between them. In fact, I was euphoric, but euphoria melts like snow beneath the harsh light of reality. I had not the slightest doubt that this love fest was temporary. Grandfather's "peaceable kingdom" existed only in his mind. Fallings-out, petty quarrels, perhaps even major ones would come. But not soon, I hoped. And with luck, maybe I wouldn't be in the middle of the next major one.

At least when they let me out of the hospital, I'd have a real home to go to. No more heading for the homeless shelter. The were house, peaceable kingdom or not, was now my home and its people my family.

ABOUT THE AUTHOR

Elenora Rose Sabin writes as E. Rose Sabin simply because people have so much difficulty spelling and pronouncing her first name. Rose is easier.

Ms. Sabin taught Spanish and language arts to middle schoolers for many years before turning to a career as a novelist. She writes what she enjoys reading: science fiction and fantasy novels. She has written novels for adults and teens and has also published a children's chapter book.

A dog lover, Ms. Sabin has two rescue dogs to keep her entertained and distracted. They make certain that she takes breaks from sitting at the computer to play with them and to let them in and out of the house.

She enjoys hearing from readers, who can post messages on her Facebook author page: E. Rose Sabin's Books. She hopes readers will also check out her web site: www.erosesabin.com

BOOKS BY E. ROSE SABIN

THE ARUCADI SERIES (fantasy):

MISTRESS OF THE WIND
BRINGERS OF MAGIC
A MIX OF MAGICS
DENIABLY DEAD
A PERILOUS POWER
A SCHOOL FOR SORCERY
WHEN THE BEAST HUNGERS
BRYTE'S ASCENT
MOTHER LODE
RELATED ARUCADI NOVEL: CAT AND COBRA

THE TERRANO TRILOGY (science fiction):

SHADOW OF A DEMON
THE GIFT OF THE TRINDE TREE
TOUCH OF DEATH

FANTASY NOVELS FOR ADULTS

DEATHRIGHT
A HOUSE FULL OF DREAMS
SEDUCTION OF THE SCEPTER
THE TWISTED TOWERS
WERE HOUSE

FOR YOUNGER TEENS:

TO THE FAR SIDE OF THE FOREST

FOR CHILDREN:

GRANDY'S GRAND INVENTIONS (A Children's Chapter
Book)

ACKNOWLEDGMENTS

Because I've been working on *Were House* for a very long time, and I've received advice and help from many people along the way, I'm very afraid that I will forget some names that should be included here. I hope those friends will be understanding and will know that any such omission was unintentional.

The idea for the novel came from a digital print I purchased from artist Mike Conrad. I told him of the idea his work had given me for an urban fantasy novel and asked if he had any objections to my using his artwork as a springboard. He had none, and I think and hope the idea pleased him. You can see the artwork here:

http://www.mikeconradart.com/Werehouse.html

My dear friend and mentor, the late Diane Marcou, freelance editor and ghost writer, helped me improve the manuscript of this work right up to the time of her death. Her sharp eye and wise counsel provided invaluable assistance, and I regret deeply that she did not live long enough to see the manuscript's completion.

Several friends did read the completed manuscript and offered helpful suggestions that brought improvements to the writing style, plot, and manuscript format. Among them were my critiquing partner, mystery author Diane Sawyer, author of the award-winning novel *The Tell-Tale Treasure*; Monique Desir, author of horror novel *Forbidden*; and long-time friend and writer Joyce Levesque, author of science fiction novels *Dominion of the Lost* and *Dominion of the Hidden*.

I also want to thank my dear friend Carol Jeffers, who produces lovely art under the name of Rubey Shea, for her unfailing support and encouragement. I would never have had the nerve to strike out on my own in self-publishing under my own Arucadi Enterprises imprint without the help and guidance of these talented friends.

Now I've put out a new edition of *Were House*, with a beautiful new cover by my very talented cover artist, Igor Dešić. He is always kind and patient with me when I request changes, corrections, or resizing, and he never fails to amaze me with the work he produces. You can see more of his work on his web site: https://igordesic.artstation.com/

And of course I want to thank my readers, who make the effort of writing and publishing my work worthwhile and a pleasure to do.